THE ADVENTURES OF CHARLIE MARLEY

MIDNIGHT'S MOMENT IN TIME

Andrew Luria

BEACHSIDE
Publishing CO.

The Adventures of Charlie Marley

Midnight's Moment In Time

First edition, 2020

TO: JACKSON, NATHAN & LUCY

GO MAKE HISTORY

PROLOGUE

"RUN FASTER!"

Charlie knew better than to keep Mrs. Cooper the Pooper Scooper waiting.

"We have to hustle," he urged again, picking up the pace toward the classroom.

Emma gave him a *no duh* kind of look.

They could hear the faint squeal of their teacher's voice from down the hallway and around the corner. Even at a distance, her voice was like fingernails on a chalkboard.

"Tennn... niiine... eiiight..."

They didn't want to know what would happen if Mrs. Cooper got to zero.

Rounding the corner, the classroom was within their sights.

A lot had changed in the short time since they'd last been in that hallway.

Like, **A LOT**.

Heck, if it weren't for them, some of the most incredible moments in sports history never would've happened. Then again, the most embarrassing play **EVER** never would have either.

"Just wait till she sees our history reports *now*," Emma insisted. "Guarantee no one else actually *met* the people they're reporting on."

They both knew for certain that no one else in their class had been through more to make it happen either. None of them had fought off intergalactic police and ridden time-traveling rocketships, all while uncovering the biggest secret of their own lives in the course of one day.

Regardless, Mrs. Cooper the Pooper Scooper wasn't one for excuses. She wasn't the forgiving kind. She wasn't the caring kind. She wasn't the quiet kind, either.

"THReeee... TWOOO... onnne..."

They turned into their classroom. If only they'd known what they were in for when they last walked out of it: an adventure that would change their lives. . . and the history of the world.

EARLIER THAT DAY. . .

CHAPTER 1

THE POOPER SCOOPER STRIKES BACK

Charlie Marley was late, as usual. He had no time for breakfast. And he certainly didn't have time to match his clothes or brush his teeth. So off he went with one blue sock pulled up and one orange sock bunched down, stumbling his way down the stairs. He slung his backpack over his shoulder and quickly mumbled a goodbye to his parents, who were not particularly surprised by his tardiness. Still, they had to pause and marvel at the colorful blur sprinting toward their front door.

"Charlie, your shirt is on backward—" his mom started. But before she could finish pointing out that his shoes were also on the wrong feet, he turned the handle and opened the door right smack into his own forehead, stunning himself momentarily.

"OWWW!" he yelped.

"Oof. You really started the day full speed a*head*," his dad pointed out as only a dad could.

"No... dad... jokes," Charlie insisted. "Not now."

He took a deep breath, focused in, and thundered on. He had to forget about the giant swelling red mark now forming above his right eyebrow. He didn't have time to dwell on details—not this morning.

"See you guys after school," he said, trailing off as he shut the door behind him.

"What about food?!" Charlie's dad tossed a breakfast bar toward him, but it hit the shutting door instead, and fell to the ground.

Charlie raced off the porch, skipped the first three stairs, and tripped on the fourth. That mishap sent his backpack soaring into the bushes and Charlie's chin crashing into the seat of his bike, which was parked on the front walkway. His hands and knees didn't fare too well either.

With no time to waste, he brushed himself off, fished his backpack out of the once-perfectly manicured shrubs, and hopped on the coolest two-wheel vehicle on earth: his *Gnarly Harley*. Yes, that's right. . . **CHARLIE MARLEY'S GNARLY HARLEY**. The bicycle was custom-designed just for him, with huge wheels and super-high handlebars.

His bike was by no means a real Harley Davidson, but *Charlie Marley's Gnarly Harley* seemed like a fitting name anyway, and it sure got him everywhere he needed to go.

2

Charlie not only rode it to school, he also rode it around town on his paper route as he delivered the daily news to the people of St. Albany. And every day before he could get to class, he had that job to do first.

St. Albany was a relatively small town, but a perfect one as far as Charlie was concerned, not that he'd been to a whole lot of others. There were plenty of playgrounds, a Little League baseball park and nice neighbors all around. It was hot in the summer, cool in the spring, leaves fell in the fall and it even snowed in the winter. He enjoyed it all, except for when he had to mow the lawn, rake the leaves and shovel the snow, of course.

Charlie's paper route had become a breeze for him, since he had been doing it for nearly two years and was a seasoned professional by now. He was the only twelve-year-old he knew of who had a job—a responsibility that made him feel quite grown-up.

On this particular day, he was especially behind schedule and knew he needed to go faster. Much faster. Charlie knew exactly what he had to do: he was going to have to use the Gnarly Harley's one and only neon yellow emergency button. When he and his dad built the bike together, they installed it under the seat.

"Now, you use The Big Boost Button only when *absolutely* necessary," he remembered his dad telling him. "Double-click it to turn on, and do it again to shut it off."

Charlie had only ever used it one time before, the day they had finished building the bike.

"*This* is absolutely necessary," Charlie said aloud to himself.

After all, the last thing he wanted to be was late to Mrs. Cooper's class, and he still had ten more houses to deliver newspapers to. If any day called for the Big Boost, it was today.

When he pushed the button, the bike sputtered and kicked, the tires squealed, and it took off in a frenzy. The Big Boost Button launched the Gnarly Harley into super-speed mode by engaging a super cool, super powerful mini motor that did all the pedaling for him. The only thing Charlie had to do, his dad had told him, was lock his feet in, and hold on tight. It was easy enough, and made his job go by much faster, but it also made his ride considerably less stable. Charlie needed to focus.

At a pace at least five times faster than Charlie could ever pedal on his own, he cruised into the final stretch of his paper route. T-minus ten minutes until the school bell was going to ring. He had only Baymeadow Court's deliveries, a few sidewalks and two flights of stairs standing between him and Mrs. Cooper's infamous **BOARD OF EDUCATION**.

The Board of Education was a meticulously-carved piece of cedar wood, shaped like a frying pan, that hung ominously behind her desk. "Don't *make* me use this," she would snarl. Mrs. Cooper loved to threaten the class whenever she had the opportunity. It made them cower like goldfish in a shark tank.

Charlie turned into Baymeadow Court, grinding the Gnarly Harley nearly parallel to the ground, which set him up for a quick and perfect final home stretch of *Daily News* deliveries. He was feeling fast, feeling powerful. But then, just when the bike straightened up, it skipped directly over a peanut-sized pebble, kicking his wheels sharply off balance like a spinning top on its final rotation. Charlie held on for dear life, wondering for a moment whether he would end up back on track or backward on his head.

Maybe engaging the Big Boost Button hadn't been such a bright idea after all.

With some quick thinking, and even quicker moves Charlie didn't even know he had, he maneuvered the Gnarly Harley just enough to regain his balance in time to fire off Mr. Murgan's paper, followed quickly by a behind-the-back shot onto the porch of the Kennedy house. Not wasting a moment to look up, Charlie tossed the Zorkers' copy toward the foot of their driveway—failing to notice that Mr. Zorker was already standing there. He also failed to notice that the newspaper he hurled was directly en route to smacking Mr. Zorker in the side of the head. The sound of the impact, however, made it abundantly clear.

WHACK!

Charlie turned just in time to see coffee flying one direction, Mr. Zorker soaring in the other, and the *St. Albany Daily News* landing safely somewhere between. But that, as he was about to find out, wasn't the worst of it.

Charlie's attention was diverted just long enough that he didn't see the giant pothole recently formed right smack dab in the center of Baymeadow Court. Neither Charlie Marley, nor his Gnarly Harley stood a chance against a crater of that depth and severity.

For the second time in less than an hour, Charlie was airborne, flailing in an uncontrollable plunge that felt—ever-so-briefly—like he was in slow motion. But it didn't last nearly long enough. He crashed down to earth with a **THUD**, landing on his backpack, crammed full of binders, notepads and one enormously oversized book of sports records. Fortunately enough, the pencils were in the side pocket.

As if the fall weren't punishment enough, Mr. Zorker's fuming glare—sent Charlie's way as he peeled himself off his now coffee-stained driveway—quite literally added insult to injury.

"Sorry Mr. Zorker," he coughed. "Again." It wasn't the first time he'd hit his neighbor with a flying paper.

Mr. Zorker just mumbled and grumbled as he shuffled back into his house.

Aside from getting the wind severely knocked out of him, Charlie seemed to have survived the fall without major injury. But, he realized with a sickening glimpse, the same couldn't be said for the Gnarly Harley. The bike's wheels were bent and wobbly, and the high handlebars were now lowriders. He picked up his damaged vehicle, and together they limped through the final deliveries on Charlie's route. Getting to school on time was now out of the question. Whether he'd get there in one piece was still to be determined.

Charlie's messy brown hair had become amazingly more out of place, and his freckled face had a few new distinctive marks since he'd woken up just thirty minutes earlier. When he turned the corner onto Churchill Road, with his bike squeaking beside him, his watch beeped. It was eight o'clock.

In the distance, he could hear the school bell ringing, and he could only imagine what the evil Mrs. Cooper would do to him once he got there. It's not like she earned her nickname for being the nicest teacher in school. No, Mrs. Cooper the Pooper Scooper would make him pay for his delay.

Finally, battered, but no worse for wear, Charlie stood in front of Eureka Elementary, home of the Fighting Dust Devils. It was a long, two-story brick building surrounded by tall oak trees and ascending stairs that led directly to the entrance.

Charlie had gone to Eureka since he was in kindergarten, and now, as a sixth grader, he felt like he pretty much knew his way around the school as well as any kid could. He only wished he knew a secret passageway that would somehow get him directly to his desk without having to open the door to Mrs. Cooper's classroom.

Charlie parked the twisted remains of the Gnarly Harley in the bike rack, trying to balance it in a spot without it topling over, and made his walk of shame up to Classroom 208.

"Here goes nothing," he sighed as he turned the handle, ready to meet his fate. He was greeted by an ear-piercing shrill.

"Chaaarlie," Mrs. Cooper squawked, as he ashamedly shut the door. She took a long hard look at him. "I can see by your face and your hands," she paused, "and your knees, too, that you probably have good reason to be six minutes and," she checked her watch, "seventeen seconds late to class today." Her speaking tone was about as pleasant as two pieces of styrofoam rubbing together. Charlie had braced himself the second he'd heard that voice screeching his name, but suddenly, he realized, no punishment had come. In fact— and he couldn't believe his ears—it seemed like she *understood*. Was she going to let him off, free and clear?

He tried to utter a response while he made his way back to his desk, though nothing coherent came out.

"But Chaaarlie," Mrs. Cooper continued, "that means your history report *better* be *especially* captivating." She grabbed the giant piece of wood hanging on the wall, and smacked it repeatedly into the palm of her hand. "Or else!"

Charlie was just getting to his desk when it hit him. No, not *The Board of Education*, but it may as well have been.

HISTORY REPORT!

He had completely forgotten to do his history report.

Just when he'd thought he was free. Just when he'd thought his lateness had been pardoned, Mrs. Cooper the

Pooper Scooper had struck again. His only reprieve was knowing he had until after recess before he would face the consequences.

The morning passed by too quickly as far as Charlie was concerned. Lunch came at 11:15, and by noon, the class was headed outside. Some of the kids wandered off to the playground. Others went to jump rope. Charlie and most of the other boys started their daily football game.

But before they could kick off, they had to pick teams: a draft, led by two captains, who selected players one-by-one. The way Charlie saw it, it was a back-and-forth battle for who *didn't* have to get stuck with him. Charlie was never captain. And he was never picked anywhere but last. While he loved football, and always gave his best effort, his hands were as good as hooves when it came to making plays in clutch situations, or in *any* situation for that matter. On this day, it was Rocky's team that lost that battle, and got stuck with the final pick—Charlie tried not to care too much.

Rocky Oakley was one of the triplets in Mrs. Cooper's class. His brothers were Buster and Dizzle, and Charlie figured each one to be more rock-headed than the next. And that was an insult to rocks. They were the toughest kids in school, and everyone learned quickly to steer clear—for more reasons than one. Rocky's lisp was nothing to worry about, unless you made fun of it. But Buster's brutal breath and Dizzle's spitting-while-speaking syndrome was enough to make most kids keep their distance.

You wouldn't know they were triplets, though. Aside from their bully sneers, the three looked nothing alike. Buster had spiky brown hair, Rocky sported slicked-back blond hair and Dizzle had nearly no hair at all—it was shaved down short enough to see his scalp. But what they lacked in physical similarities, they made up for in other areas. Namely, that their wedgie-giving techniques were nearly identical.

"You better not thcrew up thith time, Marley Charlie," lisped Rocky as he pointed a thick arm his way, reluctantly making the last draft pick.

There were a few onlookers who cared neither to hang out on the playground nor play in the football game—if they had, they surely would have been picked before Charlie too. Emma Mayfield was among them. Emma was athletic and always watched them play, but never once put herself in the pool of players. Today was no different, except that—and Charlie couldn't be sure—she did seem to have particular interest in something else on the field: him.

Charlie caught her eye as he dragged his feet—shoulders slumped—toward his team. What did Emma Mayfield want with him today of all days? She was eagerly looking toward him, waving her hand and raising her eyebrows as if she had something to say, but the last thing Charlie wanted to do was talk to a *girl* in his greatest moment of shame.

It was weird, though, considering Emma had never said much to him before. He wasn't the most outgoing kid—especially not since his best friend Archie moved away right before the school year started. Emma, on the other hand, had no choice but to be outgoing. As the lead reporter for the *Eureka Enquirer*, the school's newspaper, she was always talking to people, investigating some important issue or another. While Charlie rode his bike to school and wore whatever clothes he could slap on in the rush of the morning, Emma walked to school and wore long skirts with tie-dyed shirts. He studied NBA box scores. She studied peace rallies from the 1960s. Charlie had messy brown hair. Emma had long, straight red hair. Charlie had freckles, and Emma did too. Charlie had no idea what she could want to talk to *him* about.

And besides, even if she did have something to say to him, now was not the time. Charlie was too focused on not embarrassing himself.

The game was a back-and-forth thriller, not unlike most recess contests. Charlie only dropped three passes, and actually managed to make one spectacular juggling grab—even if the ball did bounce off his head first.

That catch came halfway through the game. With the ball suspended in mid-air, Charlie was knocked flat onto his back by "Brace Face" Chase McGee, a kid who was just about as wide as he was tall. But the collision was not as unfortunate as it could have been for Charlie, who was in perfect position for the ball to plunge right onto his chest while he lay help-lessly in the dirt. He wrapped his arms around the ball for an incredibly suspenseful, yet physically costly three-yard gain. It wasn't even enough for a first down.

The game was tied at four touchdowns apiece when the bell rang, signaling the end of recess, and setting up the fi-nal play of the day. Charlie's team was at mid-field and there wasn't much doubt as to what the last play would be. They had to score to win and avoid the most unexciting finish of all: an all-square, nobody wins, perfectly even, horrible, boreable tie.

In the huddle, Rocky gave the strategy. The lisping trip-let looked around like he was a coach delivering a legendary speech at the Super Bowl. "Boyth, it all cometh down to thith. No time left on the clock and your fanth are exthpecting a miracle." The fans he spoke of were not 80,000 strong. They weren't even eight strong. There were just a handful of kids sticking around, two of whom were already starting to head in for the second half of the day.

"We've got to go with the Hail Mary, and we need thome-body to thtep up and make a big play. I know it thoundth crathy, but here'th how it'th going to go: everybody run to the back right of the end thone. Everybody exthept for. . ." he paused and made a face like he couldn't believe

13

what was about to come out of his mouth. "Everybody exthept for Marley." The moment the words left his mouth, there were groans and eyes rolling, and heads dropping toward the ground. Charlie did a double take, not sure he'd heard correctly. *This was his chance.* "It'th the only way, team. Nobody will exthpect it, and nobody will cover it. You think you can make the catch, *Lobthter Handth*, or thould we jutht quit now?"

Inside, it felt like his guts had fallen down to his feet, but he was determined to *look* confident even if he didn't really feel like he had a hope. "I can do it, Rocky."

"Jutht put your handth out there and let the ball fall into them, okay?" Rocky pointed out the obvious as only he could.

"Yeah," Dizzle spit onto Charlie's forehead, "take off the boxing gloves and put your hands back on." Charlie did not appreciate the lack of confidence, nor the shower of saliva. What he did appreciate was the opportunity before him. This was his chance to show them his skills, his competence, his value—to prove he wasn't a total loser. Somewhere, somehow, he *knew* he could do it.

At that second, Mrs. Cooper the Pooper Scooper blew her whistle, summoning the kids to the building, giving a glare that let them know she meant business. But with one play left and the game on the line, nothing short of a bolt of lightning frying the ball into a pile of leathery ashes would stop them from getting off this last play at the buzzer.

Rocky snapped the ball and dropped back to pass. As instructed, the entire team went right, and Charlie went left. Nobody was within a country mile of him. "Here it comes!" belted Brace Face Chase, eyes fixed on the ball in Rocky's hand. It came alright, just not the way he expected. Nobody on the defense had noticed, nor cared, that Charlie was left all alone on the opposite side of the field. Rocky lofted the ball with the precision and beauty of a Tom Brady delivery and it arced directly toward Charlie. His team's victory was about to be in his hands.

As it neared, he prepared for his glorious moment. This was a chance for Charlie to show that he was as good as any of them. He reached up and braced for impact. The **"OOOHS"** and **"AAAHS"** from across the field only deepened the drama.

What happened next completely changed Charlie's depressing day. . . for the worse.

It was as if Charlie had coated his hands with grease. The ball slid right through them, slamming into his mouth, and—as if in slow motion—hit nearly every part of his body on the way down: his chest as he whiffed a second time, his leg as he tried to save it and his foot as he inadvertently kicked it. It crashed to the ground at the same time he did, and met its destiny ten feet away, coming to a rest in a muddy puddle.

Lying on the ground, Charlie stared up at the clouds above, trying to zone out the collective groan coming from the other side of the field.

There was some consolation, Charlie thought, as he tongued a now-loose lower front tooth. At least he might get a buck from the Tooth Fairy.

The players began to leave the field, some angered at a disappointing end to a hard-fought game, and others relieved. "Nithe handth there, Butterfingerth," sneered Rocky.

Brace Face Chase McGee perked up. "Butterfingers? Where?" He wasn't one to miss out on free candy. Brace Face wasn't one to miss out on *any* candy. He was the kind of kid who thought of Halloween as a working holiday.

Had Archie been there instead of in stupid New York where his dad's new job was, he would have held out both hands, helped Charlie up, and told him it was no big deal. But Archie wasn't there, and nobody offered so much as a finger.

Charlie closed his eyes, reliving his nearly-heroic play, and hoping nobody else—aside from the guys playing—saw how bad he bungled it. No such luck. Even with his eyes shut, he could tell the sun's brightness had suddenly dimmed and a shadow covered him. Opening one eye, and then the other, he saw the last thing he wanted to see: a girl. Emma Mayfield stood over him with a sympathetic smirk. "There's good news and there's bad news."

The bad news, Charlie presumed, was Emma had watched the game.

"The bad news is recess is over, and so is the fun," Emma said, looking down at him. Charlie didn't recall having fun at recess. "And it's time to face your fate from the Pooper Scooper."

"Yeah, and what's the good news?"

"You're not alone."

Charlie looked up sharply at Emma, wondering what she knew, or what she was snooping to find out.

"You didn't do the project," she declared. "I could tell by the look on your face this morning. And apparently, by the look you're giving me now, I was right." Charlie tried to hide whatever look he was giving, but that's hard to do when you can't see your own face. "As for my project," she continued, "well, I didn't think the senile old hag would even remember it was due today. Plus, it's my way of rebelling against the establishment."

Charlie nodded, as if he had any idea of what she was talking about. Emma often talked like she was about thirty-two, not twelve. "Well, whatever the punishment is, it can't be much worse than this." He pushed himself up off the ground, and they made their way up to Classroom 208 to face the consequences.

"What do you think, detention?" Emma wondered. "Maybe she'll just put us in the corner of the room and make us stare at the wall till the end of the day," she added, almost hopefully. And then she paused. "Or. . . the Board. You don't think she'll actually use the *Board*?"

Charlie was afraid any one of Emma's presumptions might be true. She always seemed to have the answers. But he really dreaded finding out.

By the time they reached their seats, Charlie still had grass clippings on his back and a small leaf in his hair. He sat down on his chair only to feel a painfully sharp prick. **"SHEESH!"** The class busted out in laughter as he stood up with a thumbtack attached firmly to his backside. Buster put up his two hands, and simultaneously high-fived his dim-witted brothers sitting on either side of him.

Mrs. Cooper, who had her back to the class, didn't even notice. Her hearing was as good as her personality was nice. She turned just in time to see Charlie removing the evidence. "Mr. Maaarley, sit down this instant!" She grabbed the Board of Education and hit it against her desk.

THWOMP, THWOMP, THWOMP!

"Now, let's get to work. These better be gooood, people." Charlie gulped, noting a decidedly nervous feeling in his stomach as the class began their presentations one by one, in alphabetical order.

A Brief History of Time was the assignment, but the specific topic was up to each student.

When the presentations neared the "M's," Charlie knew his freedom was about to be history too. "Chaaarlie," screeched the Pooper Scooper. "It's your tuuurn."

He slowly raised out of his seat. "I, uh. . . I didn't do it." The class collectively gasped. Charlie's eyes lowered to the ground. He snuck a peek up at Mrs. Cooper, awaiting her reaction.

"Oh, and hith bad day getth even badder!" announced Rocky.

"Mr. Marley, I said it's your tuuurn." Apparently, the Pooper Scooper hadn't turned up her hearing aids.

"Mrs. Cooper, I didn't do it!" he nearly shouted, just wanting the moment to be over. She stared at him for what seemed like forever, and as each moment passed, the tension grew to newer and more painful heights.

"Sit down, young maaan." The class was convinced they were about to see actual smoke billow out of her ears. "I have to decide how to punish you." She looked at the class list. "Alright, Mr. Marley didn't do it, so let's move on to Ms. Mayfield. And you, young lady, better give me an answer that doesn't make me want to smack something."

Emma stood up, plain-faced and confident. "Cooper, I didn't do it either." She knew the Pooper Scooper didn't have good enough ears to notice the lack of respect in her tone. But she also knew she was in for some real trouble, too, though Charlie admired the defiance on her face.

Mrs. Cooper was flabbergasted. She was shocked. She was outraged. "Anyone else *not* do their work?" The silence in the room was deafening. "Fine, then. Charlie! Emma! Here! Now!" She pointed to the ground directly in front of her.

They each slowly walked to the front of the room. Charlie snuck a look out of the corner of his eye and was surprised to see Emma's confident demeanor cracking a little. Neither of them, he decided, knew exactly what was to come, but both knew it wasn't going to be good.

"You two see those?" Mrs. Cooper pointed to a pile of old decrepit erasers that probably hadn't been used since the turn of the millennium. The classroom didn't even have a chalkboard anymore. Charlie had always wondered what they were still doing there, but now, it seemed, Mrs. Cooper had been saving this punishment for an especially momentous occasion. The erasers were caked with white chalk and piled as high as the top of her desk. "Clean 'em and clean 'em good. **NOW!**"

Charlie and Emma looked at each other, not exactly pleased with the prospect of carrying potentially hazardous supplies across the school. It wasn't even much of a consolation that they got to get out of that classroom since they'd probably be in trouble for not knowing what they missed while they were gone.

Chalk dust kicked up into their faces as they picked up the erasers. If you ever wondered what moldy industrial-strength sulfur-flavored chemical soot tasted like, they were sudden experts.

As they coughed their way toward the door, Mrs. Cooper shot back again. She took a pair of erasers out of her desk drawer and tossed one at each of them. "You better not forget these." They were the worst two erasers of the bunch. It was clear the Pooper Scooper had been waiting for this day for quite some time.

Charlie tried to open the door with a spare finger, his hands and arms occupied with balancing the erasers against his chest. He managed to twist the handle just enough to pry it ajar. "Oh, and you two," Mrs. Cooper added as they were halfway through the door, "this is juuust the beginning." She had a devilish smile and angry eyebrows pointed at her two victims.

Charlie and Emma hobbled out, barely balancing the erasers while trying to figure out where they were going.

They neared the stairs when Charlie turned to Emma. "Isn't the chalk eraser thingymagiggy in. . ."

"Yup." She already knew what he was asking and why it was going to be an issue. The machine they were after, known to the students only as the *chalk eraser thingymagiggy*, was in the janitor's closet located at the end of the lower hallway.

The closet was said to be haunted, and it was believed that nobody who entered had ever been heard from again. Or so the rumor goes.

"It's no big deal, Charlie. You know those are just stories." But even Emma didn't sound as confident as she let on.

When they reached the closet door, Charlie peeked over his pile of erasers, and Emma peeked back. "Are you ready?" he asked hesitantly, not knowing whether or not he could answer the question himself.

"Just open it, you big chicken."

Charlie again used his two free fingers to nudge the handle just enough. It opened with ease, but finding the light switch was going to be a whole 'nother challenge. They could see from the hallway light that the janitor's closet was big—bigger than they thought—with two sections. They saw the chalk eraser thingymagiggy in the front section on top of a long wooden tool bench. But they couldn't see much of anything beyond that.

Charlie walked in first, and tried to hold the door open for Emma with his foot behind him. But as she passed in, he lost hold of both the door and his balance, and the erasers went flying here, there and everywhere. He tumbled to the ground for what felt like the millionth time that day, catching Emma's ankle on the way down. She, too, lost her hold on her erasers and went crashing down with him. They together landed on the concrete floor, followed closely by a showering of chalk-filled felt blocks. The door shut heavily behind them.

FWHOOMP!

As they sat in the darkness for a minute, Charlie wasn't sure whether to laugh or cry, but mustered only a nervous giggle as he thought back to all the rumors he had heard. "Are you alright?" he asked.

"Yeah, I'm fine. This really *isn't* your day, is it?" Emma said, sounding like she had a smirk on her face, but Charlie couldn't see it in the pitch black. "Let's find a light."

Before either one could stand up, a noise resonated throughout the small room. It sounded like iron clanging against steel, startling them both into silence. Then, the sound of drilling. The only thing they knew was that it wasn't coming from either one of them.

They froze. The drilling stopped.

They both frantically reached for a light switch, but neither had a clue where to find it. And suddenly, the noises began again. Charlie and Emma were not alone.

CHAPTER 2

THE MYSTERY OF MIDNIGHT

The high-pitched sound of screeching metal shrieked throughout the room, until it was almost deafening for the terrified twosome. They continued to paw at the wall for a light switch, but found nothing more than flat concrete.

As suddenly as the noise had begun, it got quiet again, and Emma and Charlie both froze, unsure of what that meant.

Before either could say anything, they heard footsteps, which were rapidly coming closer and closer. After only a moment, the steps stopped with a thunderous **BANG**—the kind of sound you might expect when you drop something heavy on metal bleachers.

"Yooowwwieee!" squealed an unfamiliar voice, followed by the unmistakable sound of a **HOP, HOP, HOP.**

The lights switched on, and Emma and Charlie stood—ankle deep in erasers—blinking at the sudden brightness. They turned anxiously toward the back of the room, from where the sound had come. It took a few moments for their eyes to adjust, and for their minds to understand what they were seeing.

"Oooh, goodness! That did not feel gooood! *Why, why, why* do I insist on working in the dark?!" A man who looked about his dad's age, with a mustache and graying, wildly-erratic hair stood before Charlie and Emma. He was wearing a giant visor, which had a light shining toward them from one side, and a magnifying glass stretching across his face from the other, which made his eyes seem three times their normal size.

The giant-eyed man wore a lab coat and a bow tie and even though he was in the same room as they were, Charlie got the distinct sense that he wasn't really talking to him or Emma. And he didn't stop, even when he noticed that he had company. "I really cannot believe I just did that again. It must be the fourth time this week I've banged my darn knee into that stupid file cabinet!"

It was then that he caught Charlie's and Emma's eyes, wide and filled with fear. "Oh, no need to worry, kiddos, I'm much more of a threat to myself than to you," he assured them, before following up with, "I'm Midnight McLean," as if that were meant to make them feel at ease.

Neither of them had ever seen him before, though, when he thought about it, the name *did* sound familiar to Charlie. The more he mulled the name over, the surer he was that he had heard it, but in such a moment of sheer panic, when and where was a mystery. With Charlie lost in thought, it was Emma who was the first to speak.

"I. . . uh, I'm Emma." She said nervously, still clearly uncertain about the wild-haired man in front of them. She nudged Charlie out of his motionless stare. "This is Charlie."

"Yeeesss. . . Charlie *Marley*, I presume?" Midnight said, flipping up the magnifying lens, returning his eyes to human size. "You are just as I imagined."

Charlie was perplexed. His head cricked to the side. "How do you know who I—"

"And to what do I owe the honor of your visit?" Midnight swiftly interrupted, leaving Charlie to wonder how this strange man knew his name.

"Mrs. Cooper sent us to clean these erasers," replied Emma.

"What erasers?" Midnight looked around, as if to verify her story.

"*These* erasers!" Emma bent down, pointing at the gigantic pile before them, which was so large that it was nearly impossible to miss. Midnight's eyes had not adjusted from his magnifying glasses. "We had a decent grip on them until *Mr. Two Left Feet* over here decided to redecorate the floor with chalk dust."

"And, I have to say, it matches the walls, quite nicely," Midnight told Charlie, who felt his face turning red.

"But then," Emma continued, "we heard this loud banging noise and screeching and squealing, and we were in the pitch dark and didn't exactly have time to clean up."

Midnight's face turned serious. Were they going to get in trouble? He looked at Charlie, and then Emma. And then back to Charlie. And then back to Emma. The silence became infinitely more uncomfortable with each glance. "Well," he said after what felt like an eternity, "would you like to see what all that clattering was? I mean, you're already down here. And frankly, I'm having a hard time keeping this secret to myself."

Charlie looked over to Emma, unsure of what it was they were being invited to see. He remembered the stories about the forbidden lower hallway closet. What if every kid who came into the closet was invited to see what "all that clattering was," only to be swallowed up by some giant beast? Or worse?

Emma gave him a *stop being such a wimp* look, rolled her eyes and started toward the back of the closet to investigate like any good reporter would. Not to be left out, Charlie followed closely behind, hesitant with every step.

Midnight led the way through an open doorway they hadn't noticed before that took them into the back part of the closet. Charlie stepped through nervously, but it was only filled with school junk: old desks, file cabinets and boxes full of who-knows-what from who-knows-when. This was the big secret?

"Are you *sure* you want to see?" Midnight said, his voice somehow more ominous as he stopped and turned back toward them. Charlie looked to Emma, since she was apparently the answer-giver around here, but he could tell that even she was second-guessing her earlier decision. In Charlie's opinion, they had a perfectly good excuse to turn around and run for their lives.

"Aw, come on now, kiddos. It'll be worth it. I promise you," Midnight said, though it wasn't all that reassuring.

It was Emma, again, who made the first step, and Charlie followed as they crept around a pile of furniture and into a small side room. It was not big enough to be a classroom, but way too big to be a closet for clothes. Midnight flipped the light switch, and out of the darkness appeared the most extravagantly colorful, splendidly amazing gadget-covered golf cart they had ever seen in their lives. It had flashy wheels, two rows of seats, four doors, navigation machines, computers, monitors, furry seat covers and side view mirrors the size of basketballs. There was a roof rack on top and running boards along the sides. A pair of fuzzy dice even hung from the rearview mirror. It was the most incredible vehicle Charlie had ever seen, outside of his Gnarly Harley.

"Ladies and gentlemen, I present to you... **THE FLOGTRAC!**"

At that, the golf cart suddenly became way less cool.

"Flogtrac?" Charlie wondered aloud. "What kind of name is *that*?!"

"I take it you could come up with something better?" Midnight challenged him.

"I don't know, but anything would be better than *Flogtrac*. Call it the Superdupercart. Maybe the Golfwiz Express. Or Carty McCartface. But Flogtrac?"

"I built it, so I named it. That's it, end of story. Period. Not an issue. Let's move on." Midnight stood proudly by his invention.

Emma looked suspicious. "*You* built this? Here? In our school?"

"Well," Midnight explained, as if it were obvious, "the resources I need are right here, the rent is cheap, the walls are thick, nobody bothers me and I can listen to my music and whistle while I work."

Emma and Charlie looked over at an old CD player in the corner and the pile of discs around it. The pop-up top was open, and *Slow Jams Mix 2000* was clearly visible on the CD inside. Charlie caught Emma's eye and she sort of half-smirked, half-shrugged. He knew what she meant.

"What brought you here?" Charlie asked, realizing he no longer felt that nervous.

"Inventing is my life, young Charlie. Though," he paused, "that wasn't always the case. Like you, I was an athlete. I had an arm like a cannon, the determination of a bull, the passion of a tiger and the coordination of. . . well. . . my coordination was a little spotty. So they made me a pitcher."

Charlie didn't bother telling Midnight that his own athletic ability fell somewhat short of that. But he did wonder how Midnight also knew he was an athlete—or at least a wannabe one.

Midnight went on, "I worked my way through high school ball, then college, through the minors and even made it to the big leagues. I had the nastiest junk ball in the game, and when it came time to close down a victory, nobody could touch me. It was lights out! Hence, my nickname."

"Midnight?" Charlie concluded. Midnight nodded and continued.

"But in my greatest moment of pressure, I got trampled on."

"What, like your coach pulled you out?" Emma asked.

"No, I *literally* got trampled on! It was Game Seven. 1994 Major League World Series. We were down a run with the bases loaded. I had just shut 'em down in the top of the ninth, but in the bottom half, we were trying to make the comeback of all comebacks. I walked to the plate, with the game in my—"

"Wait a second," Charlie interrupted. "I thought you said you weren't coordinated, so they made you a pitcher? Why were you going to the plate?"

"Very good question, young man," Midnight said with a smile. "My manager's style was as unpredictable as a Midnight McLean junk ball on a howling windy day. He substituted **EVERY** single player from the bench in the first four innings to throw off the opposing pitcher. Whatever he did confused *us* more than it did them though, and it left absolutely nobody to come in to bat at the end of the game.

"So, *that* particular night, I walked to the plate with the game in my hands. But, mind you, my power with the bat was as explosive as my cannon right arm, even if my coordination wasn't great. When I knew where the pitch was coming, I could hit the ball the length of the Mississippi River. Of course, I made for a great batting practice hitter, but not exactly the guy you want up with the World Series on the line."

Charlie was starting to think that Midnight was a little full of himself by now, but when he looked over at Emma, he saw she was hanging on every word, as if taking notes in her brain. Maybe there was something to this story after all.

"I got a ball, then a strike. Then another ball, then another strike. And then, ball three set up a full count with two outs and the bases loaded. I had dreamt of that moment my entire life. And I knew exactly what was coming. It was going to be that beautiful fastball right down Broadway. He had no choice. So, he wound up and I wound back. He let it go, and so did I!

"Only, the fastball I expected took a ninety degree dive into the ground. And as I swung, the only thing I made contact with was the back of my own helmet—which hurt like the dickens, mind you—and sent me spinning around, twisting my ankle, buckling my knees and crashing into the dirt with the weight of the World Series on my back.

"The catcher jumped with joy and when he landed, it was directly on my pitching hand with the heels of his cleats. And *that's* when I got trampled on."

"Oh, that's horrible," gasped Emma, rubbing her hand.

"But that's not the end of it!" Midnight insisted, enjoying his audience now. "I was part of their celebration. As they jumped on top of one another, I played the role of the dirt. I remember lying there, thinking it was the worst moment of my life."

"So, what did you do?" Charlie asked, thinking about his own World Series dream, and how bad he'd feel if something like that happened. He could sympathize with Midnight's disappointment.

"Well, as I lay there, with my dreams shattering right before my very eyes, I realized that the pain of losing the World Series wasn't as severe as the pain I was feeling from my head to my toes. They broke me."

"Emotionally?"

"No, their cleats literally broke seven of my bones! One in my arm, two in my left leg and four in my right hand! But, not *all* was lost. I vowed then and there to *do* something about it, so I invented a batting glove with an armor padding on top and—soon after that—created armor for the elbows and shins and forearms and legs. So now, thanks to me, most ball players are as fit for a medieval jousting session as they are for a baseball game."

"So, did you ever play again?" asked Charlie, eager for more baseball stories.

"I didn't think I needed to. I had found my calling as an inventor. I could do what I wanted, create whatever came to mind, and nobody else's dreams came crashing down if I screwed up."

They sat in silence as Midnight seemed lost in the moment. Inventing might be cool, Charlie thought, but he didn't think he'd turn down the chance to play professional baseball for anything. He was imagining himself suiting up for a game and taking the field, when Midnight McLean's voice broke in again.

"Ah, I know what you're thinking, Charlie. And it's true. I haven't been able to shake those memories. Every day I work, and every day I think of baseball. And *now* it's time to do something about it!" He circled the Flogtrac, looking it up and down and checking its parts. "That's why I've invented this spectacular contraption."

Charlie turned to Emma, who looked as skeptical as he felt. What did he mean? What could the Flogtrac do, other than probably drive you through a round of golf with a little more speed and a lot more style?

Actually, Charlie noticed, there was no place on the Flogtrac for golf clubs. So it couldn't even do that.

Suddenly, Midnight stopped and turned to them, standing up straighter before speaking. "I'm taking this puppy back to 1994, and I'm going to win that World Series title like I should've the first time around."

Charlie looked at Emma just as she turned toward him.

SAY WHAT?

"So whooo's coming with me?" Midnight crowed like a ringleader in a circus.

"Wait a second," yelped Charlie. "What do you mean you're going back to 1994? Are you saying this thing can really do that? What... *is* it?"

"It's the device of your dreams—and the first of its kind. It's not what it seems. It's headed to another place and time!"

"Like, a *time machine*?" Charlie wasn't sure whether this guy was crazy or a genius or both.

"Like, *yes*, Charlie. And I could really use some help. So," he repeated louder, "**WHOOO'S** coming with me?!"

Charlie weighed his options and decided that he didn't have anywhere else to be, and he was certainly in no rush to get back to the Pooper Scooper's class either. Emma was already nodding her head in agreement.

Then, *why not*, he wondered. If this thing were for real, they might get to see history in the making; or, at least, in the *re*-making. If it weren't, as he suspected, then what could they really lose?

Charlie started to walk the perimeter of the Flogtrac, as Midnight had before. He was careful to step over the tools sitting all around the vehicle—some he recognized, some he didn't. He noticed the chrome bumpers and complex hubcaps. He even kicked the back right tire, testing its stability like he'd seen his dad do, but that caused the Flogtrac to shake and shimmer. Yes, shimmer. Charlie quickly backed off.

"Not to worry, pal, it's secure, for sure. It's perrrfecto," Midnight said, opening the back right door for his guests like a fancy chauffeur. "Shall we?"

They entered, Emma first, and then Charlie—the pile of erasers, flubbed football game, and missing history homework all but forgotten. Midnight wiped the grease from his hands, kicked the tools out of the way and grabbed a baseball glove and wooden bat from the workbench that Charlie hadn't seen before. Then, he walked around to the driver's side and took his seat.

Midnight looked in the rear view mirror at his eager passengers in the back. "Seatbelts, boys and girls."

They all strapped in.

Midnight clicked keys in one computer, and then the next. He tapped a keyboard built into the dash and pushed the screen on a navigation system. He switched a knob and punched a button and twisted a lever. Charlie and Emma watched all of it, eyes wide. "Ready for the ride of your lives?"

"Where, exactly, are we going?" Charlie asked. "It's not like 1994 is a place."

Midnight sat for a second, as if contemplating what he was about to say. "Kiddos, I know when I want to go. And I know that I've made this magnificent machine. And I know that I have to have faith in my work. But to tell you the truth, I can't say with a hundred percent certainty what's about to happen. I have no idea *where* we're going, or *when* we're going, or even *if* we're going. But I insist we give it a go anyway. What do you say?" Before they had a chance to answer, he turned the key in one fleeting motion, and the Flogtrac sputtered, kicking out a plume of black smoke and gained stability.

"Oh, great. There goes *another* layer of the ozone," Emma murmured.

Midnight tapped the accelerator. The Flogtrac shot forward and kicked back, pushing their bodies one direction and their momentum the other. They all looked at each other and laughed nervously.

"How do you think we're going to drive this thing to another time and place?" Emma said, sounding like she was now regretting the choice to go along.

"Well, based on the Theory of Bop Mucket Continuumu-mum, there should be a time continuum hidden right behind that pile of brooms and dusters and junk. Whatdya say we find out?"

Charlie couldn't think of a place that looked *less* like a secret time continuum, but before they had a chance to argue against the seemingly senseless logic, Midnight slammed his foot onto the accelerator and the Flogtrac responded with a high-powered jolt, sending them right for the cleaning equipment. Charlie and Emma braced for the worst. Midnight's eyes were as wide as they had appeared through the magnifying glasses, and the smile on his face was equally as broad.

Then, right upon the moment of impact, a bluish force field appeared behind the mops and brooms and buckets, and through it all they went.

There was a **SPARK**, a **BOOM** and a **BAM!**

They suddenly found themselves in a long winding tunnel, twisting, turning and flying along a transparent pathway at a speed they'd never experienced before.

They were definitely no longer in a janitor's closet. They were quite certainly far, far from it.

Emma tapped Charlie, whose mouth was ajar. She then nudged his head to the right, and he noticed the incredible sight out the side of the Flogtrac. They could see through the sides of the tunnel. There were stars. There were brilliant blazing bright lights. There were colors they had never laid eyes on. Midnight kept his focus on the road, and his sparkling-eyed smile never waned.

But up ahead, it wasn't all good news. A mass of enormous rocks soared from right to left, directly across their pathway. They were getting closer, and for the second time in a very short time, the three were bracing for impact.

FWOMP, FWOMP, FWOMP.

One rock, two rocks, three rocks flew by them, just barely missing taking out the Flogtrac and all of them with it.

And, just when they thought they were finally safe, they realized they had thought wrong. There was one rock—the biggest of the bunch—that was absolutely and unmistakably unavoidable. It was headed right for them.

For the first time on their short journey, the smile disappeared from Midnight's face. "Uh oh, kiddos! **WAAATCH OOOUT!**"

CHAPTER 3

WELCOME TO THE ROCK

Like a hippo about to eat a minnow, the giant rock was closing in on the Flogtrac fast, and there was nothing any of them could do about it. The closer they got, the more they took notice of its rough exterior and crater indentions—and the clear evidence that this was more than just any old rock. This rock had an agenda. They were on a collision course with a meteor!

The Flogtrac shook forcefully as the meteor hurtled to ward its path, shuddering right, vibrating left, wobbling up and jiggling on down. Midnight—Charlie noticed with a sickening **GULP**—didn't seem to be in control of their direction anymore. The gravity from the meteor was just too strong.

They all braced for impact, expecting the worst. Charlie peeked over the seat just in time to see another tiny bluish force field forming on the side of the enormous meteor, which rotated toward them the closer they got. *What was that thing?* Charlie had barely enough time to wonder before he ducked back down again, just as they were about to slam right smack into it.

But no impact came. Instead, there was a **SHWOOP!** And that was followed by a spectacle of a million brilliant lights zooming by, illuminating their atmosphere. Charlie and Emma both reached toward the seats in front of them, poking their heads back up to take a peek. Midnight was curled up in the fetal position in the front, looking shell-shocked. There was an eerie silence, and then the lights became fewer and fewer, until they were gone completely.

SHWOOP!

There it was again.

The Flogtrac stopped moving. They sat in total blackness.

"Are... are you guys okay back there?" Midnight asked. Charlie heard shuffling that sounded like Midnight was sitting back up.

"I don't know," he replied, before uttering his fear. "Are we... dead?"

Midnight didn't answer, which would have worsened Charlie's concerns, if he didn't hear more shuffling and bumping from the front seat. Suddenly, there was light and

Midnight was illuminated, holding a metal cord attached to a bulb, looking triumphant.

Once their eyes adjusted to the light, Charlie and Emma looked around and found themselves in. . . a janitor's closet. Again.

"Wow, all of that, and we're right back where we started." Emma said suspiciously.

Charlie, too, was wondering what kind of trick Midnight had just pulled on them.

But as he peered around, he realized that this closet looked nothing like the one at Eureka Elementary.

Emma, for her part, ever the journalist, remained skeptical even after Charlie pointed out his observation.

"Okay," she said witheringly, "Well, we traveled, it was weird and time passed. I'm not sure you can call that *time travel*."

Charlie turned to Midnight for an explanation—they had to have done something extraordinary, right? But Midnight didn't look at Charlie. He was busy examining the controls. Charlie heard him muttering to himself, something about how they were wildly off from his original configurations, and how the trip must have thrown off their readings. Leaning closer, Charlie heard Midnight mumble that there was something different about the dials. That in fact, there was something different about the entire inside of the Flogtrac. Charlie was just about to ask him what was going on, when Midnight spoke up.

"Hmmm, not quite as I calculated," he proclaimed aloud, scratching his chin.

That didn't make Charlie or Emma any more comfortable with their present situation.

"Do you notice anything different about the Flogtrac, other than the fact that it is very inconveniently stuck in this rinky-dinky-stinky closet?" Midnight asked, turning toward them.

Charlie tried to open the door of the Flogtrac to get a better look, but that resulted in a problem of painful proportions. The door didn't open the way every other car door had always opened for him. It opened backward, swinging toward the rear of the cart, instead of the front. And as it flung back, he swung with it, before falling onto the cold, hard concrete floor.

He gasped; both from the pain in his rear, and the sight before his eyes. Charlie was the first to find out: the Flogtrac was a golf cart no more.

"What happened to the Flogtrac?" he cried. "It looks like it morphed into a Gooberflafen!" Emma and Midnight had no idea what he was talking about, nor what a Gooberflafen was, and neither did Charlie for that matter—he didn't know where that word came from, but looking at the Flogtrac now, it oddly seemed to fit.

Emma hopped out, then Midnight, both with slightly more grace than Charlie. It was then that they, too, found that the prized invention truly was no longer as Midnight had designed it. The Flogtrac, in fact, had become not a Goober-flafen—whatever that was—but a kind of old-fashioned antique vehicle you might see at a car show, or in classic black and white photos.

The trio circled the vehicle, taking in the slick black running boards along the sides, the spare tires attached to the wall of the engine cover and the neat lights on the front that looked like they belonged in an old mobster movie. The tires, too, were black on the edges, white on the inside and the sparkly chrome rims were so polished that Charlie could see his own distorted reflection in them.

The windshield on the front was rectangular and divided in two, straight down the middle. The hood that covered the engine was nearly as long as the rest of the vehicle. And, as if it weren't cool enough already, the Flogtrac has become a convertible, although the weak yellowish light from the closet ceiling didn't exactly give it quite the gleam it deserved.

Soon, a noticeable murmur from outside the walls could be heard. They all looked at each other, wondering what other surprises they might be in for. Emma broke the silence.

"Charlie," she said slowly, "did you wear that to school?"

Emma was eyeing Charlie who knew he wasn't the best-dressed kid around, but still took exception to the comment—until he took a look for himself. He looked down and gasped, taking in the ridiculous-looking outfit that any self-respecting birthday party clown would even be embarrassed to wear. He had been so out of sorts when it came to the Flogtrac that he hadn't noticed his new red-and-white striped shirt, dark blue apron and—Charlie reached up to his head—square paper hat that made him look like he was ready to flip burgers at a fast food joint.

He turned to look at Emma. She, too, was dressed differently than when they had first stepped into the Flogtrac. Her blue blazer was strange enough, but her hat was even more bizarre. It had a brim that encircled her entire head, with a card attached to the top that read **'PRESS.'** He pointed this out to her, and then they both looked to Midnight. He appeared exactly the way he had the moment they had met him, although his lab coat was slightly more worn and his visor was turned just off-center.

"I don't know, kiddos," he said. "If I could explain it, I would. But then again, we just turned an old golf cart into a 1932 Chrysler Imperial Sedan, so I'm tongue tied." It turned out, apparently, Midnight was not just a pro baseball player and a quirky inventor. He was a car historian in his spare time too.

Whatever was going on, Charlie and Emma conceded that Midnight had at least put on quite an impressive magic act. But they were freaked out enough that they were just about done with the whole thing, even if it meant returning to Mrs. Cooper's classroom to face their next punishment—no matter what that might be.

Silently agreeing with a nod and a meaningful glance at the closet door, Charlie led the way and Emma inched closer to him, as they readied to make a run for it. Midnight peered at them, crossing his arms, but not moving. Probably wondering where, exactly, they thought they were going.

Charlie took his chances and creaked opened the closet door. Instead of seeing the dozens of students he expected in the school hallway, there were hundreds of people—most much taller than his schoolmates—walking every which way through a giant corridor. And they, too, were dressed very differently than Charlie had ever seen before.

Emma's hat suddenly didn't seem so weird, as most of the men walking by wore similar styles. Charlie's outfit, he realized with chagrin, was still incredibly ludicrous. He turned back to Midnight, who still stood by the newly-styled Flogtrac with his arms crossed and a self-satisfied smile on his face.

"What do you see out there?" he asked, gesturing toward the corridor.

Charlie quickly shut the door and put his back up against it. He turned to Emma. "I don't think we're in Kansas... or St. Albany anymore!"

CHAPTER 4

THE CALLED SHOT

Emma tried to pry the door ajar again, but Charlie remained pressed up against it, working fervently to hold it closed. He didn't know why, but he got the feeling that whatever was out there might be more than he could handle. In a moment of distraction, Emma got the door open, and Charlie went with it.

Finding the courage to peek around the door, he saw Emma's eyes were as wide as silver dollars as she got her first look out of the closet. She took in all of the people walking by with food in their hands, some holding pennants and some little booklets.

Midnight trotted over to take a peek for himself, his eyes almost popping right out of his head when he saw the scene.

"Get your programs here. Geeet your World Series programs heeere!" chanted a vendor holding up one of those booklets some of the people were carrying around.

"See, kiddos, I told you we were headed back to another place and time," Midnight said as if this were what he had meant to happen all along—although Charlie detected a hint of relief in his voice, too. "My plan has worked! Not only aren't we in St. Albany anymore, this, folks isn't even the 21st century! I've gotta get ready for my big moment. I'll see you two after the game-winning homer—or, whenever my teammates finally bring me down off their shoulders."

And with that, Midnight ran off, leaving his two travel partners alone in a janitor's closet with a giant old-fashioned car as their only transportation home. They wondered aloud if they could leave the closet. What if it weren't there when they got back, and they got stuck all the way back in 1994? Would they even know how to turn it on, let alone drive it back to the present day?

But opportunity won out over skepticism. After all, they figured, if they couldn't move the thing, nobody else from the last century could probably figure it out either. And besides, how could they miss out on Game Seven of the World Series? Weird and confusing or not, this was *historic*. So, after only a moment's worth of discussion, they left the closet and joined all the other fans who were about to witness history being made.

They got less than five feet out of the closet when someone yelled out, "Hey, you!" Charlie had a weird feeling that the voice was talking to him. "Hey, get over here!"

"Is he talking to you?" asked Emma, pausing and turning around.

"I. . . I think so. What should I do?"

"Yeah, **YOU**. Come on, son," demanded the voice, again.

"I guess you better get over there, Stripes." Emma said with a shrug, refusing to let go of just how loud Charlie's shirt was.

"Okay," Charlie said, curious, anyway. "I'll check out what that's all about. But you go get one of those little booklets. I think we should save Midnight a souvenir from his big game." Charlie turned around, and tentatively moved toward the voice, hoping Emma couldn't tell how nervous he was.

"Come on, we don't have all day!" the voice urged, and Charlie walked toward the concession stand twenty feet from the janitor's closet, where it sounded like the voice was coming from. He figured he was right, because when he got there, he was surrounded by a dozen others dressed just as outlandishly as he.

"Gee, what took you so long?" It was the voice, but Charlie still wasn't sure where or who, exactly it was coming from. They were all staring at him. He looked around the group, first to the right, then to the left. He finally looked down and saw him: a man who could not have been more than three-and-a-half feet tall if he were wearing high heels. And thankfully, he wasn't.

"You're just a little guy, but you'll do," the mini man said to Charlie, who was perplexed by the irony of the insult.

"I'll do. . . for what?" Charlie responded.

"What do you think, son? Fall into position, and listen to the colonel!"

"Colonel?" This was getting weirder and weirder.

"Yes, Kernel," the man sighed exasperatedly. "Colonel Kernel."

Charlie didn't know what the heck the guy was trying to say, but he lined up like any good army trooper would with the rest of the dorky-dressed crew, figuring he didn't have much to lose.

"Ten-hut! It's that time, team, when we go out there and give 'em all we've got." The little man paced back and forth in front of the group. "But the question is if you've got what it takes to succeed out there. They—sure as sugar—didn't give me much to work with. Most of you look like little more than butter scraping morsel poppers. But darn it, we're gonna find a way to get the job done. Now who's ready to sell some popcorn?!"

"Yes sir, Colonel Kernel. Let's do it!" yelled the group in unison—all except for Charlie, of course. And one-by-one, in sequence, they grabbed long trays of popcorn and headed off in various calculated directions.

"Well, son, what are you waiting for?"

Charlie stood there frozen after all of his matching cohorts had vanished, not sure what he was supposed to do next.

"It's simple, kid. Grab your tray and go to your position. You're in center field. I'm quite convinced you can't handle home plate." The colonel's eyebrows lowered, forming a vexing 'V.' Partially persuaded by his commanding voice, and partially hoping this would get him a step closer to returning to Emma so they could watch the game, Charlie grabbed a tray of popcorn. He swung the strap over his head and quickly left his short-legged, largely-menacing leader.

He tracked down Emma, having wildly weaved in and out of foot traffic with thirty bags of popcorn hanging from his neck, ignoring all the people who tried to flag him down for a snack. But when he neared her, he saw she stood motionless; ashen-faced, like she had just seen a ghost.

"I guess this explains the outfit," he joked, shaking his popcorn tray. But Emma didn't respond. "Everything okay?" Charlie grabbed a handful of popcorn and tossed the pieces into his mouth one at a time.

She looked up at him slowly, turning the booklet toward him. "This World Series program will tell you all you need to know."

Charlie looked at a colorful front cover. It read: *Chicago Cubs*. Underneath: *New York Yankees*. It was a World Series program, all right. It just wasn't one from 1994. It wasn't Game Seven either. And Midnight's picture was nowhere to be found inside.

Charlie squinted his eyes at the words on the top of the front cover and read: **WRIGLEY FIELD**, the legendary Chicago ballpark. Below: **1932**.

"You alright, kiiid?" asked the program vendor, as his tone dipped in his professional projecting voice.

"What game is this?" Charlie countered.

"If you look at your prograaam heeere, you'd see that it's Game Three, of course."

"How about today? What's today?"

"Uh, it's Saaaturday."

"No, what's the date?"

"It's October. Fiiirst of the month." He paused, noticing

Charlie's face turning pale faster than a chameleon on cotton, and dropped the vendor voice. "It's 1932, kid."

Charlie's sight blurred, everything spun around him and then faded to white. He passed out, stone cold.

When he came to, he saw Emma's face above his, looking helpless. "Oh, what a crazy dream I just had," he muttered as his eyes reopened. It took a few moments for him to regain total consciousness, but when he did, he first noticed the thirty bags of popcorn strewn around him, and then, slowly, the rest of the stadium, looking just as it had before.

"This is a nightmare, Charlie." Emma shook her head. "And yet, it's way too real."

He brushed himself off, wondering whether they should tell Midnight he had overshot his intended target.

They decided he would find out for himself soon enough—that he probably already had. In the meantime, they had to figure out why they ended up at the wrong World Series, and more specifically, Game Three of the '32 Series.

"Are you gonna sell that popcorn, or are you gonna just step on it?" scolded Colonel Kernel from a distance, his voice somehow just as clear booming from fifty yards away. Charlie, not wanting trouble, scooped up some of what had spilled onto the ground, and spread it freely between the crumpled bags.

"I guess I gotta go get rid of this crunched 'corn before The Munchkin Man comes over here and makes me eat it."

Charlie scurried quickly toward the interior of the stadium.

"But where am *I* supposed to—?" Charlie was gone before Emma could finish.

Emma stood there for a moment, noting the dressy outfits everybody around her wore and the proper way they all spoke, so different from what she was used to hearing. She hadn't, however, noticed the lanky man standing right next to her.

"You zeem lost," he spoke in a strong French accent.

Emma was certainly lost. Lost in another century, lost in another city and lost for words.

"Memberz of zee prezz need to go zata way for zee prezz box. Bezt zeetz in zee houze." He pointed to a small door down the corridor. "Come on now, zee game'z about to ztart."

He was a tall man with a small pencil-thin mustache and a black rounded top hat. He handed her his business card. "At your zervize, madame."

Emma took a long look at the name: *Mr. Muffin, Association of Educational Intergalactic Orbitational Unionship.*

"Mister Muffin?" she asked bewilderedly.

The man cleared his throat, rolled his eyes and projected back. "It'z pronounzed *Monsieur Moofyay,* if you want to get it right, madame."

56

"Monsieur Moofyay? It looks like *Mister Muffin*," Emma said, thinking Monsieur Moofyay was pretty ridiculous.

"Well, *madame*," he said with a slight edge to his voice, stroking his mustache, "it iz not."

"What is the Association of Educational Intergalactic Orbitational Unionship?" Emma asked, changing the subject.

"I am covering zee World Zeriez for our zcientific publication. We are analyzing zee projectionz of zee ballz and zee forzez of zee pitchez, okay?" His voice rose with the end of every sentence.

"Um, okay. I'm here representing the *Eureka Enquirer*, I guess." Emma shrugged, already thinking about the piece she was going to write about this whole experience and figuring this could only help.

"Very well, zen. Zat shall do." Mr. Muffin led the way to the press box door.

As the Frenchman turned the handle, Emma got her first peek into a real live media workshop and it took her breath away. Journalists lined the room: some typing away furiously, some writing on notepads and others simply jabbering about who-knows-what.

"Take a look around, Mizz Emma Mayfield. Zee prezz box iz your playground. Take an extra cloze look over in zee far corner of zee room, though. You zee what I zee? I'll be back." He closed the door behind him.

PRESS BOX 1

Emma turned quickly, stunned. "Wait, I never told you my name was—" but Mr. Muffin was already gone. She wasn't sure what he meant about the far corner of the room. All she noticed was a big black mechanical-looking box with white paper.

Down in the stands, Charlie was still wondering how he had ended up in an ugly vendor's outfit with thirty dirty bags of popcorn hanging from his neck.

He had maneuvered his way to the center field stands, but was so awe-struck by the sight of Wrigley Field and the ivy-covered brick that made up the outfield wall that he was barely focused on his meaningless job. A cool wind whipped Charlie's face as he tried to grasp the authenticity of a *real live* World Series and the foreignness of an era he had only read about in books.

In fact, he had books covering his nightstand; books filled with information on everything from the world's coolest stadiums, to world's best athletes. Those books were somewhere, in some future time period. But he was seeing the real thing, right here and right now.

"Hey, gimme five." Charlie was snapped out of his trance. "I *said*, gimme five," a fan repeated, with his hand up. Charlie reached out and slapped his open hand with a high-five. The guy sat there for a moment and stared at Charlie, looking as perplexed as a hamster in algebra class.

"How much for *five bags*, young man?"

It took Charlie a moment to remember why he was in the center field stands in the first place. "Oh, you want popcorn?"

"No, dumbbell, I want pumpernickels. Of **COURSE** I want popcorn. How much for five?"

Charlie looked down at the small sign pinned to his apron. "It looks like ten each, sir." He pulled out five crumpled bags of popcorn, and handed them to the fan, who gave him two quarters in return.

"Fifty cents?" he said, looking at the coins in confusion.

"You said ten each, right? Oh, well, here's a little something for your trouble." The man flipped him a nickel for a tip.

"Not what you exzpected, eh?" From behind, a tall lanky man with a black rounded top hat and a pencil-thin mustache nearly scared the popcorn out of Charlie.

"Uh, no, not really."

"I know, timez have changed, young man. Zee prize of popcorn izn't what it uzed to be." He handed Charlie his business card. "Monsieur Moofyay, at your zervize young man."

"Mister Muffin?" Charlie said, reading the small print.

The man cleared his throat and rolled his eyes. "It'z pronounzed *Monsieur Moofyay*. And I'll take zee rezt."

"You'll take the rest?" repeated Charlie with a crackle in his voice. "The rest of what?"

"Yez, I'll take zem all. It may not look like it, but if I don't have my twenty-five bagz of popcorn for lunch, my tummy doez flipz and flopz and turnz and tumblez. Zo, I'll take zem all."

Charlie thought about telling Mr. Muffin that most of the popcorn had been scraped off the dirty concrete floor in the busiest walkway at Wrigley Field, but the idea of not having to sell any more bags was too good to pass up. Besides, he figured, the faster he could finish his job and get back to Emma and Midnight, the better. "Twenty-five bags? They're yours."

Mr. Muffin handed him $2.50. "Don't zpend it all in one plaze, you hear?" Charlie gave him a sarcastic smile. He would barely have enough for a bottled water with that. "You can go pick up more in zee corridor. You zee over zere?" Mr. Muffin pointed to a walkway that led back to where Charlie had left Emma. "Zere's a door. It haz pretty picture. You'll find everyzing you need zere. Go on. Hurry up, Monsieur Charlie Marley."

Charlie didn't know who this Mr. Muffin guy was, or why he was telling him where to pick up more popcorn, or how he seemed to know so much. With a sudden realization, he stopped in his tracks. "Wait, how do you know who *I* am?" But when he turned back, Mr. Muffin and his twenty-five bags of popcorn were gone.

Before Charlie could get any sort of answer, the crowd erupted, screaming, booing and hissing like he had never heard before. Fans were throwing things onto the field—everything from tomatoes to lemons to, yes, even popcorn.

"You're nothin'!"

"The *Strikeout* King!"

"The Sultan of *Stink*!"

"The Great *Bum*-bino!"

Fifty thousand fans in unison cursed the player walking to the plate, mocking each of his mighty nicknames.

The stadium announcer boomed over them. "Ladies and gentlemen, may I have your attention. Now batting for the New York Yankees, number three, Babe Ruth!"

Charlie's head snapped toward the field. There, less than 400 feet away, was **THE** Babe Ruth! The Home Run King. The Sultan of Swat. The Great Bambino! There in the very flesh.

The Chicago crowd wasn't nearly as impressed. Its boos became deafening. According to the Word Series booklet, the Cubs were already down two-games-to-none in the Series, and Babe Ruth hadn't been shy about a prediction of a four-game sweep. It looked to Charlie like the Chicago fans despised him for it. They hadn't won a World Series in twenty-four years, he read, and it sounded like they were starting to get awfully anxious.

It was the first inning, and two runners were already on base for Ruth. It didn't take long for the crowd's fears to become a reality. The Babe sent a deep shot to Charlie's left, way out of the park for a three-run home run. And just like that, the hated Yankees were on top, 3-0.

The boos got louder with each step Ruth took, and the amount of flying food seemed to triple with each base he touched.

Unbelievable. If only they realized, Charlie thought, *most people he knew would give their right foot to see Babe Ruth hit a home run.* Most people here, though, seemed perfectly fine sacrificing their footlongs instead.

Charlie ducked and dodged the debris on his way to the corridor, still buzzing with the excitement of seeing *the* Babe Ruth hit one of his fabled homers. He came upon a perfectly good banana that had been imperfectly tossed by a fan above and picked it up, realizing only then how long it had been since he'd eaten. It would have tasted great, Charlie imagined, had he not been immediately beaned in the head by a giant bag of flying peanuts, knocking him out cold. Again.

He lay there in the walkway for two full innings, even missing—he later found out—a Lou Gehrig home run for the Yankees. Even being in the stadium, he thought, for a Babe Ruth home run *and* a Lou Gehrig home run? He felt like the luckiest kid on the face of the earth.

The Chicago fans felt otherwise. In fact, they were so focused on the game that they barely noticed—or cared—that a popcorn vendor was napping in the walkway, since they felt like their team was napping on the field.

But when the Cubs woke up, so did Charlie. He groggily arose to the raucous explosion from the crowd just as the home team put two on the board, getting them within a run at 4-3. Chicago had nearly rallied all the way back from Ruth and Gehrig's early homers.

Charlie shook off his headache and again began to stumble toward the corridor, making sure this time not to stop for any stray fruit.

The first door on his left did, indeed, have a picture on it. But it led into the ladies' room. Charlie would just as soon eat slimy popcorn soufflé than get caught in there. He quickly kept moving.

The second door read: **'TRASH.'** There was no picture on it. And besides, the staggering stench oozing from inside was enough to make door number one seem like a pretty good option.

The third read: **'AUTHORIZED PERSONNEL ONLY.'** Below, there was an image of a blueberry muffin, but a strange one. It had two eyes, a mouth and a small pencil-thin mustache. It sure wasn't *pretty*, but Charlie didn't see any other choice.

The door made a fierce creaky noise as he opened it, and only a faint light illuminated the walkway ahead. Charlie held his empty popcorn tray in front of him, slowly moving from the comfort of the crowd to the uncertainty of what was beyond.

As he headed down the hallway, the large door slammed shut behind him, echoing off the concrete walls like booming thunder, sinking him into darkness for what felt like the millionth time that day. Soon, his eyes adjusted and at the end of the long hallway he saw yet another door that appeared equally as heavy and intimidating as the first. **'VISITORS'** was the title on this one. Charlie figured he did, after all, meet that criteria. And besides, it seemed to be the only way out.

He yanked the door with all his might, surprised at its weight. He managed to open it just wide enough to slide through to the other side. It closed hard behind him, but Charlie barely even heard it. He was too distracted by what he saw.

There were lockers lining the walls. Jerseys, pants and hats hung from inside each one. Gloves, bats, balls and helmets were scattered across the ground too. There wasn't popcorn anywhere to be found though, which was a relief to Charlie.

He walked ahead, eyeing the names above the lockers one-by-one, realizing with a swell of excitement what "VISITORS" had meant.

COMBS. CHAPMAN. DICKEY. LAZZERI. SEWELL. CROSETTI. GEHRIG. RUTH.

Then there was a **BANG!** Charlie's knee smacked right into the benches out in front of the lockers, sending him flailing to the ground with a **THUD!**

"Welcome to the Yankees' clubhouse, kid." Charlie looked up through the stars in his eyes. "Gotta watch out for those seats. They'll getcha every time."

Charlie's vision cleared. He stared up at a star—just one this time—the Great Bambino himself, Babe Ruth. The home run king was wiping tomato off his jersey. "It's ruthless out there," he laughed. "But you better believe I'm gonna make it Ruth-ful next time I step to the plate!"

Charlie attempted to laugh, although between the shocking pain in his knee and the awe of the legend before him, all that came out was an awkward squeal.

"Can you believe the way they treat me out there?" Babe wondered, apparently not surprised at all to find a strange kid in his locker room.

Charlie just shook his head as if he understood, and rubbed the side of his face where he, too, had been struck by flying food.

"I wish they would just show a little respect, that's all. It's baseball, for crying out loud. And now, I've got tomato on my mighty pearl white jersey," Babe said as he rubbed the red mark. "But hey, at least it wasn't something like a big bag of peanuts. Now, *that* woulda hurt."

Charlie raised an eyebrow, wondering if it were a coincidence, or if The Babe somehow knew about his own run-in with airborne snacks.

There was a large roar from the crowd. They both looked toward the door that led to the Yankee dugout. "It ain't like the old days at St. Mary's, that's for sure. That was just baseball back in those days, ya know?"

"St. Mary's?" Charlie said, glad his voice sounded normal this time.

Babe smiled at Charlie and chuckled kind of the way Santa Claus might. "Oh, it's back in Baltimore where I grew up. I used to play ball there."

"I try to play ball at Eureka Elementary. Is it anything like that?" Charlie hoped he had something in common with Babe—a guy he always thought of as a mythical creature, more than one who was ever like him.

"I'm sure it is, kid. It's just that I went to school there, *and* I lived there too. I sure didn't want to, but my parents didn't exactly give me a choice. I felt like an orphan. But at least nobody threw anything at me when I played there."

Charlie couldn't believe what he was hearing. And he couldn't believe what he was about to reveal. "I. . . I was an orphan too, Mr. Ruth." It was a secret Charlie almost never talked about. He didn't actually know a whole lot about his real parents—only what he was able to glean from vague conversations with his adoptive ones.

"Call me Babe, son. Or Bambino. Or George. Calling me 'Mr. Ruth' just makes me feel old. I'm not all that ancient, right?"

"More than you could ever know," Charlie mumbled.

"What was that?"

"I, uh, said your age doesn't even show."

"So, you're an orphan, huh?"

Charlie was okay with change of subject. "My mom died shortly after I was born, and all I was told was that my father was off working in the diamond field and couldn't raise me, so I was put up for adoption."

"I'm sorry, kid. I have to say I do understand. Is that why you're selling popcorn? To make a penny?"

"Actually, that's just about all I've made. I'm not sure why I'm selling popcorn to tell you the truth." Charlie rambled on—decidedly unable to stop himself from saying just about anything, given the virtual out-of-body experience he was having. "It's just that this girl Emma and I got in trouble in school, you see. And we got punished and met this guy

Midnight. And then we took a trip in his machine that helped us travel through—"

"Time to bat! Ruth, you're on deck," called a voice from the dugout.

"Looks like I gotta go, kid. Duty calls. And so do 50,000 maniacs. Good luck with the popcorn business."

The slugger turned toward the entrance to the dugout with a huge red stain marked on the side of his pinstriped #3 jersey. Charlie Marley marveled at the fact that he had something else in common with the greatest baseball player of all-time—he, too, regularly had tomato sauce on his own shirt.

"Hey Babe," he called out. "You can't let them get to you. Don't let them psych you out." Charlie recited the advice Emma had given him on the football field. *Was that really only earlier that afternoon?* "You're Babe Ruth. You call the shots out there." Babe nodded. And with that, the legend stepped back in to Game Three of the World Series.

Charlie sat for a moment, realizing that nobody would possibly believe his story.

Up in the press box, Emma was hard at work, trying to figure out why they had ended up in this place, in this time and at this game in particular.

The black box in the corner that Mr. Muffin had pointed to turned out to be a typewriter: wide, heavy, and about the size of a small 3D printer. While it had a keyboard, there was just about no chance anyone would ever mistake it for a laptop. She pressed in the "E" key, and the letter popped up on a piece of paper sticking out of the machine's top. She followed with an "M," another "M" and an "A." And one-by-one, the letters popped up as she struck the keys.

She stopped typing, but before she could think of what to write next, more words continued to pop up on the page—words she definitely did *not* type herself. Below her name read: *Model 15-KSR Type-Bar Page Printer. Pleased to meet you.* Emma stared, open-mouthed. This must be a joke. She looked around to see who was tricking her. But all of the reporters were focused on the game and far enough away that none of them could've been involved.

As she peered back at the typed page, there was more: *Password please.*

Emma wondered again if she were being pranked.

The typewriter repeated itself, asking for the password. And it persistently repeated until Emma finally typed a word just to try to make it stop. But every password attempt she made failed.

She typed "baseball" and "Cubs" and "Yankees" and "World Series" and "Flogtrac" and "1932" and "Emma" and "Charlie" and "Mr. Muffin," even. But it was to no avail.

The machine finally shot back a note: *Three attempts remaining or your message will be deleted forever.*

"Message?" she wondered aloud. "From whom? For what? And why?"

It was then that a roar erupted from the crowd of 50,000 Cubs fans as Chicago tied up the game on a line drive to left field that was missed by a diving Babe Ruth. Emma was too wrapped up in the mystery before her to notice or care.

"Come on, run!" one yelled.

Emma typed in "Run" into the machine. It responded: *Two attempts remaining.*

"Here we come, championship!" blurted another.

Emma typed in "Championship." *One attempt remaining.*

"Eureka! We've found the giant hole in Babe Ruth's glove!" exclaimed a third.

Emma typed in "Eureka" into the machine. It paused.

Congratulations, password accepted.

The machine at long last furiously printed out a message, and when she read it, it nearly shocked her shoes off. "Oh my—"

"Hey," blurted one of the reporters, apparently just seeing her for the first time. "What are you doing in here, little girl?"

Emma looked up to find the entire room of eyes fixed on her. She held tight to the message and cautiously moved to-ward the door. She broke into a run, barely stopping to even open it, leaving a room full of the most articulate writers in the business completely speechless.

She sprinted down the corridor and toward an entrance-way that she hoped would lead her to center field, where she'd last seen Charlie heading. But as she turned the corner, an open door forced her to skid to a stop, just short of running right into it. She nearly had **'AUTHORIZED PERSONNEL ONLY'** imprinted backward on her forehead.

As the door closed, Charlie emerged from the other side. Emma stood there, out of breath, relieved to see a familiar face.

"Just in time, Charlie! You have to see this. I know you'll never believe me, but there was this machine in the press box. And it typed back at me. And it gave me this message. And—"

"Don't worry, Emma," Charlie broke in. "I believe your story—whatever it is. But I don't know if you'll believe mine."

Emma shoved the paper toward him, wordlessly. It was mostly crumpled from her tight grasp.

"It tells us what will happen if the Yankees win the World Series. And what will happen if the Cubs win," Emma explained. "And either way, one of them is doomed."

Charlie examined the message.

The winner of this battle will go on to great riches.
And the other will run into nothing but hitches.
To the victor goes 20 more championships by century's end!
To the loser: a terribly miserable failing trend!

"We've gotta go find Midnight," Emma said. "What if something happens that's not supposed to, and we get trapped in 1932?"

Charlie's eyes widened. "You really think that could happen?"

"I don't *know*, Charlie," Emma cried, exasperated. "But why else do you think we ended up *here* of all places?"

"Oh no, what if we— or the— and I get— I've got to let Babe know!"

Emma looked at him, confused, but there was no time to waste asking questions. She ran off toward the closet where they had left the Flogtrac, hoping she might find Midnight. But when she looked behind her, expecting to see Charlie following, she saw no one.

Charlie started toward the field, hoping he could find Babe Ruth.

"Wait just one moment there, soldier," a familiar voice boomed behind him. It was Colonel Kernel. "Where do you think you're going with that empty tray of popcorn? I thought we made a pact?" Charlie stood stiff as a board. "I thought we were going to go out there and fight, fight, fight! Are you with me, son?"

"Ye. . . yes, sir," muttered Charlie, not sure if he had any other option.

"Aaaalright, then get loaded up." The crazy colonel re-filled his supply. And once again, he was bound for center field with thirty bags of ten-cent popcorn weighing him down by his neck.

He heard the boos exploding from the stands as he neared, which he knew by now, meant there was a star Yankee up to bat. "Ladies and gentlemen, may I have your attention. Now batting for the New York Yankees, number three, Baaaaaaabe Ruth!"

Charlie started to run to the center field bleachers where he might be able to catch The Babe's attention. With every step, the bags of popcorn danced wildly, shedding their contents one buttery piece at a time.

He had made it to right field when Babe got his first strike. The Bambino never even tried to swing, holding up his index finger, indicating the one strike against him.

Charlie was in right-center field by the time strike two had passed him by. The Babe held up two fingers this time, indicating the two strikes against him. *So cool*, Charlie thought as he ran.

Two pitches later, Charlie had made it to center field, with the count reaching two balls and two strikes.

He again found himself dodging fruit and vegetables, popcorn and peanuts. He was waving his arms at Babe, trying to somehow indicate that the history of the Yankees depended on him. And that Charlie, Emma and Midnight's fate just might too. Babe would go down as a colossal fool—not the heralded hero—if he and his teammates let their guard down and allowed the Cubs to rally.

Babe stepped away from the plate to take a practice swing, and the boos grew to deafening levels. Charlie was still trying to get his attention.

"Hey, kid, I'll take two." Popcorn Charlie had a repeat customer in the center field stands. "Hey kid, **NOW!**" The last thing Charlie wanted to do was to give the man more ammunition to throw onto the field, but his tone told Charlie that he might not even make it back to the Flogtrac in one piece if he didn't deliver.

With a scowl and in a hurry, Charlie started down the stairs to the fan. But he barely made it halfway there. His foot caught on the tip of a cane somebody had left sticking out in the walkway, and he tumbled head-first down the stairs.

Popcorn spewed everywhere, landing in large part on the man who called for it in the first place. Charlie flew past him, coming to rest near the bottom of the bleachers, covered in bruises, bumps and butter. This really was *not* his day, was it?

Babe Ruth, it turned out, saw the whole thing from the trip, to the toss, to the tumble and called attention toward Charlie. The fans' boos and hisses increased as he pointed his finger toward center field. And the debris doubled.

"Is that little guy okay out there?" Babe asked.

Charlie peeked over the outfield wall toward home plate. He could hear Babe's voice, oddly magnified in his head. Looking around, he realized he was probably the only one who could—from this far away, anyway.

"Which little guy?" the umpire responded.

"That little guy up there in center, Doofus," Babe pointed again. "Did you see the fall he took?" He emphatically shook his finger toward the center field wall, but the umpire couldn't care less.

"I don't see anything, let's play ball!"

"Yeah, that's a surprise," muttered The Bambino, "A blind ump. Who woulda thunk it?"

Charlie watched Babe step back into the batter's box just as the pitcher wound back and delivered the ball. As quick as the pitch came, it took even less time to leave the park.

CRACK!

The ball exploded off Babe's bat with the force of a launching rocket. He sent it farther than any ball that had ever been hit in Wrigley Field's history.

It traveled nearly four hundred fifty feet straight to center field—directly over Charlie's head and into the bleachers behind him.

Charlie got up and brushed himself off as the fans scrambled for the ball. It was then that he realized he had done it—he had somehow ensured that The Babe hit his legendary home run, and that he'd pointed exactly to where he was going to send it.

The **"BOOS"** turned into **"OOOHS"** as the fans noted not only the unbelievable distance of the home run, but also how Babe had just called his shot with his definitive and energetic point to center field.

As Charlie got back to his feet, he saw The Great Bambino look right at him, winking as he rounded second base and headed for third.

"Did that just happen?!" Charlie said aloud to no one in particular, not that he would've been heard anyway. The raucous crowd made it hard enough for him to hear himself.

But he could see plenty, including Colonel Kernel angrily waving his arms and charging toward him from the left field stands. He must have seen the fall, Charlie thought. And he must have seen his popcorn blanket the center field stands, too.

Charlie started to inch the other direction. He was out of popcorn and just about out of his mind if he didn't think he had to move quick. He headed toward the corridor, where Emma and Midnight appeared, out of breath and waiting.

"Did you see what just—" Charlie blurted.

"We don't have time, Charlie," interrupted Emma. "I think we have bigger issues."

Midnight stood next to her, wearing a Yankee uniform. "I know what you're thinking Charlie. But no, I didn't hit that great home run."

"That's not exactly what I was—"

"I know, I know. I was just standing by in case the old coach needed an extra bat or an extra arm in the clutch. You know."

Emma rolled her eyes, and shook her head, leading the way back toward the janitor's closet.

"Midnight found something that might be of major importance," Emma told Charlie as they ran.

"I was working on the Flogtrac," Midnight explained, "checking on the electrosensogram and the uberbooger-mover, trying to figure out exactly why we kinda missed our target."

"*Kinda* missed our target?" repeated Charlie. "We overshot it by more than six decades! That's more than 'kinda.'"

Midnight glared at Charlie like he'd just sneezed in his snow cone. "Well, kiddo, I was working on *fixing* our little mishap, when I noticed that my beeper was flashing and the timer was counting down. I think it means we better get outta here." He pulled up a small, but complex machine that was attached to his belt.

"Where did you get that?" Charlie asked, looking at the strange little box.

"Some funny tall dude gave it to me. He told me to treat it well and it would do the same to me. I'm not sure what he meant, but I like the way it sparkles."

Charlie stopped in his tracks, much to Emma's annoyance.

"Can I take a look at that?" Midnight handed the mini machine to Charlie and he noticed that the sparkles and lights were actually indicating a new message.

He pressed the flashing button.

Move on. Time is running down. Move on to another time and town!

"What did the man look like who gave this to you, Midnight?" Emma asked, having come to inspect the message, too.

"I don't know. He was tall and lanky with some silly round black top hat and a cane."

"Did he have a small pencil-thin mustache?" asked Emma.

"Oh yeah! And boy, a silly one at that."

"How about a weird French accent?" asked Charlie, with realization rising in his chest.

"Oh, unforgettable! I could barely understand a word he said. Why, do you know him?"

Charlie looked at Emma and Emma looked at Charlie. They cried out together and at once, "Monsieur Moofyay!"

Who was that guy?!

CHAPTER 5

THE BEAT OF A DIFFERENT DRUM

harlie, Emma and Midnight rushed toward the janitor's closet. Charlie's popcorn tray banged against his belt with each step he took.

CLANK! CLANK! CLANK!

Emma's top hat nearly flew off her head. And Midnight's not-so-snug jersey flapped wildly in the wind.

They were just steps away, when one of Charlie's feet crossed with the other, and he flailed out-of-control into Midnight, causing both of them to tumble. They slid to a stop six inches away from the room that held their ticket home.

"SAAAFe!" announced an umpire, who was walking by on his way to the concession stand.

Emma hopped lightly over the Charlie Marley-Midnight McLean tangle and pushed open the door.

Charlie scrambled up and peeked inside the room first. He saw nothing there.

Emma bravely walked into the blackness and pulled the cord from the ceiling. Once again, there was light, which shined down on the Flogtrac sitting in the middle of the room and also revealed Emma's smug expression.

"Oh," said Charlie, feeling himself turning the color of a ripe tomato.

"Let's get a move on, kiddos," Midnight said, shutting the door behind him as Charlie and Emma took their seats in the back of what was once just a souped-up golf cart. The Flogtrac was ready for its next journey, which Midnight swore would land them on target once and for all.

He flipped the dials. He punched the computer buttons with more fervor than before. "I think I've got it this time. Let's buckle up. Seatbelts, boys and girls!"

He switched a knob, twisted a lever and turned the key in the ignition. The Flogtrac roared like a famished tiger. "Here we go!" A plume of black smoke rushed out of the back of the car filling their nostrils with the smell of a dirty chimney stack.

The mop buckets, brooms and cleaning equipment that they needed to go through were in the corner of the closet, very inconveniently *not* directly in front of them.

"Hang on, kiddos. We'll be there before you know it." Midnight looked over his shoulder at the blank wall behind

Charlie and Emma's heads. He backed up ever-so-slightly, moving the Flogtrac just two inches back. He quickly looked to the front and moved it barely three inches forward. Again, he looked back over his shoulder and reversed the steering wheel, backing up another couple inches. And again forward. And again back.

The beeper rang out. Emma crossed her arms and gave Midnight her best *Can We Hurry This Up?* look. He turned away, and continued the thirty-three-point turn to get the Flogtrac facing the right direction.

"Alrighty! Here we go. Are we ready?" Before Charlie or Emma could even think to respond, Midnight hit the accelerator, again trusting the Theory of Bop Mucket Continuumumum.

There was no time to react. They hit the corner and flew through that familiar bluish force field, producing a **SPARK**, a **BOOM** and a **BAM!**

They were back in the long winding tunnel, twisting and turning at an incredible rate of speed with the astonishing multi-colored scenery serving as their backdrop, as it had before. Midnight, however, was more concerned with the vision *ahead* of him—the double-vision, that is. The winding pathway was about to divide in two, and the split was quickly approaching.

"What to do, what to do?" he yelped. "Which way should we go? I haven't a clue!"

Charlie and Emma snapped out of their wonderment, suddenly focused on the dubious dilemma.

"Wait, what's up?" asked Emma.

"Goodness, if I only knew!"

"Whatever direction you choose, we're down," Charlie offered in support, sounding more certain than he felt. Wasn't Midnight supposed to know where they were going?

"Up? Down?" Midnight swerved the Flogtrac, nearly jackknifing it at the fork in the road. But by some intergalactic miracle, they stayed in one piece. "You went left, right?" Emma asked.

"Wrong!"

The tunnel ended abruptly as another bluish force field appeared seemingly out of nowhere and swallowed them up.

SHWOOP!

They wondered if that right turn were really the correct one.

The incredible number of sparkling lights that zoomed by let them know they appeared to at least be on the verge of *some* destination. But whether they'd wind up in the *right* place, *left* in limbo, *up* a creek, or *down* the drain remained to be seen.

SHWOOP!

They were there. Somewhere. In pitch blackness. Again.

There was something different this time, however. "What *is* that smell?" Charlie asked disgustedly, posing the question that each of them was thinking.

"That *is* gnarly, Charlie," Emma agreed. Her voice sounded like it was coming from the inside of a balloon as she pinched her nostrils closed.

"Do you guys see where the light string is?" Midnight asked.

"We don't see *anything*, Midnight," Charlie said as he reached around for a pull string to turn on the light.

"I don't feel anything either," said Emma, her voice back to normal as she took her fingers off her nose long enough to search.

"Looking for this?" asked a scratchy voice from the dark. The lights turned on and Midnight, Charlie and Emma blinked, as they struggled to adjust to the brightness, their arms still suspended in the air. "Are you guys doing the Thriller dance? If only, like, we had a totally radical boombox to rock out on."

They all lowered their hands, and looked around for the source of the voice.

"D'ya have a permit to park there?" the voice uttered with a chuckle. As their vision cleared, they saw a man wearing headphones and an aged rainbow visor with a neon green see-through brim. He walked away from the light switch and back to the pile of uniforms he'd apparently been folding.

"For heaven's sake, sir, what *is* that stench?" griped Midnight, stepping out of the Flogtrac.

"The name's Coach Stinkysox," the man said in a voice that was both gruff and tough. "That stench is yesterday's laundry. And the day before that's laundry. And the day before that's, too."

Midnight looked around at a room full of dirty jerseys, pants, pads and helmets. Emma returned her fingers to her nose.

"Killer car, dudes and dudette," noted Coach Stinkysox. "I've been hoping to get one of those Trans Ams myself." It didn't seem like he cared that a giant car had just landed in his equipment room.

Midnight did a double-take and turned back toward the Flogtrac. It was no longer the incredible vintage 1932 Chevy Imperial with wheels atop the sideboards, nor the golf cart he intended it to be in the first place. It was a much sportier fire-red Pontiac Trans Am with a giant bird painted across the front hood.

Emma took one look at Charlie and collapsed to the floor in laughter before Midnight could find an answer to how the Flogtrac had, yet again, transformed. She was snickering and snorting and rolling around like she had just swallowed a crazy pill.

"What is it?" asked Charlie. "Have you lost your mind?"

"If you could only see yourself!"

Charlie peered down cautiously, noticing a bright-red jacket that nearly matched the color of the transformed Flogtrac. The apron was gone. The popcorn tray was too. But in their place was a flashy blazer, bow tie and—he reached up yet again to his head—a tall, white fuzzy hat atop his messy brown hair.

"What happened to me, now?!" he cried, wondering why he was always the one stuck with the worst outfit.

"I don't know, but you look like the Nutcracker," she snickered. "BUM ba ba ba bum bum BA BA BA BUM!" She mimicked The Nutcracker March, waving her fingers back-and-forth like an orchestra leader.

"Yeah, well what about you? You look like you're one of the Men in Black."

Emma stopped humming on the spot and discovered the black tie, black pants and black round hat atop her own head.

"You guys all look like you're a little behind schedule," interrupted Coach Stinkysox.

"Schedule?" Emma repeated.

"And what, exactly, makes you think that?" asked Midnight suspiciously.

"Well, the second-half kickoff's just minutes away, and looking at Nutcracker boy over there, I'd assume he's got somewhere to be."

Charlie tried to keep his big hat from toppling over.

"Kickoff?" asked Midnight. "Don't you mean *first pitch?*"

"Well, if you're looking for the first pitch, then you're early," the coach replied. Midnight let out a deep sigh of relief.

"By about four months."

"What do you mean, Stinkybooty?"

"It's Stinky*sox*," the old coach replied, shooting an angry look at Midnight. "And what I mean is that the only season that matters around these parts right now involves the old pigskin." He handed Midnight a damp newspaper from under a pile of dirty jerseys. "Baseball season's quite a ways away."

Midnight's eyes watered at the sight of the paper. It may have been because of the revolting scent in the room. Or, it may have been because of the date above the headline: *November 20, 1982*. They'd missed their target yet again.

The headline read: **THE 85ᵀᴴ BIG GAME**

"How could this be?" he wondered aloud.

"Well, it happens every year, dude. The Stanford University Cardinal. The Cal Bears. It's called 'The Big Game' for a reason. The best college football rivalry in all the land, if you ask me."

"I didn't ask you, Stinkyfeet. What I want to know is how we could have missed 1994 again."

Nobody had an answer for him, although a loud commotion from outside the room overtook the silence. Charlie curiously strolled past Coach Stinkysox and reached for the door handle. "Shall we?" he asked as he turned toward Midnight and Emma. An increasingly noisy swishing of shuffling feet came from the other side of the door.

"What do you think, Stinkyshoes?" asked Midnight.

"I think you guys better get out there before you miss The Big Game altogether."

"Well, we wouldn't want to do that, now would we?" sniped Midnight, visibly disappointed. "Go for it, Charlie.

What have we got to lose, but time? And our minds? And our way?"

Charlie, stoic in his blazer, bow tie and tall hat, cranked open the door to the sight of people marching by: some dressed in Stanford cardinal and white, and some dressed in California gold and blue. Midnight and Emma inched up behind him.

"Who's going first?" Charlie asked, already knowing that the answer would be him.

Emma quickly responded, "I think The Nutcracker should have the first act. All in favor, say 'aye.'"

"I—" Charlie started to protest, but before he could finish, he was nudged helplessly into the flow of the crowd and swept away like a tiny piece of driftwood in the rapids of a flooding river.

"AYE, YAI YAIIII!" Charlie's voice disappeared as fast as he did.

Emma and Midnight tried to keep Charlie in sight, but it was no use.

"Wait a sec," said Midnight, as if a light turned on in his head. "*The Big Game?* 1982? The band?! Oh, I wonder if Charlie knows what he's getting himself into."

Emma looked at him, wondering what it was that he was realizing about this game in particular.

"It's a zoo out there," muttered Coach Stinkysox before she could ask, as he folded another jersey.

"Yeah, well it *smells* like a zoo in here, Coach Stinky-poo. I honestly don't think I can take it anymore." Midnight jumped through the doorway, and just like Charlie, was whisked away by the crowd, leaving Emma alone in yet another decade, with yet another mystery to unravel. What was their purpose *this* time?

"What about you, little lady? Aren't you gonna hop out of here too?"

"I'm not quite sure," Emma said, still holding her nose and sounding like a munchkin chipmunk. "Any suggestions?"

"If you want the grand look. . . the best seat in the house . . . the big view of The Big Game, then I've got the answer to all your problems. The answer is. . ."

Emma waited for Stinkysox to finish his thought, impatiently. "Yes?"

"Great. Right this way, then." The coach dropped a pile of neatly-folded uniforms and led her to the opposite side of the room. He pushed a little green button on the wall and—like a secret passageway—a section of bricks raised up right before them. Behind it, two sliding glass doors opened horizontally, leading to an elevator. "Ladies first."

Emma tentatively stepped in first and he followed.

"Going up!" He pressed one of the dozens of buttons on the wall, and the doors shut them in. The elevator shuddered, then rocketed up and Emma finally took her fingers off her nose in order to hold on for dear life.

"Take a look." Coach Stinkysox pointed behind her.

The back wall of the elevator was all glass, and through it they could see a packed stadium with tens of thousands of fans waving pennants, banners and signs.

Emma looked down to the cheerleaders, marching bands and mascots. The elevator came to a screeching halt, and she held tight to the railing before the momentum could shoot her right through the roof.

"We're here," Stinkysox announced.

"Well, you're right. This probably is the best seat in the house, Coach," Emma said, marveling at her surroundings.

"This isn't your seat. *That* is." He pointed through the opening elevator doors. She turned around to a now familiar, yet still awe-inspiring sight. "Enjoy the game. Just make sure you check out that super-cool gizmo over there. It's brand new. Most awesomely radical thing since the answering machine." He nodded over to the corner at a large rounded monitor attached to a keyboard below. "And one more thing: don't forget where you came from, Ms. Mayfield. And don't forget who helped you get here!"

Emma stepped out through the doors to the press box. She was still taken aback by the massive room of reporters: some furiously punching away at typewriters and others mulling through papers and media guides.

She flipped around. "Wait a second. Now how did *you* know my name was—" But the doors had closed, and Coach Stinkysox had disappeared behind them. This had a familiar feeling, she thought, as she headed toward the old-fashioned computer in the corner of the room.

The momentum of the crowd had led Charlie down the corridor of the stadium like a leaf in a flooded gutter, until he was finally able to work his way out of the flow and into an opening. Finally able to catch his breath, Charlie adjusted his hat, straightened his jacket and turned down a walkway, which had a light at the end of the tunnel.

With every step he took, the sound of a roaring crowd amplified. And with every step, the walkway became brighter, too.

JINGLE... JINGLE... JINGLE.

His movement also had a certain ring to it. Charlie looked down at his shoes to find both covered in bells. He shook one foot:

JINGLE... JINGLE.

And the other:

JINGLE... JINGLE.

It had been too loud in the corridor to hear them before, but now he took a few steps forward and shook each foot around.

Charlie was still looking down when his fuzzy hat rammed right into what felt like a brick wall. Looking up, Charlie realized that it was, in fact, not a brick wall. It was the backside of a giant.

The giant turned around. "Watch it there, kid."

"I'm so sorry. It... it was an accident," stammered Charlie.

"Eh, just watch where you're going, huh?" The giant man was wearing colossal shoulder pads, holding a football in one hand and a white helmet in the other that seemed about the size of Charlie's entire torso. There was a number 7 on his chest. "Sorry to be so jumpy," he continued, easing his tone. "Just a little on edge, that's all."

Charlie suddenly realized he was face-to-face—or, more specifically, face-to-hip—with the quarterback of the Stanford football team. *Wow.*

"Elway, you ready to lead us?" barked a coach from the end of the tunnel that led out to the football field.

"Ready to go, Coach!" he responded.

Elway, Charlie thought. *Elway...* Is this *the* John Elway? He looked up again, and recognized the guy he'd seen on television countless times, only now looking a lot younger than Charlie remembered.

"So, what exactly are *you* worried about?" Charlie wondered, pushing his fuzzy hat up off his eyes.

"It's my last game of my senior year. I just want to go out a winner, that's all. Didn't help that we couldn't even score in the first half. But to come back on these guys will make it even sweeter." John began to pace back-and-forth, visibly itching to return to the field.

"Then what are you waiting for?" asked Charlie, still unable to believe that this was now *two* pep talks he'd given to legends he'd only read about in books, or seen on TV.

A voice rumbled over the stadium loudspeakers. "Ladies aaaaand gentlemen, the Stanford Cardinal!"

"*That's* what I'm waiting for!" John said, giving Charlie a tap on the side of the shoulder that nearly knocked him off his bell-covered feet. "Just make sure you do your part! I'll lead my guys on the field. You lead your guys on the sidelines." The Cardinal quarterback skipped and took off out of the tunnel.

"Do *my part?*" Charlie didn't know what the big guy meant, but had little time to think about it before a new stampede of comparably-sized giants charged into the tunnel, making the Running of the Bulls seem like the Westminster Kennel Club Dog Show. Charlie clung to the wall as they took their spots, ready to return to the field.

He turned around and stood eye-to-eye with a golden-colored thigh pad. He looked up to another monster-sized mass of pads and helmet.

"Are *you* gonna try to stop us now?" laughed the man behind the gear. "I guess *they* couldn't do it out there, so *you're* their only hope."

Charlie swallowed hard as he stared up at a group of men, each of whom could have crushed him with a pinky.

"Don't worry about him," boomed another player from Charlie's other side, as the rest of the team distracted themselves by slapping hands and smashing their helmets into each other.

"Who are you?" asked Charlie, trying to understand what he'd gotten himself into.

"I'm Kevin Moen. It's my last game playing for the Cal Bears. That guy's still got more football ahead of him," he said, pointing at the especially-intimidating player. "Another year here for the school. Maybe a shot at the pros. For some of us, though, this is it." Kevin wore a large gold number twenty-six across his chest and a blue helmet that matched the jersey.

Charlie looked up, still overwhelmed by his size. "Well, I guess when you get to the end, then it's all behind you, huh?"

"Yup, it'll all be behind me, that's for sure. Let's just hope we get the job done here."

The announcer's voice again boomed over the loudspeakers. "Ladies and Gentlemen, *your* California Golden Bears!"

The grunting and cheering from the players became as rowdy as a pack of actual wild bears.

"You keep up the good work," added number 26. "I can't tell you I like your songs, but I do like your energy. After all, the band makes the game what it is."

And with that, the pack of University of California Golden Bears dashed through the tunnel, sending much of the crowd of 80,000 into a frenzy.

Charlie gripped the wall, yet again, clinging on until the very last player had stormed by.

And then it hit him: **THE BAND?!**

Charlie walked toward the football field, where it became quite clear he was going to have to lead the Stanford band. A young woman, who looked as outrageously dressed as Nut-cracker Charlie, made her way right toward him. It truly was a fashionably-frightful sight.

"Where've you been?" she asked. "I've got the band all set. The halftime show was a hit, and the second half is on. Let's get out there, Disco Charlie."

"*Disco* Charlie?" he shot back.

"Well, it'll be more like *Dead Man* Charlie if you don't get out there quick," she insisted. "The band is getting restless. They just started playing *Itsy Bitsy Teeny Weeny Yellow Polka Dot Bikini*. I don't even want to know what's next!"

"As long as it's not *Who Let the Dogs Out*, I don't care" Charlie said, staring up at the band.

"Dogs? What dogs? I didn't let out any dogs. Who let what dogs out?"

Right, thought Charlie, *it's 1982.*

They walked around the field, inside the sea of blue and gold California fans. Charlie looked across the stadium to the red and white section of Stanford fans, noticeably fewer in number, but loud and spirited nevertheless. Their colors matched those on Charlie's outfit.

An earsplitting roar came from the left, as a section of fans stood up and threw their arms into the air. Then, the section next to them did the same. And group-by-group, the raucous flurry neared them, until it passed by and on in the other direction.

"Weird, huh?" the assistant asked. "It's the cool new thing to do at ballgames. It's called *The Wave*."

"The Wave? Of course I know—"

"Look," she interrupted, "I've gone over all the signals with the band. Remember, hands on the head means we play the fight song. Reach your hands out to the sides and flutter your fingers for *All Right Now*. That comes after we score."

"Flutter my fingers?" Charlie repeated. He had only been half listening, as he watched The Wave move around the stadium.

"And don't forget, put your arms up in 'V' for victory. That's when we all go onto the field to celebrate our win," she explained. "Come on, Disco Charlie. You know this stuff. Time to be part of Stanford history. After all, this is The Big Game!"

"So I've heard," Charlie said absentmindedly.

She gave Charlie a friendly shove in the back, inadvertently sending him tumbling to the ground. Again. And in a cloud of dust, he rolled to the base of a staircase leading up to a platform that rose above the band. For the second time, Charlie was actually glad he was wearing that tall fuzzy white top hat. It saved him quite the headache.

Being a drum major wasn't as hard as Charlie anticipated. The band virtually played on its own. It played when he itched his head. It played when he stretched his arms. He wasn't exactly sure why, but his job appeared mostly effortless.

Charlie waved his hands up and down and in and out, like how he had seen in the movies. Sometimes the band would play for what seemed like forever. But he went with it. His arms would eventually tire out, and the songs would subsequently end, usually trailing off in a hodgepodge of mishmashed static.

Up in the press box, Emma was on a mission to again figure out why they'd landed where they had.

The *gizmo* that Coach Stinkysox urged her to check out was an old-school computer. It had a large monitor attached to a keyboard, but looked more like it belonged in an antique shop. She noticed the digits on the screen in large white font on a blue background. She read the top of the keyboard: *Commodore 64*. Coach Stinkysox insisted it was brand new. Oh, how times had changed.

As Emma reached for the letters on the keyboard, the screen sent out a message of its own. *Welcome to 1982, Emma.* She jumped back. She still wasn't used to these talking typing machines. *Password, please.*

Emma remembered the password from the 1932 World Series: *Eureka.* It had taken her a while that time, but she was on top of it this go-round. She typed the word in.

Sorry, try again. She tried *eureka* in all lower case. Then, in all UPPER CASE. Then, oNe LeTtEr LoWeR aNd OnE lEtTeR uPpEr. That didn't work either.

She remembered what Coach Stinkysox told her: *Don't forget where you came from. And don't forget who helped you get here.* They'd come from Chicago, and Mr. Muffin had helped along the way, but it was Babe Ruth's heroics that made it all possible.

So, she entered *Babe*, and that sent the large printer sitting next to the Commodore into a fury. The printer screeched and shrieked and shook, painstakingly printing out. . . one . . . single . . . page.

Emma took a close look at the printout, discovering another potentially dubious fate. This time, the message focused on the quarterback for Stanford. Number 7. The Heisman Trophy candidate. John Elway.

A sudden eruption from the crowd diverted her attention from the sheet in her hand. Elway had just led Stanford to a touchdown. She had to act quick.

With the rest of the media men distracted, Emma made her escape through the press box elevator hidden behind the brick wall. Only as the doors closed did she get a perplexed glance from a confused reporter. "Good giggly grapes! Stop the presses! Did that girl just—"

The door shut before she heard another word.

The elevator took her to field level, where she looked to track down Charlie. She scoured the sidelines, searching for the red jacket and white fuzzy hat. It wasn't as hard as she thought it'd be.

An entire section of Charlie clones were standing together playing their music at the base of the Stanford cheering section. Each was dressed in Cardinal red and white, though most wore smaller white hardhats covered in duct tape instead of Nutcracker fur. But that wasn't even the worst part. From short ties to bow ties to polka dotted plaid ones, each person's neck decoration was worse than the next.

Emma went toward the odd-looking group where, sure enough, Charlie stood on the platform, paying noticeably more attention to the game than to the band he was supposed to be leading.

"Charlie! We have to do something."

"Well, hello there, Emma. Have you got the beat? Because, I sure got the beat. I've got the rhythm. I've got the music!" He waved his arms up and down and threw them around, and the band began to play. "And, by the way, it's *Disco* Charlie to you."

Emma sighed. What the heck had gotten into him? She gave him one of her patented piercing looks, impatient with his antics. "You have to take a look at this, *Dorky* Charlie." She handed him the paper from the Commodore 64.

The senior QB has gotten this far,
But can he become a true superstar?
Take note, you must.
A win for the Cardinal, and Elway's a bust.
But if it's a loss in the Big Game, you see,
Cue the band. Big John's a Hall of Famer to be.

"Elway: a bust? A Hall of Famer?" Charlie blurted out. "I can't say there's a better quarterback these eyes have ever seen." Of course, Charlie's basis of comparison was lisping Rocky on the Eureka Elementary playing field.

"It looks like if John Elway leads Stanford to a win here, he could ruin his entire career. But if he doesn't, he's bound for greatness."

"That makes about as much sense as untying your shoe-laces so you *don't* trip," said Charlie, using an analogy he understood better than anyone.

"A win here," interrupted a familiar scratchy voice, "and they're headed to a bowl game. Elway will win the Heisman Trophy. He'll have hit his peak." Coach Stinkysox stood right behind them. He was leaning up against the wall of the stands, staring out at the field. "But if he loses today, it will be another story. Another year without a bowl game. A crummy future for the program. He'll fall short of the Heisman. And. . . he'll have even more reason to prove himself in the pros."

"Well, we can't let him win," Emma insisted. "It will ruin him. Do something, Dopey Charlie."

"I won't do a thing if you don't get my name right." Charlie righteously pounced back up the stairs to his podium, leaving Emma behind.

She turned to Coach Stinkysox, but he was gone.

"I guess we're on our own, Emma. What do you expect me to do, anyway?"

"You'll think of *something*," Emma said, and she believed it—after all, Charlie had already come through in the clutch once before, for Babe Ruth. Then again, technically that was 50 years ago.

There was less than a minute on the clock—fifty-three seconds to be exact. John Elway and Stanford were down on their own thirteen yard line, trailing by two points, facing 4th down and 17. As far as Charlie was concerned, they didn't stand a chance anyway.

But as he watched, what once seemed impossible suddenly became doable. The Stanford quarterback dropped back to pass, firing over the middle to a receiver at the forty yard line for an extraordinary first down to keep their hopes alive.

Charlie couldn't believe it, and neither could the other 80,000 fans in the stadium. He gripped his head with both hands in disbelief. And, in response, the band let out its loudest version of its favorite earsplitting fight song, nearly shocking the jingling bells right off Disco Charlie's shoes.

In the midst of the drive, the last thing he was expecting—or wanting—was any more music out of his band.

After two more plays, Stanford was all the way down the field, inside the twenty.

Charlie couldn't stand to see Elway win the game and ruin his future. He quickly turned to his band. "Taps!" he yelled out. "Hit it!"

The band members turned to each other in shock. Even this, it seemed, was too weird for them.

"I said hit it!" On cue, they broke out into the rowdiest and most rambunctious version of a song more fitting for a funeral than a football game. He thought it might send the right message to the star quarterback.

Disco Charlie turned to wave his arms at Elway, but it was too late. The QB was already headed off the field, yielding to the field goal kicker to come on and finish the job. He had led a remarkable drive, leaving only eight seconds on the clock.

The future of the guy with the golden arm rested on the leg of the kicker. But that fate seemed sealed as the ball was booted, and sailed right through the middle of the uprights. The field goal put Stanford up, 20-19 with just four seconds remaining.

"Why? Why? Why?" asked Charlie, looking up to the sky; his arms extended at his sides, accentuated with fluttering fingers. The band started its famous post-scoring celebration song as they all moved forward from their seats and down to the edge of the field.

The fans of the Cardinal jumped up and down, dancing and singing, celebrating what would be a sure victory in just four tiny seconds.

The ball was kicked off, and four seconds turned into three, two, one and zero. The kick went short, ending up in the hands of Cal's #26, Kevin Moen, who Charlie recognized from the tunnel. This was to be the final play of his football career, but he had no plans of going down without a fight.

Moen took the ball forward like he was ready to run through a brick wall. But when that brick wall—made up of Stanford's entire eleven—approached, all he could do was toss the ball behind him to another Bear in gold and blue. The teammate took it ahead just a few feet before he, too, was about to be tackled. He tossed it back, and one lateral toss turned into another. And then another. It was a game of cat and mouse, and Cal's team was doing its best job of playing keep-away.

Each Cal player, just before getting tackled, threw the ball backward to keep the play—and their microscopic hopes of winning The Big Game—alive.

Charlie, like everyone else in the stadium, could barely believe the sight in front of him. He threw his arms up in the air in anticipation of what might be a miracle in the making, but the 'V' formation of his arms did more than just that. It sent yet another unplanned signal to his band—this time, that a victory was to be celebrated.

'V' for victory was not what Disco Charlie had intended, but as the band started to move past him, he was reminded of his assistant's advice: *That's when we all go onto the field to celebrate our win.*

The latest Cal ball handler ran toward their side of the field. And the band moved ahead, oblivious to the fact that they were on the playing field. Thanks to Charlie's order, the band—one trumpet, trombone and drum set at a time—was on the football field, and **RIGHT IN THE MIDDLE OF THE ACTION!**

Disco Charlie's arms remained in the air, frozen in fright.

It became quickly apparent that if the Stanford football team couldn't tackle Cal's returners, maybe Charlie's musical team could. The band members advanced through the playing field like lemmings on a cliff. Regardless of their fate, they were going to follow their leader's orders.

The sea of Cardinal red and white band members, and the wild goose chase developing with the Cal kick return team, made for a setting of astonishing anarchy.

A perfect storm was brewing, and the two disasters were about to collide. The only consolation for most of the band members was that they were at least wearing their own headgear.

Nearly tackled, the latest Cal player with the ball blindly tossed it over his head in one final hope of desperation. It could have landed out of bounds. It could have landed on the ground. It could have landed in a French horn. But almost magically, the ball dropped directly into the hands of Kevin Moen once again.

Moen had just twenty-five yards to go now, and the only thing that was going to stop him was maybe a sidestepping saxophone or a ferocious flute. He had surpassed the Stanford team, but still had to get through the Stanford band. He navigated right through the sea of Cardinal red blazers and shiny musical instruments, and zigzagged in for the touchdown, finally colliding with one of Charlie's trombone players in the end zone.

As it turns out, Trombone Gary was just about as close as anyone to tackling a Cal player on the play.

Charlie quickly shuffled his feet toward the tunnel to exit the field, trying not to call any attention to himself. The jingling of his shoes didn't help, but the deafening cheers and jeers from around the stadium drowned everything out anyway, including the **BOOM** of a cannon shot that celebrated the Cal score.

"Did you see that?" Emma crowed, halting Charlie in his tracks. "That was unbelievable! Elway has his future. Can you stand it?!"

Charlie had turned the color of a snowman with a milk mustache.

"What is it, Dippy Charlie?"

"Nothing," he muttered, looking over at the pandemonium he'd caused on the field. "It's just. . . I think I did *that*."

"Maybe we should get out of here," Emma suggested, grabbing his arm. It was more than a suggestion, really.

As they turned in to the tunnel, they saw a familiar face. Midnight had wide eyes and an even wider grin. "Oh my goodness!" he shouted. "That was seriously like the most amazing, sensational, dramatic, heart-rending, exciting, thrilling finish—"

"Are you done yet?" Charlie interrupted. "I'm not quite sure it was supposed to happen that way." His eyes remained almost glazed over, as if he had just seen a ghost. "And it was my fault."

"Oh, let me assure you, it *was* supposed to happen that way," Midnight insisted. "It's been many years, but I've seen that play before. I never imagined what it would be like to see it in person though. It was **UN-REAL!** And it was spectacular! And now we know *you* are the reason why!"

Looking over at the chaos still rampant on the field, Charlie wasn't convinced he hadn't majorly screwed up.

"Midnight, what are you wearing?" Emma interrupted, realizing he had a Cal Bears' jersey with a giant number twenty-six across his chest.

"I grabbed it off that Cal dude running off the field," Midnight announced proudly. "Looks pretty snazzy, huh?" He pointed at his chest and nodded in hopes that they would agree.

"It looks about seven times too big," said Emma with a raised eyebrow.

"Yeah, well so does Charlie's hat, but we're not telling *him* that, now are we?"

The tunnel was jam-packed with players, coaches and officials, all immersed in the same debate. Nobody listened. Everyone spoke. Each of them with an opinion about what just happened. It looked like the floor of the New York Stock Exchange.

Through the sea of people, a security guard was giving them an evil look. Before anyone could say anything, Midnight's pager screamed out a piercingly-loud alarm that was audible even over the blaring arguments before them.

Ready for a bam, or a spark, or a boom?
Time to return to the smelly, smelly room!

"Saved by the bell. Off we go, kiddos!" Midnight shouted, grabbing Emma and Charlie by the elbows and giving the security guard a nervous look.

The guard continued to stare intently in their direction as they made their way back to the Flogtrac. It appeared their work there was done.

The time traveling trio scooted through the crowd in the tunnel and back to the odorous equipment room.

They held their noses as Midnight opened the door to the closet. It still smelled like it might be doubling as a toxic waste dump. The Flogtrac sat in the middle of the room, just as they had left it. Coach Stinkysox was stacking shoulder pads in the corner and dancing to whatever was playing on his headphones.

"*Should I stay or should I go?*" he sang off key, apparently oblivious to their return.

Midnight strapped himself in the front seat of the Flogtrac and immediately began punching buttons and turning dials. Charlie and Emma hopped in the back and prepared to leave 1982 behind, hopeful that they might get to a more intentionally-desired year for once.

"*If you go, there will be trouble. But if you stay, it will be double!*" Coach Stinkysox sang, still in his own world. He turned toward the travelers and addressed them directly. "Really, I'm not just saying that. You've got to get outta here!"

"Well, that isn't very nice," Emma responded.

"Yeah, Stinkysinger," added Midnight, not even looking up from the Flogtrac computer.

"Listen, dudes and dudette. You've got trouble on the way, and you don't have much time. So hit the road, Jack!"

There was a loud **BANG! BANG! BANG!** coming from the outside corridor. Coach Stinkysox leapt to the door, holding it closed with everything he had.

"Quick, Midnight, hit it!" yelled Charlie. His tall headgear nearly toppled over as he jutted forward.

"Seatbelts, boys and girls!" Midnight tapped the keyboard, pushed keys on the navigation system, switched a knob, punched a button, twisted a lever and turned the key in the ignition. The huge puff of smoke that discharged from the back of the Flogtrac shot right at Coach Stinkysox, who struggled with the door, as it began to open.

"Get going! Quickly!" His voice went high-pitched, and combined with a smoky cough, sounded something like an angry alien elf.

They started straight for the mop buckets, vacuums and brooms piled right between two piles of dirty jerseys that stacked up to the ceiling.

"Thanks for everything, Stinkycheese."

"For the last time, it's Stinky*sox*!" the old coach shouted, just as he lost control of the door. It flew open precisely as the fire-red Trans Am Flogtrac shot through the time continuum.

There was a **SPARK**, a **BOOM** and a **BAM!**

And with that, they were back in the winding tunnel, zooming up and down and through the passageway surrounded by brilliant colors and stars.

"You guys alright back there?" Midnight asked as he turned back to Charlie and Emma. Before they could respond, Midnight's eyes widened. Charlie followed his gaze and noticed that something wasn't right. Off in the distance behind them, there was a speck growing rapidly closer and closer.

It wasn't a meteor. It wasn't anything naturally intergalactic, either. It was a vehicle, and it was gaining on them by the second.

"Are you going to watch the road, or what, Midnight?" asked Charlie, anxiously.

"Um, don't freak out my little friends, but Stinkypants was right. There's definitely trouble. Take a look behind us. We've got company."

CHAPTER 6

THE RIDDLE ROCKET

Midnight put the pedal to the metal, but the Flogtrac engine sputtered like an old cat choking on a hairball. **RRRR PUTT PUTT PUTT... RRRR PUTT PUTT PUTT.**

The mysterious vehicle speedily approached, and with every inch it gained, it became clearer and clearer that it was heading not just *toward* them, but *for* them. Their chance of escaping was drastically declining by the second.

"Step on it, Midnight!" Charlie pleaded.

"I'm giving it all I've got," Midnight grunted, sweating and swerving in the front seat.

"Well, find a way to give it more!" Emma commanded.

Everything Midnight could give wasn't going to be enough to get the Flogtrac to go any faster. It coughed and wheezed its final gasps, making them an easy target for the approaching rocket, which they could see now was covered with flashing red, white and blue lights on its top. The twirling pinwheels and whirligigs along the wings—not to mention the sparkly streamers that hung from them—made it look more like a techno disco party than a time traveling rocket ship.

Smoke burst from the back boosters as it buzzed by Charlie, Emma and Midnight, before coming to a screeching halt sideways in front of them. The Flogtrac sputtered to a stop just inches short of ramming into the cluster of shiny horns that lined the rocket's side.

The three sat frozen in fear staring at the tinted rocket ship cockpit, realizing they were at the mercy of whomever or *whatever* was about to come out of it.

The cockpit opened, and out first stepped a monster-sized foot that, Charlie figured, could only belong to Bigfoot. After everything else that had happened that day, a Bigfoot sighting wouldn't be all that surprising. Another giant foot followed, and Charlie held his breath expectantly.

But the Bigfoot comparisons ended there. The body attached to those enormous feet looked like it belonged more at a string bean convention than in the intergalactic power craft he piloted.

A miniature man—no more than four feet tall—with a long white bushy beard and ears that looked to be almost as big as his feet, hopped out of the shiny ship, eyes laser focused on the trio of anxious onlookers.

He wore a red baseball hat, turned just slightly off-center, and one of those tuxedo t-shirts that—at least from a distance—made it look like he was wearing an actual tux and bow tie. He wasn't.

Walking with a stick in hand, the string bean man proceeded toward the Flogtrac. His giant feet flopped with every step. The stick made for a mystifying medley.

FLIP FLOP DOINK, FLIP FLOP DOINK.

When he reached the Flogtrac, he could barely see over the side of its door. But his eyes just made the cut, and he stared at Charlie. Then at Emma. And finally, at Midnight.

The uncomfortable silence was broken when he used his cane to vault up to sit on the driver-side door, right next to Midnight.

"License and rrregistration, please," he blurted, rolling his tongue.

"I... uh.... I don't have—" Midnight stammered, turning out his pockets.

"Of course. Just as I expected." He had a crackly voice. "Then what exactly are ya doing in these parts, might I ask?"

"We... uh.... We were just coming from—"

"It doesn't matter where you were coming from. It matters where you're headed. Where, exactly, *are* you headed, sir?"

"We're—" started Midnight.

"And you two," the petite patrolman interrupted, turning his attention to Charlie and Emma, "shouldn't you be in school?"

They sat like statues in the back seat. "We started there," protested Charlie.

"And then we were sent to the closet," continued Emma.

"With a chalk eraser thingymagiggy."

"And we found Midnight."

"We didn't want to go back to Mrs. Pooper Scooper's class, so we went with him."

"We didn't even know where we were headed—we still don't!"

"And the next thing we know, we're like a million miles and a million years away."

"And—"

"Alright, that's enough out of you. What is it, exactly, you're doing traveling on . . . lemme see here." He shuffled through a notepad that he pulled out of his sock. ". . . Frequency 3.14159 of this intergalactic system?"

The tiny mystery man was sliding his lumpy little rear end along the door of the Flogtrac. Charlie snuck a glance at Midnight, who was watching with a horrified expression on his face.

"I *suggest* you be straight with me," the man said to Midnight with V-shaped eyebrows. "Or I'll *have* to put my foot down," he threatened, not realizing what a giant threat that really was.

Midnight looked back to Charlie in the rearview mirror, then over to Emma. He proceeded with caution.

118

"We're headed to the hmmm hee hsss," he finally muttered.

"Sorry, lad," the little man's tongue rolled. "I didn't quite catch that."

"We're going to the wrrrd seee huss," Midnight repeated, no more clearly than the first time.

"Still not getting it."

"We're going to the **WORLD SERIES!** 1994. Game Seven. Okay? I'm going to take care of some unfinished business." Midnight's face turned a dark shade of red.

"Ell-way, ou-yay are in rouble-tay!"

Midnight shot right back, "We're in trouble? O-nay ay-way!"

"Yes way! So, I see you speak fluent Pig Latin too, huh?" The man stared at Midnight and squinted his eyes, focusing intently like he was looking into his soul. "Wait just a second there." He pulled his notebook back out of his sock and flipped through a few more pages. "Oh, yes. . . **YES!** I've been expecting you. Case number 112679. My goodness, where have you been? I'm glad I caught you while there's still time."

"Time for what?" asked Charlie. Maybe they were finally going to find out what it was everyone had been warning them about.

"Time before *they* get here."

Emma, too, was on the edge of her seat. "Who are *they*?"

"*They* are the TTT. The **TIME TRAVEL TROOP**."

"The Time Travel Troop? What's *that*? And who are *you*?" asked Charlie.

"I'm Cornelius, young man. The best travel troll around these parts. And lucky for you, I'm on your side. But I used to work for the TTT myself. Ah, those were some interesting days in the Time Crime Unit."

"Time Crime Unit?" asked Charlie. More inter-dimensional police forces?

"Yup, they're part of the top governing body out here." Cornelius raised his little arms and looked around at the endless surroundings. "It's the law enforcement wing of the Einstein Institute for Extraterrestrial Integrity and Operations. And they run a tight ship."

Charlie looked to Midnight and Emma for answers, but they looked as confused as he felt.

"Einstein Integers of Extra Terrible Institution. . . Operations," he repeated, trying to put the words together.

"The E.I.E.I.O."

Charlie nodded his head in bewilderment. "Got it."

"So, the TTT are part of the Time Crime Unit of the E.I.E.I.O.," repeated Emma, who did, in fact, get it.

"The TTT takes its work very seriously, you know. That's how most of the Time Crime Unit is. And if they find you breaking the time travel rules, they're merciless."

"What will they do to us?" Emma wondered, sounding more worried than Charlie had ever known her to be.

"Oh, not much. Maybe just send you to Dung Geon forrr about a hundo each." Cornelius' emphatic tongue rolling was starting to grate on their nerves.

"What's a hundo?" asked Emma.

"And what's Dumb Gee Uh?" added Charlie.

"Let me just tell you there's nothing *dumb* about Dung Geon. And there's nothing fun about a hundo. A hundred years in a galaxy farrr, farrr away is no easy stretch. Not in a place like that, especially." Cornelius paused for a moment, staring at his pointy fingernails. "So, if the TTT gets you, there's *that* option. Orrr, you could just follow the time travel rules."

"Yes, that's a good option. We'll do that. What are the rules?" asked Midnight desperately, with little consideration of what Cornelius might say next.

"They're rather simple, actually." Cornelius reached under his tuxedo t-shirt and pulled out a rolled up paper. He grabbed one end of the sheet, and the rest unfurled out in front of him. He read off the rules, rolling his tongue with more vigor, the more excited he got.

1. YOU CAN'T CHANGE HISTORRRY
2. YOU CAN'T TAKE ANYONE WITH YOU FRRROM ONE TIME AND PLACE TO THE NEXT
3. YOU CAN NEVERRR, NEVERRR, EVERRR, EVERRR RR-REVEAL YOU'RRRE FROM THE FUTURRRE

"Check, check and check!" said Charlie, hoping he was right. He still wasn't convinced he hadn't completely messed everything up with the band debacle.

"Perhaps you haven't broken any rules. *Yet.*" Cornelius raised an eyebrow at Charlie. "But that's just because my associates have seen to it."

"Your associates?" repeated Emma. "Like Mr. Muffin?"

"And Coach Stinkybutt?" added Midnight.

"My people are looking after you. We can leave it at that. But you're still going to have to keep an eye out for the TTT. One wrong step, and they'll be on you like spots on a ladybug. There's just about no way to shake 'em."

"So, how are we supposed to know who the TTT are?" asked Charlie.

"They're chameleons," Cornelius answered, as if it were as obvious as the sky being blue.

"They're *reptiles?*" Charlie was more confused than ever. Were they being chased by space lizards?

"Don't be ridiculous. They're men. They're women. They're boys and girls. They're whoever they need to be to catch you. They just have a way of morphing, and blending in. And they do any number of jobs."

"Like?" asked Midnight.

"They're security guards."

They all turned toward Midnight, remembering the evil eye the security guard had given him back in the football tunnel.

"And they're vendors. Players. Ushers. Fans," Cornelius continued.

Charlie, Emma and Midnight exchanged puzzled looks.

"And that's just to name a few. The TTT can fit in anywhere and everywhere, and they're *always* watching," Cornelius advised. "Just remember: one slip up, and it's Dung Geon city."

"Why so strict?" Charlie wondered. "We just want to go to a baseball game."

"One change in the past; one wrong move; one person who knows too much, and you could alter the course of history forever. Oh, and there's one more thing," Cornelius remembered. "You *must* watch out for their patented move: THE

FRAME-AND-BLAME. Even if *you* don't change history, they'll try to make it look like you did. These guys work on commission. For every misguided time traveler they send to Dung Geon, they get a big-time bonus. And they'll do *anything* to earn it."

Emma looked puzzled. "So they can change history, but no one else can? And we can follow your rules, but *still* get punished?"

"Let's just say they have a way of cleaning up the evidence and making things look right. Corruption at that level knows no bounds," Cornelius assured her. "But that's where my associates come in. It's our job to keep them in line."

"So, what if we run into these TTT quacks?" asked Midnight.

"You will. But know this: distance yourself from those who avoid the cracks. The TTT are afraid of very few things. But one mightily frightful thing is sidewalk cracks."

Just when Charlie thought this couldn't get weirder, it got weirder.

"And," Cornelius continued, "their Jawbreakers."

"WHAT?!" squealed Charlie. "They're going to break our jaws? What have we gotten ourselves into?"

"No, *they* are not jaw breakers. They have a *weakness* for Jawbreakers. . . you know, the candy?"

Charlie felt himself turning red with embarrassment. "Oh, right—yeah, totally," he said, trying to play it off.

"It's their Achilles' heel. Like kryptonite to Superman. Sidewalk cracks, Jawbreakers and. . . one other thing make them weak in the knees."

"What other thing?" Charlie asked, not sure if he really wanted to know the answer, and hoping it wasn't something like chainsaws, or dynamite, or anything else he didn't particularly want to get his hands on.

"Tall redheaded women with pigtails."

"*Huh?*" all three travelers said in unison.

"I know, I know. It's been a mystery for centuries. But there's just something about tall redheaded women with pigtails that distract the heck out of the TTT. I wish I understood it myself. But this is not for understanding. It's for using."

"How are we going to find these things when we get stuck in some odd place in some odd time? Not to mention, I'd imagine tracking down a tall woman with red hair and pigtails doesn't come at the snap of a finger, either. And Jawbreakers? What if they haven't been invented yet?" Emma sniped.

"Relax, young lady. Haven't we gotten you all this far?"

"So why did you stop working for them?" asked Emma bluntly.

"Creative differences. I wanted to rehabilitate wayward time travelers. They wanted to send as many as they could to Dung Geon. Whatever, I'm glad I left them. Truly I am. I was too darn good looking for them, anyway," he said, as if trying to convince himself it were true.

"Too good looking?" Charlie whispered to Emma, "He looks like he's 700 years old!"

"Actually, I'm 457. And in great shape for my age, I must admit." Cornelius flexed his stringy right arm, admiring a physique that even a piece of pasta wouldn't think much of. "Listen folks, I'm on your side. The TTT gave me the boot. So now, instead of enforcing the rules of time travel like those goobershnobles, I'm helping travelers learn the way of the roads. That is, as long as their missions are honorable."

"Well, we're trying to get Midnight back to his big moment in time—when he struck out in front of the world, ate dirt and got trampled on over and over again. Is that a good enough mission?" Charlie ventured.

Cornelius looked at Midnight, who shamefully shrunk down in his seat, as if the emotion of his failure was swarming back to him all at once.

"Is it good enough for me?" asked the travel troll. "Embarrassment of that severity should allow for an exception to the rrrules. But I must insist that they be followed nonetheless."

He glanced again at Midnight and then muttered out of the side of his mouth toward Charlie and Emma, as if Midnight couldn't hear him. "Trampled on, huh? Like a doormat?"

"Like the streets of Pamplona," laughed Charlie, imagining the Running of the Bulls.

"Like the front door of a Walmart on Black Friday," added Emma.

They bantered on as if Midnight weren't in the same solar system, much less the same vehicle. It was too funny a story to stop.

"Enough!" he finally exploded, having heard more than he wanted to about *the incident*. "So, can we go now, or what?"

"Well, you can go, but you won't make it far." Cornelius said. "*They'll* get you, that's all."

"Then what are we supposed to do?" asked Midnight, who for once looked like he didn't have a plan.

"You need to *prove* you can follow the rules."

"Why? And what happens once we do that?" asked Emma.

"Then you earn your Time Travel Wings. They're your free pass to travel wherever and *whenever* you want."

"And why, may I ask, would you allow that?" Midnight wondered. "Why can I go back to the '94 World Series *then* and not *now*?"

"It's our job to teach you the rules of time travel, Mr. Mc-Lean. "It's your job to do things right with that awesome responsibility... *if* you earn your Wings. We're confident you'll see the big picture in the end."

"So where do we get these time Time Travel Wings you speak of?" asked Midnight, taking a closer look at Cornelius, as if to see where he might be hiding them.

"I can't just give them to you, I'm afraid to say."

Cornelius hopped off the Flogtrac door and marched away from the trio, back to his own rocket ship.

"So, that's it?" wondered Midnight. "Not even a tow to the nearest galactic service station?"

"Yeah, I'm sure there's an Exxon-Terrestrial right around the corner," said Emma sarcastically.

Charlie quickly realized Cornelius wasn't about to leave them behind. The travel troll reached into his rocket ship, pulled something out—about the size of an iPad—and turned back toward the Flogtrac with the device in his hand.

FLIP FLOP DOINK, FLIP FLOP DOINK.

"What have you got there?" asked Midnight nervously, as Cornelius returned and catapulted back up onto the driver-side door.

"Well, young man, you've earned your keypad. It's called the **EMC2**. Now, all you need to do is find The Code to enter into it." Cornelius held up a pyramid-shaped electronic screen that he secured to the front dashboard of the Flogtrac. It had a keyboard underneath, and the screen was sectioned off in six triangularly-placed squares: one on the top row, two on the second and three on the bottom.

Midnight inspected it closely. This had been the missing piece in his development of the Flogtrac all along, and only now did he realize it. Charlie could see the amazement on his face, as Midnight looked intently at every inch of the device.

"If this is the EMC2. . . what happened to the EMC1?" Charlie asked cautiously.

"That prototype didn't seem to have quite the right formulaic equation. We're still hoping to find that crew of space monkeys one of these days," Cornelius muttered under his breath. "But I'm growing increasingly confident that the EMC2 is a relatively trouble-free operation. If you can show that you can honor those three rules of time travel, you'll have the chance to enter The Code—six magic numbers—into the EMC2, and when you fill out all of them, you'll have earned your Wings and can travel freely through the massive expanses of space and time at your leisure. Easy breezy."

"And how will we find this Code?" asked Charlie. "Are these numbers just supposed to magically appear out of nowhere?"

Cornelius looked at him with raised eyebrows, as if he'd been waiting all day for the very question to be asked. "Just remember this: Since **E**mma equals **M**idnight times **C**harlie to the power of **2**, time and space is relative to you. To find your code, just figure on your *hero*. He might be a *three*, a *two*, a *one* or a *zero*. Just be careful to know your answer for sure-sy, 'cause one wrong slip, and you might get stuck in New Jersey!"

The time traveling trio all had blank looks on their faces—as confused is if the instructions had been given in Chinese.

Cornelius handed them each a walkie-talkie. "Here, these come with an interminable lifetime warranty. They should work for you from here to eternity.

"Oh, and one more thing." He looked each of them in the eyes to make sure he had their full attention. "Lose that pager and you're in danger. The clock's begun and it's on the run. Twelve hours is what you've got. After The Babe and the band, I'd say you better get hot to trot!"

And with that, the self-proclaimed *best travel troll around these parts* hopped off the Flogtrac door, flopped his way back to his rocket ship and sped off faster than a bolt of lightning.

"Now what?" asked Emma. "We're stuck in this tunnel with a busted engine and an impossible riddle. And even if we get out, we have to run from the TTT, whoever they are. And one little mistake, and we're bound for a life of dung. And—"

"Eureka! I've got it!" exclaimed Midnight. "*Since Emma equals Midnight times Charlie to the power of two, time and space is relative to you.* If we can just clone ourselves, we can go to wherever this thing takes us *and* to 1994. And maybe," he continued, while Emma and Charlie stared open-mouthed, "we can even make it to New Jersey, too!" Midnight was a brilliant inventor. Riddle-solver? Not so much.

Emma pointed out that the keypad on the EMC2 had only numbers and no letters. "*Figure on your hero. He might be a three, a two, a one or a zero.* Maybe we need to plug in the numbers of our heroes. First it was Babe Ruth. What number does he wear?"

"Three," answered Charlie, glad to be able to contribute something.

"And then who scored the winning touchdown back at Cal?"

Midnight looked down at the uniform he was wearing, which he'd taken from Kevin Moen. "Ninety-two!"

"What about if you look at it right-side-up, Midnight?" asked Emma, raising her eyebrows.

"Oh, twenty-six!"

"Yeah, three and twenty-six," said Charlie, his adrenaline rising. "Plug it in!"

"Are you for sure-sy?" asked Midnight. "Afterall, we don't want to get stuck in New Jersey!" He was starting to get it.

"I'm sooo sure-sy," said Charlie.

Midnight tapped on the first box, and typed in the number three. It lit up, flashing like a strobe light. He tapped the second box, typing in twenty-six. Again, more lights, more flashes.

There was nothing for a moment. But as they sat in that uncomfortable silence—and just as Charlie was about to accept his fate of being stuck in this intergalactic tunnel forever—the Flogtrac engine roared like a hungry lion, shooting out from zero to 60,000 in barely half a second.

"AAARRGIIIIIII! BRRRAAGHHH! GBBAARDDD!" The sounds they were collectively making were not understandable, nor flattering.

"Where. . . are. . . we. . . going?!" Charlie finally yelped out in a somewhat coherent way as he gained control of his body against all the force. His back was suctioned into his seat and his face was flat and wrinkly, as he fought to hold up his head against the sudden jolt of energy.

"I don't know," Midnight shouted over the earsplitting super-engine, "but time is *not* on our side!"

"And neither is *that*!" Emma pointed ahead to a gap in the tunnel floor. At their speed, it was unavoidable. Midnight tried to slam on the brakes, but it was like the Flintstones trying to stop a bullet train. Dropping through a bottomless hole in the windy tunnel was inevitable.

In no time at all, the Flogtrac free-fell like it were plunging from the top of a roller coaster. Suddenly, another one of the now all-too-familiar forefields appeared, and swallowed them up in an instant.

SHWOOP!

That was the good news.

But what they saw next was the most horrifying sight they ever could have imagined.

CHAPTER 7

THE PERFECT SOLUTION

"**W**e're heeere!" exclaimed Midnight, just as the Flogtrac came to an abrupt stop at their new destination: a smaller, yet significantly less-stinky closet. "Wow, what a trip!" He stretched his arms up, unbuckled his seatbelt and turned to Charlie and Emma, smiling broadly as if the whole ordeal with Cornelius had never even happened. "Don't get me wrong, that hole was the scariest thing I've ever seen. And the free fall almost made me lose my lunch. But the colors and the lights and the—"

Midnight paused upon noticing the terrified looks on the faces of his two passengers, frozen as if they were covered in ice. Their hands were clenched on the seats in front, and both of their mouths were agape. A drop of drool dribbled out of Charlie's mouth directly onto his lap.

"What is it?" asked Midnight. "What? Do I have something on my face? Do I have a boogie in my nose?"

Charlie shook his head, staring at Midnight, who reached up and felt around his face, his hands continuing down to his shoulders, then to his arms and stomach, before looking down at where his lab coat should have been.

"EEEK!" he screamed, as high-pitched as a whistling tea kettle. "Who did this to me? I mean. . . who would. . . why. . . what the. . . huh?!"

Midnight was wearing the tightest-fitting, brightest-colored, and frankly the most hideous pure-elastic leotard that any of them had ever seen. He looked like a flying trapeze artist. Or a bulky ballerina. Or a super-sized silky-smooth gymnast. Its glossy texture stretched from his shoulders to his hands, from the top of his legs to his feet, and everywhere in between.

Midnight resembled a misshapen rainbow with red, white and blue stripes running up his arms and across his stomach. The tightness in his tummy area was evidence of his unfortunate obsession with banana splits, hot fudge sundaes and chocolate milkshakes with whipped cream and cherries on top.

"It's not *that* bad, right guys?" he asked, reaching out a hand to each of them, looking for a couple of high-fives. Instead, he got a pair of zeros as Emma jumped out of one side of the Flogtrac, and Charlie the other.

They froze again once they saw the Flogtrac. Then, they looked at each other and gasped in unison.

"*Now* what is it, you two?" Midnight asked, still rubbing his hands on his belly.

Charlie pointed at the Flogtrac. "I think we found something uglier than your skin-tight leotard."

"I'd prefer the term 'body suit,' if you don't mind," Midnight said defensively.

"Well, then what do you want to call the Flogtrac?" Charlie said, staring at the vehicle's new comically-stumpy features.

"What has it become now?" asked Midnight.

"Lemme see here," Charlie said as he examined the decals on the side of the Flogtrac. He found the brand. "Yugo," he announced.

"No, you first," countered Midnight.

"I said, *Yugo.*"

"*I'll* tell you what I'd *like* to call it right after you tell me what it really is!" insisted Midnight.

Charlie was getting frustrated. "No, the Flogtrac—it's a, it's a... Yugo!"

"Charlie, just tell him what type of car it is so we can get outta here," said Emma, already by the door.

"Emma, are you not listening to me? *Yugo!*" Charlie wondered if they had both gone deaf. "Y-U—"

"*Why I* what? Why I say that? Why don't *you* just tell us, huh?" Emma was shouting now.

"Argh! The type of vehicle the Flogtrac has become is a *Yugo*! For example, Midnight might say, 'I'll take my hot fudge sundae and chocolate milkshake *to go* in my *Yugo*,'" Charlie shouted, exasperated.

Midnight's hair frizzed up and he cracked an awkward smile. "Oh. Okay. Why didn't you just say that in the first place, geez? Hey, I had a Yugo once. It may not be the prettiest thing in the world, but it gets you from one place to the next. I mean, it got us here, right?"

"Let's just hope it gets us home," said Emma.

Charlie was just glad to not have to explain anymore. He turned to open the closet door, keeping a close eye on Midnight with his colorful attire in his tiny blue wimpy-looking time traveling machine.

"Alright, Charlie, let's find our hero," said Emma.

"Midnight, maybe you should stay here," Charlie added. "Make sure the Flogtrac is still in working order." He still wasn't convinced the Yugo Flogtrac could get from here to tomorrow, given twenty-four hours. "Plus, we don't want anyone outside this room to see you."

"Because of the Time Travel Troop," Midnight presumed.

"Because of the totally terrible embarrassment," Emma corrected.

Charlie scampered out from the closet with Emma closely behind.

"It's okay, guys. No problem," Midnight shouted toward them as they got farther and farther away. "I'm fine. I was going to stay here and work on the Flogtrac anyway. Maybe try to figure out this EMC2 thing." The slamming of the closet door left Midnight alone with his excuses.

"So where in the world are we?" Charlie asked Emma. They were amidst hundreds of people in yet another stadium walkway.

"And *when* in the world are we?" Emma added.

Before Charlie had a chance to explore further, he got smacked in the side of his head by a large white towel that stuck to his face and wrapped partially around to his other ear.

"I guess this answers our questions," he said, peeling it off and noticing the large logo on the towel which read:

WeLCOMe TO THe 1984 OLYMPICS

THe GAMes OF THE XXIII OLYMPIAD

And below that: **LOS ANGeLeS, CALIFORNIA**

"Nice hands, shorty. Where've you been?" asked a tubby man in a bright white shirt and even brighter white shorts, both of which were *way too small for* him.

"I've been, uh, in space," Charlie said boldly.

Emma nudged him, "That's *rule number three!*" she whispered loudly through her teeth, trying to fake a smile to the tubby man, hoping he didn't hear her.

"Spacing out? Can't do that on this job. Not with all that's weighing on us. Now listen: you're needed on the floor. The all-around event is just getting good."

"All-around event?" asked Emma.

"Yeah, little lady.   No American has ever won the all-around gymnastics gold medal, and we've got one who's *really* close. Now get to the floor," he instructed to Charlie. "Your country needs you, towel boy!"

As he stormed off, his short shorts slid farther and farther down his rear, brimming on the verge of splitting at the seams.

Emma and Charlie looked away, afraid of what they might see next. Midnight's outfit had been enough torture for one stop, after all.

"Gymnastics, huh?" asked Charlie. "I wonder if he's on the team."

"Let's hope not," Emma grimaced.

"I guess I'd better get to work. You heard him. My country needs me."

"What do you think might come of it?"

"Of what?" asked Charlie. "That guy's shorts? I think they might come apart."

"I mean of our stop. We've already seen how things can turn upside down depending on who wins," said Emma. "What do you think our mission here is?"

"We better find out soon. You heard what Cornelius said. We only have twelve hours to fill out all those spots on the

EMC2. And now with the TTT after us, we have to make sure things happen exactly the way they're supposed to. If the wrong team wins, or we help the wrong person, *we're* going to be history."

"Not to mention all the other outcomes the computers have warned us about." Emma started heading on a search for the press box. "I'll let you know what I find, Charlie. And I'll let you know what to do. You've got to make things right. You've got your walkie-talkie?"

Charlie reached down, but there were no pockets to be found. For the first time, he noticed that he, too, was wearing bright white short shorts and a bright white shirt.

Feeling something on his hip, he reached into his underwear, and pulled out his walkie-talkie.

"Ewww," screeched Emma. "Better talk at it from a distance."

Charlie gave her an embarrassed look as she turned and walked away. He thought about those computer warnings at the '32 World Series and at The Big Game. "All that we've seen on the line is one team's championships. And one player's future. Whatever happens here can't be *all* that big a deal. It's gymnastics, for crying out loud."

He started toward the arena floor.

Midnight had remained in the closet to tune up the stumpy Yugo Flogtrac.

He was tinkering around under the hood when he was nearly knocked to the floor by the closet door suddenly flying open. He tried to cover his legs and chest and arms, unwilling to show off his outrageous outfit.

"Well, there you are, I've been looking all over for my prototype," a short old man said as he approached. He wore a red, white and blue cowboy hat that covered his slicked gray hair. His voice was slow and crackly, but he seemed surprisingly energetic for his age.

"Who are you?" asked Midnight, thinking about Cornelius' warnings about the TTT.

The old man mustered a raspy chuckle. "Heh heh heh. You know me, son. Everyone knows ol' Tex the Tailor from the deep south of Texas. Boy, I've been doing this since near the turn of the century."

Midnight wondered which century he was referring to.

"And I'm here to help. Some crazy fool thought it'd be a good idea to test out uniforms for bigger gymnasts."

"Bigger? Wouldn't you want—" started Midnight.

"Yeah, you're telling me. Gymnasts are supposed to be small and supple. But that ain't for me to figure, anyway. So, how does it fit there, partner?"

"A little tight in the tummy, but my arms feel surprisingly stretchy. In fact, if not for the obvious humiliation, I have this urge to sashay through the hallways in this thing."

"Well isn't that just perfect. I got me a crazy giant gym-nast on my hands. Hold still, will ya? I have to make a little adjustment here, and a minor fix there." He poked and prod-ded Midnight's elastic leotard with tiny pointy safety pins. "Now, don't you think about goin' nowhere. I'll be back in a jiffy." He waddled out of the closet, leaving Midnight frozen in place.

Barely two seconds after the door shut closed, it shot back open again. A janitor entered with a broom cart and gi-ant trash bag. He looked awkwardly at Midnight before grabbing a small trash can in the corner and emptying it into the big bag.

Midnight tried to think of a way to explain his outfit. "There's a tailor. He's tiny. He poked me with safety pins. I'm his prototype. Okay?" He smiled nervously.

The janitor just looked at him blankly, creating a painful silence. "Nice little piece of machinery, huh?" he finally said in a deep baritone voice, referring to the Yugo Flogtrac with surprising admiration. "Brand new model. I'm thinking of getting one myself. It's efficient, cost-effective, and flaaashy, if I may say so."

Midnight wondered what this guy would think if he knew what the vehicle could *really* do. He just nodded anyway.

"Where'd you get it?" the janitor asked.

Midnight racked his brain for an answer and noticed a poster on the wall: *Los Angeles Auto Expo 84.*

"Auto Expo. Yeah, it's on loan. Just giving it a little spin, that's all."

"Then, how on God's green earth did it end up in this closet?"

Midnight wasn't sure how to answer that one. He tried to change the subject. "So, this leotard breathes pretty nice. Ever try one on?"

The janitor grunted as he neared the Yugo Flogtrac, eyeing it keenly as he went to the other side. "Hmmm," he grumbled. He kicked the back tire and moved on.

The Flogtrac shuddered. And then, right on cue, the tire's hubcap opened up and a robotic foot came out, kicking back at the janitor, hitting him swiftly in the butt.

The janitor turned around, but the hubcap had already closed back up and the robotic foot was nowhere to be seen. Midnight had to restrain himself from bursting out in laughter, happy to see that the Hubcap Backside Slap 2000 worked just as he had created it to.

The janitor gave him a perplexed look. And then, an angry one. He grabbed the Flogtrac key out of the ignition, adding it to the keychain on his belt that already had dozens like it. He reached for his wristwatch and pushed a button on its side, pulling it up toward his mouth. "We've got some *trash* that needs to be taken out," he intoned, raising an eyebrow at Midnight.

Midnight, horrified, stared at the Flogtrac's key, now lost amongst all the others. He didn't know who was on the other end of that message. And he wasn't sure he wanted to.

"Just taking care of business," the janitor insisted as he took his cart and slowly backed out of the closet. "Stay right there, Mr. Spastic in Elastic."

Midnight panicked. This felt like it could be the TTT that Cornelius had told them about.

Maybe the janitor was onto the fact that the Yugo wasn't really a wimpy Yugo at all, and was really a butt-kicking time traveling machine. Or perhaps he had realized that no reasonably sane man would drive to a sporting event dressed in a skin-tight multi-colored leotard. And shouldn't such a man be able to find parking somewhere better than a closet, anyway?

Midnight looked around for another way out of the room and found an air vent. It wasn't ideal, but it was his only chance.

He locked the closet door, took the cover off the vent and climbed through. Thanks to his leotard, he fit. Just barely. The vent's smooth metallic texture helped him slide through the passageway, like a super-slow-motion head-first luge.

Charlie, meanwhile, had followed orders from his tubby towel boss and made his way down toward the stadium event floor. Thousands of fans lined the arena but nobody seemed to give him much notice, despite the fact that his bright whites made him stick out like a marshmallow on a fruit cup.

His head still swiveled around as he kept an eye out for the TTT. He didn't know what, exactly, he was looking for. But just as he reached the bottom of the stairs, the evident gaze of a janitor—maybe twenty feet away—was just enough distraction for him to lose track of the steps.

He tripped, catching his feet on the final stair, launching forward like a belly flopper.

BOMP!

His plunge was cushioned by something, which was good news for Charlie; not for the poor soul who was his padding.

"Hey, watch it there," said a soft voice.

Charlie got up and dusted himself off.

Below him was a girl who wasn't all that much older than he, wearing an outfit incredibly similar to Midnight's. It looked and fit much better on her, Charlie was certain.

"I. . . I'm sorry. I was a little distracted, I guess." His face was as red as a radish.

"Well, you would certainly never make it in *this* sport," said the girl, as she got back on her feet.

She must have noticed Charlie's look of humiliation, because she eased up, and gave him a giant smile that could have lit up the entire arena. "Well, hey, nobody's perfect anyway."

A man yelled toward her from a distance. "Mary Lou, you're up next on the floor exercise. And you'd better be perfect!"

"Who's that?" asked Charlie.

"That's my coach," she answered. "I'm on Team USA."

"Oh," Charlie said, making the connection. "My mom loves floor exercise."

"Your mom—she's a gymnast?"

"Hardly. She puts on her workout video, grabs a bowl of ice cream, and lies next to her dumbbells and a bouncy ball. When I ask her what she's doing, she says she's exercising. And I ask her, 'On the floor?' She says it's her floor exercise."

"That's not exactly the same thing," Mary Lou smiled. "This is more about running and jumping and flipping around. And then, at full speed, landing perfectly still without moving an inch," she explained.

"Ah," said Charlie. "Mom barely moves an inch, too. But I'll have to ask her about that when I get home."

"Where's home?" asked the gymnast.

"Well, the question isn't *where's* home. The real question is *when*—"

"Charlie!" Emma's voice squealed out of his walkie-talkie. "I need your help!"

"I think your shorts are talking to you," pointed Mary Lou.

Charlie's eyebrows furrowed as he laughed nervously. He pulled the walkie-talkie out of his shorts. "What *is* it?" he grumbled.

Before he could get an answer, the announcer came over the loudspeaker.

"Now up for the United States of America, on the floor exercise, Mary Lou Retton!"

"Well, that's me. Gotta go," Mary Lou said, putting on her giant smile. "Charlie, was it?"

"Charlie who? Charlie. . . uh, me? Oh, yeah, that's me. Marley Charlie. I. . . I mean Gnarly Charlie. Er. . . Charlie Marley." He blushed.

"Nice to meet you, Charlie Marley," Mary Lou said as she turned to wave to the crowd.

"Waaait!" demanded Emma's voice through the walkie-talkie. "Don't let her go!"

Emma had been hard at work, sneakily tracking down the crystal ball computer: this time, a model Apple IIe set just outside the broadcast booth. It was big and slow and clunky, but it was an advanced workstation by 1984 standards.

"Charlie, you have to stop her," she said sternly through the walkie-talkie.

"How can I?" his voice crackled back. "She has the weight of the country on her shoulders right now."

"You bet she does. This time it isn't about championships or football careers. It's about national history!"

"What do you mean 'national history?'" Charlie said, sounding confused.

Emma, frustrated, read him the message that the Apple IIe had spit out moments before:

> *The American gymnast knows it's up to her,*
> *Her medal, her country; its entire future.*
> *But if she fails to be golden, you see,*
> *No other American ever will be.*
> *She better be strong, she better be bold,*
> *Or the U.S.A. will lose the war that is cold!*

It must be perfect, times two,
Anything less, and the U.S. is doomed.

"Perfect times two? What's that supposed to mean? And how am I supposed to make sure that happens?"

"Snap out of it Charlie. There's still time. Looking at the scoreboard, she needs. . . um. . ."

Emma squinted, doing the math in her head.

"She needs what, Emma? She needs what?!" Charlie squealed through the walkie, just as Emma came to her answer.

"I don't know how to tell you this, but she needs a perfect ten in the floor exercise."

"Okay. . . maybe she can get lucky once," Charlie said, sounding hopeful.

"And," Emma continued, "she needs a perfect ten in the vault, too. Or the USA can kiss the gold goodbye, forever. And the Cold War, apparently, too."

Emma heard a muted **THUMP**, like Charlie fainted—again.

"Charlie? Charlie!" Emma spoke into the walkie. "Your country really does need you!"

It took a few moments and the roar of the crowd, but Charlie came to, just as Mary Lou tumbled, twisted and flipped her way up and back across the floor mat. She stuck a breathtakingly perfect landing, sending the fans into raucous shouts of approval.

Charlie was just getting off the ground as the judges' marks flashed on the scoreboard: **ten...ten...ten.** Perfection!

That sent the crowd into an even wilder outburst of excitement.

"Halfway there," Emma's voice blurted through Charlie's walkie-talkie.

Mary Lou walked back toward her teammates, passing Charlie with a huge smile before shrugging her shoulders and rejoining her team in preparation for her final event.

"Nice jo—" Charlie started to call out before he was interrupted by a figure in a green uniform.

"Well, there, young man." Charlie's view of Mary Lou was suddenly obstructed by the janitor from earlier, now holding a mop in one hand, balancing it up against his shoulder.

"Shouldn't you be folding towels? Or wiping up sweat? Wait, lemme guess. Your job is to come over here and bother the athletes before the biggest competition of their lives. Bother, bother, bother away. Am I right?"

Charlie couldn't imagine why this janitor cared whether he was folding towels or wiping his nose with them. But the sight of the man and the sound of his baritone voice still scared the socks off him.

Meanwhile, on the other side of the arena, Midnight squeezed his way through the air vent, finally exiting into the main corridor, where more than a few fans stopped to gasp at the sight. After all, it's not every day that a grown man in a skin-tight leotard slips out of a vent onto the concrete floor in front of you.

He brushed himself off, shook his hair back, and moved down the walkway like nothing was out of the ordinary.

He knew there were things to do, keys to retrieve and janitors to evade, but all of the traveling and excitement had made Midnight hungry. He found a concession stand and ordered a pretzel with mustard, a hot dog with ketchup, ice cream with fudge and a soda with lemon and lime. The leotard, he hoped, was the extra stretchy kind.

Midnight wasn't sure if it were his order, or if it was something worse, but the evil look he got from the vendor made him even more uncomfortable than the spandex did.

"Hungry, huh?" asked the cashier, leering as he handed Midnight his change.

"Uh, it just feels like snack time."

"Why so much? With this kind of meal, it's like you haven't eaten in *years*." He raised his eyebrow at Midnight, who cracked a smile and slowly backed away from the counter with his large tray of food.

Still in a locked stare with the man, Midnight turned to get away. But just as he did. . .

SMACK!

Emma, in a rush to get down to Charlie on the stadium floor, was also paying little attention to her whereabouts. And thanks to their synchronized distraction, Midnight's leotard was now completely covered in mustard, ketchup and fudge. Although, truth be told, it really didn't make the outfit look much worse.

"Why don't you watch where you're going?!" Emma blurted out, before realizing who she had slammed into. Midnight was lying on the floor with food splattered everywhere, including his ice cream, which had conveniently landed half on his forehead and half on the rest of his face.

"Midnight! How could you be eating at a time like this? We've got to get downstairs and make sure our country doesn't lose its golden touch. Or the Cold War!"

Midnight was in a daze. "Lose its golden touch? Cold War? What in the world are you talking about?"

"I can't explain it now. We just need to help Charlie make sure our American girl wins."

"Which girl?" asked Midnight.

"Mary Lou Retton."

"*America's Sweetheart*? Of course she wins. I remember these Olympics like they were yesterday," Midnight recalled. "Or, like they're today, I guess."

"But now we're here. And so is the TTT. You remember what Cornelius said. They'll do *anything* to send us to Dung Geon. We can't let our country down. She's only behind by five one-hundredths of a point and there's only one event left," insisted Emma.

"You're right," Midnight said as he leapt up. "Let's go!"

Emma led the way, with Midnight close behind. And with every step he took, a wake of ketchupy mustard fudge dripped off, creating a trail of bitter sweetness behind.

"Janitor!" growled the food cashier, transmitting a message into his wristwatch. "We have a big mess that needs cleaning up. Now!"

Emma and Midnight hustled down the corridor.

But they screeched to a dead stop when a familiar old man with a red, white and blue cowboy hat stepped out in front of them.

"Now didn't I say not to go far?" barked Tex the Tailor in his crackly tone. "Hot diggity, Sonny. I'm gonna have to start my measurements all over from scratch."

"Who are *you*?" asked Emma.

"Everyone knows ol' Tex the Tailor from the deep south of Texas, Girly," Tex said as he took the measuring tape that was hanging around his neck and held it up to Midnight's leotard. "What in goodness sakes almighty have you gotten on my get-up here?"

Tasty condiments were clearly not part of the leotard's intended design features.

Midnight, helpless to Tex's measuring tape, saw Emma getting impatient, and he knew why—every second was crucial if they were going to find their hero, escape the TTT and continue on their quest.

"Don't worry there, little lady," said Tex, noting the concern in her eyes. "It's all under control. But these measurements must be absolutely *preeecise* if this thing is going to be perfect. Mmmm hmmm. Like a big Texas moon was made for the great state of the south, this suit was made for you!"

Emma folded her arms and tapped her foot, yet to be convinced there was no reason to worry. Was she the only one with any sense around here?

"Now," said Tex, finally, "*these* measurements are just right. But if you're gonna find what you're looking for, there's another measurement that needs adjusting."

"What do you mean?" Emma asked, suddenly wondering if this tailor could be of help to them after all.

"You two need to move like the Texas Twist to make this fix. She doesn't know it, but your girl downstairs has a bigger hurdle to get over than she thinks."

"Yeah, she needs a perfect ten. We know that, Mr. Tex," Emma said, itching to get going.

"Sure, she needs that perfect jump. But it's gonna be hard with a vault that's dimensions need fiddlin' with," Tex said with a meaningful look. "She don't know it. Nobody does. But there's an evil-doer or two who's got it in for her. Make sure your crony down there knows what he's doing. Got it, partners?"

"Somebody's messed with the vault? Why would they do that?" asked Midnight.

"I reckon someone who wants to win bad enough to cheat. But you get that fixed, and your girl will flip, twist and turn sweeter than homemade Texas Tea. And that gold? It'll taste better than Texas Toast straight off the griddle."

"Now up on the vault," a voice boomed through the loudspeakers, "from the United States of America, Mary Lou Retton!"

"Well, then, let's *go!*" Emma shouted as she grabbed Midnight's arm.

"After all, y'all, you don't want to end up with the wrong hero. Get some odd number, and you might land in Rio de Janeeeiro!" Tex shouted as they quickly moved away.

Emma turned back, wondering how he knew what he did, but ol' Tex was nowhere to be found. A sewing kit and measuring tape on the floor were the only indication that he had been there at all.

She wanted to ask Midnight if he knew any more than she did, but they had no more time to waste. Mary Lou was making her way to the start of the vault runway. "Charlie! Charlie!" Emma shouted into her walkie-talkie.

Charlie shifted his two freshly-folded perfect piles of towels so he could respond to Emma's call. "Yeah, I know, she's up. Do you think she can do it?"

"Charlie, she can't."

Charlie balked. "What kind of attitude is that? Mary Lou's amazing!"

"No, Charlie, you don't understand," Emma urged. "There's trouble."

"You're telling me," Charlie said, fired up now. "There's trouble with common courtesy. I've been folding towels here, handing them out there and wiping up sweat everywhere. But do I get any thanks? All I get are angry looks from the big guy, and everyone else telling me weird things like 'danke,' or 'gracias,' or 'merci.' I mean, the least they could say is 'thank you!'"

"Charlie, our problems are a little bigger than that. Somebody's—"

Suddenly, the walkie-talkie cut out. Nothing but intermittent static as she tried to explain that somebody had rigged the vault.

All that Charlie heard were bits and pieces of the message.

"Somebody's. . . pushed. . . us. . . there's trouble. . . Midnight's. . . stuck. . . help. . . do something!"

Charlie was on the far side of the vault from Mary Lou, as she readied for her attempt. But he quickly decided he couldn't stick around to watch. Not while his friends were in trouble. He was sure she'd be fine—she *was* amazing. He tossed his pile of towels at Mr. Tubby and took off directly across the runway.

He was at full speed down the pathway, looking like an albino antelope in his bright white shirt and shorts, not caring that he was definitely breaking the rules of the Olympics by being there. There was an **"OOOH"** and an **"AHHH"** from the crowd.

But then came a collective gasp—and not the good kind.

In the midst of his sprint, Charlie's shoe caught on the landing mat, sending him in a tumble that would actually have been incredibly impressive if he were actually *in* a tumbling event.

Charlie rolled once, twice, three times, and was stopped only by the vault itself. He slammed smack into it like a little bird into a clear glass window.

He lay there for a moment, stunned and sprawled out, wondering where in the world he was.

"Charlie? Charlie?!" Emma's voice broke through the walkie-talkie. "Are you alright?"

Through the fog clearing in his brain, Charlie thought she must have witnessed the stumble from above, heard the rumble and saw him crumble. All Charlie could muster was a mumble: "Oooh." And a bumble: "Uhhh."

He rolled off the mat, away from the vault.

"Can I offer you a towel, *sir*?" Mr. Tubby lurked over him looking furious. "Perhaps you can wipe up your dignity off the runway so someone else can use it?"

Charlie pushed himself up and hobbled away from the vault, dazed, looking for Emma.

Mary Lou, not one bit bothered by the ruckus, started down the runway with a head of steam. She built up to full speed just as she approached the springboard. The crowd held its breath as she jumped on the board with all her might, pushed up into the air and braced the vault with her hands, sending her even higher into a twisting spectacle. She turned once, twice, and landed, hitting the ground perfectly on her feet. She fired her arms up into the air in triumph.

Mary Lou Retton had done the impossible, nailing her vault in the moment she—and her nation—needed it most.

Her giant smile said it all. She jumped up and down, slapping her hands together. As she ran past Charlie, she gave him a pat on the shoulder. Perhaps it was in approval. Perhaps it was in thanks. Or perhaps it was just in sheer excitement.

Emma and Midnight reached Charlie, who was still woozy from his nose dive.

"Did we win?" asked Charlie. His eyes seemed a little crossed.

"Not sure yet. Are you okay?" Emma wondered.

"Sure. Never been better." He paused, and looked at them, confused. "Hey, I thought you guys were in trouble. Aren't you supposed to be stuck?"

"We could've all been stuck here, if you hadn't done what you did," said Emma.

"Yeah, that vault was all out of whack until you masterfully threw yourself right into it," Midnight noted. "Probably jarred it right back into place, just in time."

"I. . . did? I mean, yeah, **I DID!**" Charlie boasted. "So now, all we need is the number to put into the EMC2."

"Bad news," Midnight realized, looking down at his own outfit. "Gymnasts don't wear jerseys. Exactly what number are we supposed to get?"

There was silence for a moment as the trio pondered this.

While the moment seemed to last forever, the crowd put an end to it with one prompt roar in unison.

They looked up at the scoreboard and the score from the three judges: **Ten**... **Ten**... **Ten**. A collective "aha" rose from the group.

"I guess we've got our number," said Charlie.

"And I guess we've still got the golden touch, too," added Emma.

"For now," Midnight noted. "But we've still gotta get out of here. The closet's locked, the Flogtrac's a stinkin' Yugo, some janitor took the key to it, and I'm still dressed like a ballerina in a pig pen. Other than that, everything's just perfect."

"The janitor took the Flogtrac key?!" Charlie repeated.

"Not to worry my little friend," Midnight assured him, looking like he had it all under control.

Then, he turned on his heel and led the trip up the stairs, through the corridor and to the air vent through which he had escaped the closet.

Midnight boosted Emma in first, and then Charlie. He looked both ways for trouble, and jumped through himself.

"Hey, you!" shouted a voice from behind. But Midnight ignored it. He grabbed for the vent and pulled himself through. The chocolate fudge helped slide him along as smooth as syrup. "Hey! You're in big—" The voice trailed off as they slid through the vent.

Emma was first to get to the other side and back into the closet. Charlie followed. And Midnight—now in a panic—came through in a rush, landing head-first on a wooden desk below.

He shook off the ache. There was no time for pain. If he had to guess, he'd bet the janitor would be there any second.

A knock on the locked door confirmed that urgency.

"Quick! Into the Flogtrac!" Midnight shouted.

The closet door jiggled.

They hopped in the Yugo Flogtrac quicker than their ol' tailor could do the Texas Two-Step.

"What's the number?" Midnight cried, blanking under the pressure.

"Ten! Ten! Ten!" answered Charlie.

"Actually, just one ten will do," Emma assured him.

Midnight tapped the third box in Cornelius' EMC2 screen. He typed in a *one*, and then a *zero*. The box flashed like a strobe light.

"Now, time to find a way to start her up," he thought out loud.

"What do you mean *time to find a way?*" Charlie and Emma shrieked simultaneously.

"Well, that janitor guy took our key out of the ignition before he disappeared."

They heard a jingling of keys through the closet door. One entered the handle, but it didn't turn. Wrong key, apparently.

"Lucky for us, I invented this," Midnight said, reaching under the dashboard and fluttering his fingers. The Flogtrac shuddered, and a compartment opened, spitting out a brand new key into his hand. "It's the TICKLE ME SPARE KEY 323. Only a perfect tickling touch can break a new key free."

Charlie and Emma didn't know whether they should be impressed or horrified.

Midnight stuck the new Flogtrac key in the ignition, popped buttons on the computer and tapped into the navigation system, switched a knob, punched a button and twisted a lever. But the Flogtrac would not start up.

Midnight tried again. The Flogtrac sputtered for a moment, but died again. "Piece of junk!" he yelled.

Another key jiggled into the closet door. No turn. And then another. No turn. Whoever was on the other side had what seemed to be a whole ring of keys; just like any janitor might.

"Let's go, Midnight!" Charlie shouted, anxiously.

"Start this thing!" Emma repeated, impatiently.

Midnight tried again. It started.

And then it died.

One more try. The Yugo Flogtrac stammered, shook and bounced.

"Come on, Yugo!" yelled Charlie.

"I think we should *all* go!" corrected Midnight.

162

The next key from the outside fit into the closet door, and the handle turned. The door creaked open. Charlie, Emma and Midnight, sitting in the idle Flogtrac, were trapped.

CHAPTER 8

BREAKING THE BARRIER

"**G**o go, you yo-yo!" Charlie shouted frantically. "STEP ON IT!"

Midnight gave a final desperate shot, and he certainly did step on it. He stepped on the accelerator so hard, in fact, he put it right through the floor, ripping a gaping hole in the bottom of the Yugo Flogtrac. He had, quite literally, put the pedal to the metal.

The janitor burst into the room, closing in one deliberate step at a time. His frame cast a long shadow toward them and his footsteps echoed like thunder as he approached.

But just as he reached out for the Flogtrac door, the vehicle sputtered, wobbled and in a flash, shot forward, sending its passengers straight through the brooms and mops in its path. They entered the time continuum, leaving nothing behind but jet-black skid marks and an empty-handed clean up man.

There was a **SPARK**, a **BOOM** and a **BAM!**

But that paled in comparison to the **BOLT**, the **FLASH** and the **WAVES** suddenly swirling around the Flogtrac and down the path of the twisting time tunnel.

"Sweet crazy currents!" bellowed Midnight. "Look at those vectors and flows."

Charlie stood up in the back of the Flogtrac to get a better look at the curving lines and as he rose, his shirt was sucked right up off him to the top of the tunnel.

He quickly sat back down, reaching to cover himself, hoping Emma wouldn't see.

But she saw plenty. Giggling, she pointed at his wardrobe malfunction. Although as she did, her bracelets flew right off her arms and out of the Flogtrac.

Up front, Midnight's hair was wildly pulled in every direction, which, truth be told, really didn't make it look much more out of place than usual.

"It's an electromagnetic field, kiddos. It's pulling us this way and that."

"Hey Midnight," Emma spoke up. "What if that janitor was trying to give us something? He could've been trying to help."

"Not unless he had a magnet neutralizer," suggested Charlie. "Or a magnet polarizer. Or a magnet demagnetizer. Or—"

"Or a chick magnet," interrupted Midnight. "Now, *that* would have been something."

Before Charlie and Emma could roll their eyes, the front right wheel did some awkward rolling of its own. It, too, was pulled away by the magnetic force. The back left wheel went the other way. The rear license plate went down. The front one went up.

"But I don't think he had any of those," Midnight continued, sharing his suspicions. "The only thing he had for us was trouble, as far as I could tell."

Pieces of the Flogtrac started splitting off like flashes off a sparkler, zooming away with the magnetic force.

The numbers in the EMC2 jumbled, and soon, all of the processors on board looked as scrambled as a digital omelet with a side of smoked computer chips.

"Hold on to everything you've got! Everything's going haywire!" yelled Midnight, clutching onto his pants—which had thankfully replaced the leotard.

PSHEW! PSHEW! PSHEW!

There went the doors, the hood and the bumper.

Before they knew it, all that was left of the Flogtrac were the two bench seats—one with a cowering Midnight atop, and the other with an anxious pair behind—traveling through the tunnel in tandem, bouncing with the magnetic pull.

Emma wore a more wowed look than a worried one.

"What is it?" asked Charlie.

"I'm not sure Midnight stands a chance—not with *his* metal brain."

"I always thought him more as Spam-brained," guessed Charlie.

"Spam? Where?" asked Midnight, suddenly distracted from their dilemma. "Or did you say ham? Or was it jam?"

"I wonder what kind of magnetic pull they would have," wondered Emma to Charlie.

"What a sham!" groaned Midnight.

It didn't take long to find out. Whatever-brained Midnight was, it must've been magnetic enough. Seconds later, he too was yanked off the flying seat with the force.

SHWOOP!

Emma and Charlie looked up to see a bluish force field appear in the top of the tunnel as he was pulled away. They looked toward each other so fast, it was as if their eyes were magnetized. But the look only lasted for a moment, because they were also yanked away from the Flogtrac—in opposite directions. Emma flew off to the left side of the tunnel into her own bluish force field, and Charlie to the right into one made just for him.

SHWOOP! SHWOOP!

Bright lights zoomed by at seemingly a million miles an hour. Emma was both terrified and mesmerized. The lights disappeared, and momentarily, she wasn't sure she'd ever see Charlie or Midnight—or anyone, for that matter—again.

SHWOOP!

Emma's worries continued once all the action stopped. She looked left to see brooms and buckets and mops, which seemed on par. But when she looked right, she saw a giant cartoon-like bird staring back at her like it was about to eat her for lunch. *That* certainly seemed strange.

"HIYYYA!" she yelled, giving the giant bird her best improvised karate chop. **"AND HOOOA!"** she followed, with another hack.

"What in the world is going on back there?" a voice called, and Emma turned to see Midnight, sitting in front in what appeared to be a reassembled reconfigured Flogtrac. "What is all the commotion?"

He turned and saw the giant bird, whose feathers were suddenly floating through the air like leaves off a tree.

It was so discombobulated by Emma's attack, its head was spinning. It was literally pointing in the wrong direction.

Midnight looked just as surprised to see an oversized multi-colored bird in the back seat of the Flogtrac as Emma felt—about as surprised as a surfer might be to see the Loch Ness Monster on the back of his board.

"Wait, let me—" started the bird. But before it could say another word, Midnight gave him a thump on the thigh, a whack on the wing and a knock on the knee. The bird adjusted its head back to the front just in time for a bop on the beak and let out an ear-splitting shriek.

The bird plunked open the Flogtrac door with what oomph it had left, flopping to the ground like a boxer knocked out for the count.

Midnight peered back to Emma with a look that somehow combined *What have we done?* with *Do you think we hit him hard enough?* with *Why in the world was there a giant feathery bird in the back of the Flogtrac?*

"oooh," groaned the bird as dust and feathers settled together on top of it. It reached up and pulled off its head. Emma gasped and covered her eyes, only opening them when a familiar voice called out angrily.

"What did I ever do to you?!" asked Charlie, struggling with the head of the bird costume. He might have had steam coming out of his ears if they weren't covered in bird feathers.

"Charlie!" shouted Emma.

Midnight was equally flabbergasted. "Why are you— what is the— how did— when— where— who—?"

"I don't know. All I know is after the tunnel split, I didn't think I'd ever see you guys again. Then, when I did, you two beat the bird brains out of me."

"Well, to be fair, I think we beat the bird *feathers* out of you."

Midnight's analysis wasn't much comfort.

They were interrupted by a rowdy rustling that sounded like somebody trying to juggle pots and pans inside a coat closet.

CLANG! PLOP! BANG! BOP!

"Who is it there?" wondered Midnight anxiously, almost certain that another member of the TTT was going to try to serve them each a one-way ticket to Dung Geon. He placed his hand on the ignition, ready to make a run for it.

"Oh, well, top of the mornin' to ya, laddies. I didn't see ye over yonder."

"Who you callin' ladies?" demanded Midnight.

"I think he said '*laddies*,'" Charlie corrected.

"Well it's the bloody crummiest day as eva was, huh chaps?" said a man in a funny sounding British accent who popped out of nowhere. "So, I figured I might spend a little time looking for the scalpel I lost last week in that wild game of Hide and Go Seek." He pushed around a few more items in a bin, making more clanking noises. "Oh, splendid! I think I've got it here. Off to surgery I go. Cheerio!"

He turned to walk out, holding a tennis racket that he'd pulled out of the bin, which looks absolutely nothing like a surgical scalpel.

Charlie tilted his head with a concerned look. "So, what's with the racket?"

"Oh, yes," said the man, looking over his shoulder. "Sorry for all the hullabaloo over here. Ye never know where you might lose these things."

"Um, I didn't mean the noise racket. I meant the *tennis* racket. . . you know, the one you've got there in your hand."

The man turned, visibly embarrassed, and hid the racket behind his back. "Oh, uh, well. . . tennis. . . yes. Who doesn't love to hit the courts after a daring day in the operating room?"

Charlie was pretty sure a tennis match was nowhere in the man's future. After all, his eyeglasses had to be the biggest and thickest any of them had ever seen before. If he could make contact with a tennis ball the size of a disco ball, they'd be surprised.

The man wore blue surgical scrubs, although they were inside out—probably, Charlie guessed, not on purpose. Underneath, he wore a short, thick purple polka-dotted tie, a pocket protector and the brightest and whitest nurse shoes you could ever imagine. They matched the color of his hair, which was short up top and quite long in the back, reaching almost down to his shoulders. It was partially covered by a green-and-white surgical mask that hooked around his ears and sat atop his head.

He looked the part, but Charlie was having a hard time believing that a crazy-eyed, goofball super-klutz might have much success as a surgeon.

"So, uh," the man hesitated, "where did ye venture from, after all, might I ask?"

"Far, far away," said Charlie.

"Far, far, *far* away," followed Emma.

"Farther than far away, really," added Midnight.

"Well, then, chaps, let me be the first to welcome ye to Ebbets Field—the finest Major League facility in Brooklyn."

"Ebbets Field?" repeated Charlie, thinking back to a book he read on stadiums. "Isn't it the *only* Major League facility in Brooklyn?"

The man ignored the clarification and cleared his throat, as his accent became more eloquent. "I'm the distinguished and dignified Dr. Dilbert Dinglehopper, chief surgeon here in town."

Chief surgeon? It was even worse than Charlie had thought.

The doctor reached out his hand to shake. Midnight obliged and reached his out in greeting, but Dr. Dinglehopper missed the exchange by a good six inches. Midnight tried again, and again Dinglehopper missed.

This was going to be a lost cause. After all, the man's glasses were thicker than ice cubes fresh from the freezer.

Dr. Dinglehopper turned to what he clearly thought was the direction of Emma and Charlie, although with his terrible vision, he was actually looking at the blank wall, pretty far off from where they were standing. "Where'd you bloody find this guy?" he asked.

"In a closet," Emma answered candidly.

The conversation was interrupted by a piercingly loud alarm roaring from Midnight's hip. Everyone covered their ears, eagerly awaiting the new message on the pager display.

Chickens to fly, barriers to break. Hurry on up, for crimeny's sake.

"I get the feeling we don't have much time," Midnight figured.

"Indeed you don't," Dr. Dinglehopper assured them. "And nor do I. I'm off like the Queen's crown at bath time. I've got surgery to do!" He started toward the exit.

"We should go too," said Charlie, knowing they didn't have time to waste either. After all, the quicker they could figure out *why* they were where they were, the quicker he could get out of that feathery bird suit he was inexplicably stuck in.

Dinglehopper and his super-thick spectacles skipped to the door with the coordination of a turtle on a tightrope.

Charlie, to his credit, tried his best to follow, but his feet weren't exactly known for being compatible with one another, either. It didn't help that they were webbed now, and the size of flippers. And as he reached the exit, he tripped and stumbled forward.

Dr. D, seeing as clearly as a blind bat, noticed nothing in his pathway, skipping mindlessly and humming carelessly. If only the doorway were big enough for the both of them.

WUMPTH!

They arrived simultaneously, budging into the doorway precisely side-by-side, leaving Charlie suspended halfway in the air, only able to kick his webbed feet against the wind.

The bird boy focused his momentum on pushing through to the other side. Meanwhile, Dinglehopper wiggled and wobbled, but it was as if the doorway had been designed with Charlie's bird frame and the doctor's scrubby shoulders as its perfect width. They were wedged like sardines in a tin can.

"OHHH!"

"GRRR!"

"Hmmm!"

"I've got an idea!" announced Midnight, looking back to the Flogtrac.

Charlie wasn't exactly convinced the plan wouldn't turn them into Charlie Chicken Stew with a side of Dr. D Dumplings.

"If my calculations are correct, and the kickback force of the projected trajectory is perfect-a-normous, we just might have something here." Midnight hopped into the Flogtrac and began banging on buttons and turning handles. "This is a 1947 Ford Woodie Wagon. From this distance, and with this power—"

"Wait!" yelled Charlie. "What exactly are you planning to do?"

Midnight didn't answer. He turned the ignition, revved the engine, and floored it. The Flogtrac did not, as Charlie had feared, rocket toward them, but instead let out a blast of energy that shot Charlie and Dinglehopper right out of the door frame like champagne corks.

The sight of a bird flying through a stadium walkway wasn't typically head-turning stuff. The sight of a giant feathered fowl with a boy's head was a decidedly different story. Charlie flapped his wings, thinking for a split second that it might actually work. He might as well have been flapping anvils.

"Read all about it! Robinson goes 0-for-4... **AGAIN!**" shouted a newspaper boy nearby. "Read all—**OOF!**" He never saw the giant bird boy coming. Charlie landed on the front page of the newspaper; just not in the way he had always hoped he would.

As the dust settled, Charlie brushed feathers off the newspaper, and saw a picture of a baseball player with his head lowered on the front page. The opposing team in the picture cheered. The date on top: **MAY 1, 1947**.

Before Charlie could see more, he was shoved to the side as the newspaper boy emerged from beneath him.

"Read all about it! Giant bird boy baffles Brooklyn! Read all about it!"

Charlie rolled away from the newsboy right into a steel door and another cloud of dust.

COUGH! COUGH!

Two people walking by covered their mouths. "Oh no!" one of them cried as they picked up their pace. "I'd hate to catch bird flu." But they weren't the only ones to take notice. Others started to gather around him, having never seen such a bizarre sight before.

Charlie stood up and took a look at the steel door. **DODGERS PERSONNEL ONLY.** He wasn't Dodgers personnel, but he was starting to get cornered by the curious crowd. He looked around the group of people, but neither Emma nor Midnight were visible in it. He decided his only option was to go through that door, no matter what it said.

But as it screeched open, he realized the path ahead was so zigzagged it might as well have been a corn maze. It just might be impossible to navigate.

"Midnight?" he blurted after fishing through his feathers to find his walkie-talkie, which thankfully had made it there with him. "I need some direction."

"Don't we all, kiddo?" Midnight responded, quick as a flash.

"I just got tossed toward a door that said it's for Dodgers personnel only. I'm going to see if I can figure out what we're doing here. But this hallway is like a maze, and I don't know where to go. You've played the Dodgers here at some point, I'm sure, right?"

"I've played the Dodgers, but I haven't played here."

"Is this some sort of riddle?"

"Oooh, I love riddles. What's big and bulky, can fly, and goes 'beep, beep' like a birdie?"

"I don't know, *me*?"

"No, silly. The pager. And it's got a message."

"The pager can't fly, Midnight," Charlie said, rolling his eyes as he heard the pager beep in the background.

"It can if I throw it. Do you want to hear the message or what, Bird Boy?"

Right on, Mr. McLean, you and your genius mind.
You've left your post and your Flogtrac behind.
Left the closet to the likes of who-knows-who.
Just remember right who has a copy of the Flogtrac key now too.

"You're not with the Flogtrac? Where did you go?" Charlie asked.

"Can't a guy get a little batting practice in while he has the chance? So, like I said, I don't think I can help you with your maze mess. It may be to your chagrin, but I know Dodger Stadium in Los Angeles, not Brooklyn."

Emma broke in through her walkie-talkie. "Yes you can."

"I can?" Midnight asked.

"You just did," she said.

"He did?" asked Charlie.

"I did?!" said Midnight.

"Are you both blurry brained? Look at the message again. *Right* on. *Left* your post. *Left* the closet. Remember *right*." She paused while Midnight and Charlie put it all together for themselves. "You two wouldn't even know what direction to put your shirt on if the label didn't tell you."

Charlie had made that mistake plenty of times, label or not.

"So, right, then left, then another left, then right again?" he repeated.

"That's what the message said."

"Exactly." Midnight was suddenly more certain. "Just as

I said, little buddy. Don't ever doubt the great Midnight Mc-Lean. I am the smartest, brightest, brainiest, bestest—"

"I think that's enough," Emma interrupted. "I'm just outside the press box now. I'll let you know when I—" she hesitated.

"When you what?" Charlie asked.

"When I, uh. . . I lose my train of thought."

"That doesn't make sense," insisted Charlie, but Emma didn't answer.

Just as she found the press box, Emma had made an unexpected discovery that took her focus. Leaning along the wall was a boy about her age—maybe even thirteen—who looked like he belonged on a billboard or in a movie, instead of in front of her.

He had spiked blond hair, was tall—at least five feet—and wore a bright red sweatshirt and baggy jeans.

"Uh, hi," she said, as he looked up, suddenly feeling nervous.

"Hey," the boy responded, sounding about as cool as he looked.

"There doesn't seem to be a lot of kids like us up here," she said, wondering what he was doing near the stadium's press box.

"Yeah, that's true. So why are you here then?" he asked, almost annoyed.

"Oh, my friends and I are just, you know, hangin' out," she answered, hoping she sounded cool, too. "We're just chillin'. Like a villain. Like Bob Dylan."

"Who?" The boy turned to her and she faltered again.

"You know, from the 60's. . . uh. . . never mind." She was rambling, distracted by his strategically untidy hair and flawless features. She had never met a model before, but this boy had to be one. And if he weren't, then some magazine cover somewhere was certainly missing out.

Back downstairs, Charlie, still in his brightly colored bird suit, carried his big bird head—bent beak and all—under his wounded wing and shed countless feathers along every uncertain turn he made.

His steps reverberated off the wall.

Right, left, left, right, he thought.

He made one turn right. Then a turn left. Another to the left, and a final turn right. Then, as if out of nowhere, a dark looming figure jumped in his path, nearly scaring the chicken fingers out of Charlie.

"Well, *there* you are," the man said.

Charlie swallowed hard.

"I've been looking everywhere for you," the man continued.

Charlie took a step back.

The man moved forward and reached out, grabbing for Charlie's shoulder.

Charlie leaned away, but couldn't avoid his grasp.

"Son, you can't run away this time. It's out of your hands now. We've been looking all over for you."

"I know, I know," Charlie said sullenly, ready to turn himself in. "I just wanted to finish the job."

"You haven't even *started* the job."

"Huh?" Charlie blinked up at the man, confused.

"The regular mascot went home sick with a wicked cold. So, we're relying on you now. Plus, since he took his costume, the one you've got on will have to do. Got it?"

"Uh. . . got it. I guess." *Another odd job for old Charlie.*

"Perk up. This is your big shot! You're up after the top of the third inning." He released his grip on Charlie's shoulder and walked past. "Oh, and kid," he said as he turned back, "break a leg. Not that it should be too tough with *those* chicken stems."

Charlie moved toward the lone door at the end of the hall, listening to the man laughing at his own joke behind him. He pushed open the door, which had the Dodgers logo painted in dark blue and white, leaving behind the nearly-desolate concrete hallway for a vibrant energized clubhouse full of players moving all around the room.

Charlie tried not be noticed, but there weren't exactly a lot of other giant birds in the Dodgers locker room to help him fit in.

"Hey!" one player yelled out.

Charlie froze in his tracks.

"What's it called when the pitcher starts his windup, then stops in the middle?"

"A balk?" answered another player.

"A balk! Balk, balk, balk! Balk, balk!" he screeched in his loudest toned squeal, flapping his arms and hopping around like a chicken. "Balk, balk!"

Charlie turned as red as a cardinal. But, as he wasn't in St. Louis, that didn't help him blend in either. He plopped his bird head back on to try to hide his embarrassment.

"It isn't easy being different, is it?" asked one of the other players, as the rest grabbed their gear and shuffled out of the locker room taking their chuckles toward the field.

"Not really," Charlie said, his voice muffled by the giant beak.

"Come over here, kid. You got a rough start. I'd like to take you under my wing—" the player hesitated, "uh, you know, in a manner of speaking."

"Well, Mr.—"

"Robinson, Jackie Robinson," the player said. He was

strong—about 200 pounds of pure muscle, with smooth dark brown skin, but looked about as comfortable in that locker room as Charlie the Chicken did.

"I stick out like a sore thumb everywhere, Mr. Robinson. I mean not just here, either—let's just say I'm not the most popular guy in school, even when I'm not wearing a giant bird suit." Charlie was surprised at how easy it was to open up to the famous ballplayer.

"Young man, everybody is unique. But when people hold it against you, that's when it hurts. Tell you the truth, I think it's just because they don't know any better, or they're really just jealous."

"I seriously doubt they're jealous of my feathers, or these webbed feet," Charlie mumbled.

"Shoot, kid, if I had feet like those, I could steal second base faster than you could say 'Polly wanna cracker!'"

"Polly wanna cr—?" Charlie started. But before he could finish, Jackie had already darted across the locker room and back. He laughed in spite of himself.

"And that's even without those wily webbed feet. Just think what I could do *with* them. No matter what makes you who you are, you have to figure out what it is that makes *you* special, kid. What makes the bird man unique?"

"It's Charlie, Mr. Robinson."

"What makes bird man Charlie unique?"

"Well, I'd have to say my hands," Charlie said, holding

up his wings. "Yup, all the kids back at my school say I have hands of gold," he lied. "Good ol' *Golden Hands*. Yeah. That's what they call me."

He guiltily looked at Jackie. "No, no, no," he confessed, shaking his head. "Who am I kidding? They don't call me *Golden Hands*—not at all. No, they call me *Butterfingers*. Hands of butter, *that's* what I have. I couldn't catch a cold at the north pole. I couldn't catch a minnow in a fish bowl. I couldn't catch a beach ball with hands the size of soccer goals."

"Charlie, it's okay. I know a little bit about what you go through."

"Really? You couldn't catch a minnow in a fish bowl either?"

"Uh, well, I know what it's like to have high expectations, and feel like you can't achieve them. I thought I was ready for this. Ready for the big leagues. But, kid, it doesn't seem like I'm good enough for these guys, no matter what I do."

"What, are you not fast enough for them?"

"No, I—"

"Don't have a good enough arm?"

"No, I'm—"

"Not strong enough for them?"

"No, Charlie, I'm not *white* enough for them."

"Not white enough? That's ridiculous, Mr. Robinson. You're not white at all."

"And that's the problem, kid."

"Why's that a problem?"

"I don't know what warped time zone you come from, son, but Negros aren't exactly treated as first class citizens around here."

Charlie realized then that he hadn't seen any other black players on the team.

"But wait a second," he challenged. "You just told me to be proud of my differences, webbed feet and all."

"You're right, Charlie. It just seems that no matter what I do, I'm hated for *my* differences." Jackie grabbed his things from his locker and started to pack his bag. "The color of my skin—to them—makes me inferior. Period. No matter how fast I run."

"So, just because of what people say about you, you're giving up?" Charlie asked.

"Well, it doesn't help anything that I'm 1-for-my-last-20 at bats, and people scream and yell and tell me they want to *kill* me. You think you could play through that?"

Charlie thought for a moment. "I . . . I guess not. I mean, I get called a name or two, and sometimes get tacks put on my seat at school, but nobody threatens to *kill* me, that's for sure."

Jackie continued, "So, you see, Charlie, I just don't think I can do it anymore. It's not that I even care if they like me or dislike me. All I ask is that they respect me as a human being. And right now, they don't."

Jackie grabbed a few things from his locker and picked up his bag to head for the door.

186

Back upstairs, Emma was with her new friend, showing him how she could peek into the future with a few swift keystrokes and some technological magic. She knew she wasn't supposed to talk to anyone about their mission, but what harm could there be, *really*?

"See?" she said, grabbing the printout from what looked to her to be an antique typewriter. "And then I tell my friends what's going to happen so they can do what they have to do."

"And what, exactly do they *do*?" asked the boy.

"That depends," she said, coyly.

"On what?"

"On where we are, or *when* we are."

"*When* you are?" he asked. "Very interesting." He ran his hands through his spiked blond hair and squinted his eyes. Emma nearly melted.

"You know what? You never even told me your name," she realized.

"Oh, uh," the boy hesitated. "Right. I'm Don. Don Ginmaster."

Emma's eyes sparkled. "Oooh, how cute," she whispered, not realizing that she was saying it out loud. "How about if I call you Donny? That's a sweet name."

"Sure, whatever. So, tell me what that paper says," Don instructed, a little bit more callously than she would have liked.

Emma looked down. "Oh my," was all she could muster. She picked up her walkie-talkie.

"Is that a handheld transceiver?" Donny asked. "I've heard about those, but I haven't seen one yet."

"It's a walki—uh, yeah. It's one of those." She focused back on the paper and picked up the walkie-talkie. "Charlie. Are you there? Here's what I've got."

"I can't believe he's about to walk out of the clubhouse," Charlie answered.

"Who?"

"Jackie Robinson. He's just gonna quit."

"Well, stop him!" she said, and quickly read Charlie the latest typewriter printout:

History will change as one man takes the field,
Even if he can't do it without a shield.
Just for the color of his skin, he'll be heckled at any cost,
But if he walks out, all opportunity will be lost.
A little patience and pride and strength to persevere,
If your hero doesn't quit, he'll be Rookie of the Year!

"Rookie of the Year?" Charlie repeated. "But he's 1-for-20, and three feet from the door."

"Rookie of the *what?*" Jackie said, turning back as he gripped the handle. "There's no such thing."

His whole life, Charlie had watched as the best first-year players got the Rookie of the Year Award. Then again—he had to remind himself—this was 1947.

He put his faith in the message Emma had read him. "I promise you there is, Mr. Robinson. You can't walk out. Doesn't a promise mean anything to you?"

Jackie thought for a moment, and his face changed ever so slightly before he spoke. "Sure, Charlie, it does," he said, his voice softer now. "The promise I made to Mr. Branch Rickey means everything."

Charlie wasn't quite following what was going on, but he sensed it was a good thing.

"Mr. Rickey is the general manager of the Dodgers. He brought me in here to break the color barrier. No more white-only leagues and negro-only leagues. Segregation is supposed to end with me playing here in Brooklyn with the Dodgers. And he told me things would be tough. That people will show their prejudice and hate. And not only the fans from other teams. *Our* fans, too. And even my own teammates, if you can believe it."

Charlie shook his head, unable to comprehend how people could be so awful.

"There's a lot of hatred out here, Charlie. But I promised Mr. Rickey I would never lash out. I would never take my anger out, no matter how bad it got, because all that would do is show people that I don't belong here. And if *I* don't belong here, then *no* black players belong here. I have to hold up my end of the bargain."

"So, go on out there and keep your promise, Mr. Robinson," Charlie said, feeling relieved.

Jackie slowly removed his grip from the door and walked back toward Charlie.

"I just keep thinking I'm making a mistake," he said, reluctantly placing his bag back in his locker before grabbing his #42 jersey.

"This ain't fun, kid, but you're right. I have to get it done."

"Robinson, get on out here!" came a voice from beyond the clubhouse. "The dang game's about to start. And *you*, chicken boy," the man demanded, peeking his head around the door and pointing at Charlie, "you best be flawless. These fans want a show, and a show they best-be-gettin'!"

"I don't even know what I'm—" Charlie faltered, but the man disappeared, grumbling his way toward the field.

"Go get 'em, Chicken Charlie," Jackie said, slapping his back as he moved toward the dugout.

It was enough to throw Charlie's balance off, still not used to the weight of the costume. Jackie made it out of the room just about the time Charlie hit the floor: head down, tail up.

He wiggled and he wobbled, but it still took him nearly two full innings before he could right himself. When he finally became vertical again, Charlie realized he wasn't alone.

From across the room, Dr. Dinglehopper called in his British accent, "What in the bloody blue birds are you doing down there?"

"How long have you been sitting there?" Charlie asked, just as confused to see him.

"Oh, Charlie, it's you," he said. "I tell you, for the longest time, I was convinced you were either an anteater or an ostrich with your head in the ground like that."

"You couldn't have gotten a little closer to find out?" Charlie gritted his teeth as he stumbled forward toward Dr. D. "And maybe lent me a hand?"

"Lent you a hand?" Dr. Dinglehopper laughed. "Oh, my boy, I need these two babies for my most important life skill." He fluttered his fingers.

"Ah, surgery, I presume," Charlie scoffed.

"Nope, cooking."

"Cooking?"

"And making sweet music."

Charlie just stared blankly before shaking his head. "Look Dr. D, I'd love to hear more about your artistic passions, but I need to get out of here. This costume's too big, too bright and too birdie."

"You do need to get out of here, indeed," Dinglehopper agreed. "Out onto the field. Time's-a-wastin' and the people are-a-waitin'."

He pushed the bird boy toward the exit. Before Charlie knew it, he was standing in the Dodgers' dugout, with the door swinging shut behind him, and the most incredible sight in front.

Charlie fished his walkie-talkie out from under his wing.

"You guys wouldn't believe what I'm seeing."

"And you wouldn't believe the service around here," Midnight said, figuring whatever it was that Charlie was yammering on about could wait. He put his walkie-talkie down and tapped on the bell in front of him.

RIIING! RIIING! RIIING!

Nothing. Nobody. No response.

"Can I get a little service out here?" Midnight eventually reached across the counter in front of him toward the equipment cage. Jerseys, pants, hats, balls, bats and gloves were scattered throughout. "Geez, I'm on a tight schedule here, people," he said, even though nobody seemed to be there to hear him.

Midnight grabbed a jersey that was about three sizes too small for a six-year-old, and pants that were tighter than bicycle shorts on a sumo wrestler, but he squeezed in anyway, and then plopped on the first cap he could grab, which was quite the opposite fit. It was so big, his ears fit under the sides, and he had to hold the brim up to keep it from completely covering his eyes. "Hmmm," he thought as he found a mirror. "Not quite as I calculated."

He reached for another hat, but as the brim briefly blinded him, he missed the next cap on the shelf completely. His hand was grasped in mid-air by another's.

"Hat-way in the orld-way?"

"*What in the world* are you doing, I ask?" came a voice.

Midnight used his free hand to lift the brim. "Dr. Dangledinger? What are you doing here?"

"I would ask you the same, bloke, if you weren't already wearing the evidence."

"I just thought I'd get a feel for the threads, that's all," said Midnight.

"And that's *all* you had planned?"

"Sure," Midnight paused, sensing that Dr. D knew more than he was letting on. "Or maybe I was hoping to get into the lineup. A pinch hit or something. Nothing big," he laughed nervously.

Dr. Dinglehopper let go of Midnight's hand and pulled himself up and over the counter, more like a gymnast than an over-the-hill uncoordinated buffoon. He pulled Midnight close.

"Listen, Mr. McLean. I may look like a doddering old doctor, but I know what I'm doing. You better follow the rules if you want to travel at will. You better follow the rules if you ever want to get back to the World Series. And you *better* follow the rules if you want to stay out of Dung Geon. There's only so much we can do to protect you if you're messing with the prime principles of time travel."

"No, *you* listen, Dinglepooper. I wasn't—, I won't—, I'm not—" Midnight tried to save face.

"Forget it, McLean." Dr. Dinglehopper pulled Midnight even closer by the collar, and Midnight felt him slip something into his pocket. "And for goodness bloody sakes, mate, it's *Dinglehopper.* Not Dingledopper. Not Dingledipper. Not Dinglepooper. Got it?"

"Geez. Got it, Dingle. . . hopper. Take a chill pill. Just one. You can call it a single-popper. And then maybe you can go to a store at Christmas time and be a jingle-shopper. Or you can get a job working rooftops, and become a shingle-popper."

"Bloody enough! Why, I oughta—"

But before Dinglehopper could finish the thought, Midnight quickly skipped off and out of the room, with whatever it was that Dr. D had slipped into his back pocket.

At that precise moment, the stadium started to shake like an angry earthquake. The final out had just been made in the top of the third inning, meaning the Brooklyn Dodgers' rookie first baseman, Jackie Robinson, was coming up to bat.

The boos rained down like the opponent's most hated enemy was about to hit. But it wasn't the opposing team that was up. It was *their* team, and their own first baseman.

"You bum!"

"You can't even get a hit!"

"Send him back to the minors. Better yet, send him back to the Negro Leagues—where he belongs!" another fan screamed out in disgust.

Charlie watched as Jackie readied his bat and toed the first step of the dugout.

"Wait, Robinson," said one of the coaches. "Before you're up, it's bird boy's turn." The team turned toward the other end of the dugout.

Charlie had tried to avoid their attention, but he was hard to miss. He stuck out like an armadillo on an ant farm.

"Better beat those Brooklyn boos out of 'em," the coach commanded. "We don't want to deal with these horrible heckles no more. Dang, it's bringing us down."

Charlie looked over at Jackie who simply lowered his head at the base of the stairs. It wasn't *his* fault people were so hateful. Charlie just didn't get it. How could his own team-mates complain about being *burdened* by the taunts. If only they knew what Charlie knew. If only they would just *talk* to Jackie and treat him like a person.

"And kid," one of the players directed, breaking Charlie out of his thoughts, "don't disappoint us. We'll be watching you like a hawk." The team broke out in laughter.

"Don't act like a dodo," added another. "They'll all think you're cuckoo! Cuckoo!"

Charlie slowly stepped up to the top of the dugout stairs, hearing the crowd's tone turn to excitement. Fans all around the field pointed toward the brightly colored bird stepping out of the Dodgers' dugout.

He could hear cheers growing with each step he took. But that all changed right about the time he reached the top one. Maybe it was the weight of the suit. Maybe it was the webbed feet. Maybe it was just Charlie being Charlie, but his chicken feet caught the top stair, sending the bird boy flying forward like no bird should.

He smashed his beak flat into the dirt at the edge of the dugout.

"OOOH," groaned the fans.

"I guess what we've got is a dirt-pecker here," said one of the players. Much of the rest of the team snickered.

Charlie raised his bird head along with his crooked bird beak, which now looked more like a squiggly zigzag than a piercing point.

He heard laughter and taunting, but it was no longer meant for Jackie. It was meant for Charlie. He pushed himself up angrily.

"Always mocked. Everybody thinks it's funny when I fall on my face," he grumbled, walking away from the dugout and toward the field. "Why does everyone think it's okay to laugh at Charlie, huh? So maybe I tripped on the step and fell on my face. Who hasn't done that before?"

The angrier he got, the more animated his actions on the field. Of course, nobody could hear him from beneath his costume, so all they saw was Charlie running toward first base, looking out at the crowd and furiously shaking his arms. Simply, a bird flapping its wings and a perma-smile on its bird face.

Charlie ran out toward second base and faced the center field crowd.

"Yeah, it's so stinkin' hilarious to see little old me go face-first into the dirt. Like I *meant* to make out with the muck. As if I like to get down with the dirt." He raised his arms up in anger, yelling louder the farther he went.

But again, all the crowd saw was a berserk birdie shaking his head, his wings and his tail. And the more fired up Charlie got, the louder the heckling drowned him out.

He ran toward third base, and the stadium sounded like it was about to explode with exuberance. The taunts and the teases flew through the air like spit at a lisping convention—all aimed toward the bouncing bellowing bird.

"I'll show you! Laugh all you want, but it won't stop me from being the best bird you've ever seen!" He flapped his wings all around, pumping up the crowd even more. "Yeah, that's right. When I'm gone, you *all* will miss me!" A moment later, somebody hit him square with a ripe red tomato.

SPLAT!

"Oh, well *now* you've done it. You think you can make fun and throw tomatoes at me?" He ran down the third base line toward home plate. "Come on, crazy people. Give me all you've got. Because *nothing* can stop the great Charlie—"

CRUNCH!

Charlie tripped over a lonely wood baseball bat that nobody had thought to remove after the last half inning. He tumbled onto his head through the batter's box, landing flat on his bird back in a heap of feathers on home plate.

"Well," he groaned, "*almost* nothing can stop the great Charlie. . . chicken."

"Alright," said the umpire, as if a flailing bird mascot in the middle of home plate was of little concern, "outta the way, birdbrain. Batter up!"

Charlie rolled himself over, looking up to see Jackie Robinson tapping the dirt off his cleats with the barrel of his bat. He gripped the handle and walked toward the plate. Jackie looked focused, but still paused for a moment to give the dirt-covered Charlie-bird a wink and a nod.

The bird boy limped over toward the visiting team's dugout as Jackie approached the batter's box.

"Now batting for your Brooklyn Dodgers, Number 42, first baseman Jackie Robinson!" said the announcer over the loudspeaker.

The crowd's reaction was lukewarm at best, but grew increasingly nasty.

Jackie dug into his spot by home plate. More boos filled the crowd in disapproval of the only black player in the Major Leagues. Charlie couldn't believe the hostility. He also couldn't believe that Jackie simply ignored it, no matter how hateful the words were. Heck, the crowd hadn't shouted anything half as hateful toward Charlie. But *he* had reacted like a lunatic. In fact, he was *still* angry about it. Jackie, though, Jackie was the picture of calm.

Charlie couldn't just stand there and let them say those things. He pulled himself up onto the backstop wall and stepped up on top of the dugout.

"Move outta the way, you featherbrain!" shouted one fan.

"Yeah, haven't you done enough?" cried another.

But Charlie hadn't. He paraded up and back across the top of the dugout, riling up the fans even more. As a mascot, he knew it was his job to excite them. He didn't think it was his

199

job to make them want to tear him to pieces, though. He was successful, nevertheless.

On the mound, the pitcher gripped the ball, looking angrier than a swatted wasp. Jackie focused in.

The pitcher wound back and delivered. Jackie swung with all his might.

"STEEERIKE ONE!" yelled the ump.

The crowd booed with the ferocity of an angry mob, continuing its fuming objections.

Charlie kicked up the dust off the dugout roof, trying to electrify the fans with some distraction. You could call what he was doing tap dancing, but then again, you could just as accurately call a rock a fruit. And you'd be wrong on both accounts.

He was tapping nonetheless, and it was enough to get the fans' focus off Jackie momentarily again.

"You better move, or I'll come over there and move you myself!" bellowed a fan in the third row, whose view was blocked.

He didn't have to. Another fan took care of the problem with a swift toss. His mustard, ketchup and relish-covered hot dog nailed Charlie right on the beak, knocking him back on his birdie booty. Everyone behind the dugout cracked up so hard, they lost focus on the action on the field.

On the mound, the pitcher looked to home plate with an infuriated eye. Jackie dug in for the 0-1 pitch.

Another mighty swing from #42.

"STEEERIKE TWO!" cried the ump.

The crowd again turned its anger on Jackie, who stepped out of the batter's box to regain his concentration. It wasn't easy with thousands of his own fans yelling at him, telling him how terrible they all thought he was.

"Can't you hit anything, Robinson?!"

"Yeah, you can hit the road, Jack!"

Charlie was running out of ideas. He wondered what else he could do, raising his wings to the air. Waving them forward, he flapped them up and down. Charlie knew he had to distract the fans from Jackie.

"What in the world is the bird doing?" asked one fan.

"It looks like he's losing his mind," said another

Charlie wiggled his tail feathers all around and clapped his wings together.

"By golly, he's doing some sort of chicken dance."

The fans were spellbound by the moves. They slowly began to repeat Charlie's ridiculous actions, clasping their fingers, flapping their arms, shaking their tails and clapping their hands. Each time they cycled through the movements, they went faster and faster.

And by the time the organist chimed in, the crowd had transformed from a resentful mob to a fully-synchronized dance team with a few jerky jiggles and a couple wacky waves. Charlie could almost feel the tension in the stadium dissipating. But was it enough?

Another windup and pitch. Jackie turned on the inside ball and ripped a wild line drive foul ball toward the visitor's dugout.

"Duck!" yelled a fan, somewhere between flapping his arms and wiggling his tail.

"Yeah, I get it," started Charlie. "I'm some sort of bird. But I'm not a du—"

He turned just in time to see the seams of the baseball hurtle toward him, thumping into his bird forehead with the velocity of a freshly fired cannonball.

Charlie hit the ground with a thud. Again.

The fans stopped their chicken dance, falling into an anxious silence.

"Awwwk!" Charlie howled like a crying crow. He was pretty sure he saw little birdies floating around his own head.

"Oh, the bird's fine," said a fan.

"Yeah, birdie, don't be a wimp!"

"Bird boy hurt his *wittle* head," another fan mocked. "We came here to be entertained, not to see you fumbling and bumbling." He took an egg out his pocket and threw it at Charlie.

SPLAT!

"That *had* been for Robinson, but I think you deserve it more."

Another fan followed with a piece of pepperoni pizza, which stuck unflatteringly to Charlie's feathers.

"Here, enjoy!" That one threw a chocolate mousse pie.

202

PLUNK!

The crowd had turned again. But with the focus on Charlie, it wasn't on Jackie, which was all that mattered. He dug in for the 0-2 pitch. The pitcher wound, reached back and delivered.

It hadn't seemed there was much that was going to stop the verbal and culinary assaults on Charlie as he woozily wobbled around, but if there were one thing that could do it, it was that **CRACK** of the wooden bat.

Jackie connected flush with the pitch, sending a soaring, deep, sharp shot straight to center field. It was sky-high, sailing toward the clouds like a rocket. The outfielder ran back, reached for the wall and pulled himself up. He extended for the ball, but it was simply out of his reach, flying well over the fence for a home run.

The fans froze for a moment, unsure what to do. Some behind the dugout near Charlie stood still in mid-food-throw.

"WOOO HOOO!"

They erupted in hysteria, going wild like they never had before for Jackie Robinson. Jackie rounded the bases, flashing a smile for the first time since he had started playing for the Brooklyn Dodgers.

Charlie regained his balance, and wildly flapped his wings in approval—excited that the slugger was finally able to break through, and excited that the fans had finally stopped tossing their cookies—and other things—at him.

Jackie rounded third and took in the joy of support, which he had yet to experience since making it to the big leagues. He was greeted at the top of the dugout by his teammates— not all of them, however, but more than had been there before to support him.

Charlie gazed all around the stadium, wondering how the fans could turn so drastically. All it took was one crushing hit, and one terrible turkey. Or chicken. Or whatever the Charlie-bird was. It was a start.

He looked at the fans in the lower section, and the fans in the upper deck. And then his eagle eyes were drawn to the press box where he could barely believe what he was seeing.

Emma was giggling with some blond spiky-haired boy, clearly not focused on the game in any capacity, whatsoever.

Then suddenly, a pair of hands grabbed Emma's shoulders from behind and whisked her away, leaving the blond boy standing alone, and Charlie helpless below.

Who could he call? Where should he go? What would he do? He did the only thing he could. Charlie Bird went to save Emma.

There were steel cables hanging from the stadium façade, which held the backstop net upright and led all the way to the press box. Could he do it? Charlie leapt up, grabbing onto the cable and one of the clips attached to it. He had no choice. He fastened his bird suit and pulled himself up toward the press box like he was Superman.

"Look!" cried out a young fan. "It's a bird! It's a plane! It's. . . uh, no, I was right. It's a bird."

The crowd, again enthralled with the amazing bird boy, **OOHED** and **AAHED**.

Charlie was just about halfway up, focused on rescuing Emma, when he heard a fan scream out below.

"Quick, does anybody have any eggs left?"

CRUNCH! SPLAT! BOINK!

Apparently, they had more than just eggs.

CHAPTER 9

THE FLOGTRAC'S NEW COMMANDER

C harlie pulled himself up through the window of the press box; his feathers soaked in tomato juice, yolk and even a little bit of Coke, surprised that his plan had actually worked.

Every reporter in the room's jaw dropped so low you could've rolled a bowling ball right in. They, it turned out, were even more surprised than Charlie.

"Where is she?" demanded a sweaty, dripping Charlie. "Where's Emma?"

Nobody answered the food-covered, multi-colored bird boy.

"You!" Charlie charged with an angry tone, pointing to the blond spiky-haired kid he'd seen from the ground. "Where'd she go?"

"Who?" he said, with feigned cluelessness.

"Emma, you bozo!"

"Red haired girl?" the kid wondered, holding up his hand to shoulder level. "About this tall? With the freckles?"

"Yeah," replied Charlie irritably. "That's the one."

"Never seen her."

Charlie noticed a look in the boy's eyes—not unlike the janitor had given him at the '84 Olympics. His suspicion grew to anger. *What was this guy up to?*

"You've never seen the girl you just perfectly described, who you were *just* talking to until someone grabbed her and took her away?" Charlie asked, sarcastically.

"Ohh," said the kid. "*That* Emma. Yeah, I remember now. I'm pretty sure I know where she is." He panned up and down at the bird costume.

"Well, aren't you gonna tell me?" asked Charlie.

"I'll do you one even better. I'll take you to her."

Down at field level, Midnight pulled open the clubhouse door leading to the dugout. Hoping nobody would notice his entrance, he pulled his hat down low and quietly tiptoed over to the corner, taking a seat on the bench.

The crowd applauded in approval as Pee Wee Reese, the Dodgers' shortstop, ripped a line drive to left field. The go-ahead run was on base, and the team's slugger, Dixie Walker, was stepping up to the plate.

"Come on, Walker. Let's get another one here," cheered one of the Dodgers' players.

"Big shot here, Dixie. Look for that fastball!" shouted another.

Midnight was quickly taken in by the excitement. "We want a pitcher, not a belly itcher!" he yelled out.

The whole dugout turned to him in shock, and Midnight, realizing he might have just blown his cover, pulled his hat lower, clapping his hands like all was good.

Dixie Walker swung mightily at the first pitch, sending it high and deep to left. The crowd rose to its feet, screaming in anticipation. But as it rose higher and higher, the ball curled farther and farther left.

"Foul ball!" shouted the umpire, as the stadium let out a collective groan.

Midnight paused, realizing just who was in front of him and around him. Pee Wee Reese, *Hall of Famer*. Duke Snider, *Hall of Famer*. Arky Vaughan, *Hall of Famer*. Jackie Robinson, *Hall of Famer*. He'd played in the big leagues for years, but this was something else. These were legends from a whole different era.

"Man, can Dixie rip that fastball," noted the player sitting next to Midnight, shaking him out of his wonderment.

The next pitch headed right at Walker, but then took a sharp turn over the plate. He swung with all his power at the ball. But this time, he missed. By a lot. He flailed around and dropped to the ground like a pile of bricks, knocking himself out cold.

"But he sure can't hit a curveball to save his dang life," the player said again.

"Dad gum it! What are we gonna do now?" the manager bellyached. "There goes our biggest slugger." He turned to the players on the bench. "I need a pinch-hitter."

"Oh, oh! Pick me! Pick me!" Midnight sat on the edge of the seat, flapping and twisting his raised hand like a kindergartner.

The manager grumbled under his breath, looking at his options, and Midnight waved his arms even more wildly, realizing it might be a once-in-a-lifetime opportunity to get on the field with this group of legends. And to get in a few reps before his own big moment in time comes again. Finally, the manager turned his way.

"You? *You* want to pinch-hit for the great Dixie Walker?"

"Uh," Midnight paused, not believing he was about to get picked. "Yup."

"Alright," said the manager.

Midnight excitedly hopped up off the bench.

"That is, if you can tell me one thing."

"Sure, coach. Anything. You name it."

"Alright then. By golly, who the *hoppin' hammerin' heck* are you?!" He turned from laid-back to on-the-attack in the blink of an eye. "Security!"

Midnight started backing up slowly toward the stairs.

210

"I'm— We're— Let's—let's not be irrational here."

As the manager closed in, Midnight skipped up the stairs, hopping out onto the field and down the right field line. *Had he just screwed everything up for the mission?* He was starting to regret his decision. After all, how would Charlie and Emma get home if he wasn't still in this galaxy to drive them there in the Flogtrac? He feared what was about to go down, but he wasn't ready to give up.

Security wasn't slow to respond. Three officers appeared and chased him like bears after a honey-covered bunny. Midnight noticed as each of them hopped, skipped, and jumped over every little crack in the concrete walkway next to the field. Just as Cornelius had warned them about the TTT.

Midnight didn't have the fleetest of feet, but he did have a plan. He zigzagged toward the right field fence, and that slowed his pursuers just enough.

"Get him!" the manager yelled to the guards from the top of the dugout stairs. "Come on, **Tony, Tommy, Timmy**. We don't pay you guys for nothing!"

As they gained on him, Midnight started shedding pieces of clothing, hoping less weight would mean faster running.

First went the Dodgers jacket, which he tossed back toward the chasers. Then his hat, his belt, his spikes and his socks. But it wasn't enough. He felt around, reaching into a pocket to find something unexpected: a handful of Jawbreak ers. *Huh. Where did those come from?* Midnight didn't have time to ponder that at this very moment, and as he reached the bullpen, where more than a few befuddled pitchers sat—some with half-made gum bubbles stuck in mid-blow—he held the Jawbreakers up in his hand, thinking quickly. He knew he had to get them into the mouths of the TTT security guards.

"Hey, you bums!" he heckled at the pitchers, raising their attention. "See those three stooges?" He pointed to the wheezing security guards. "They've got this trick, you see. Throw something, and they'll catch it in their mouths. Throw some gum, they'll catch it. Throw pizza dough, they'll catch it. Throw a rock, and—well, they'll probably break some teeth. But you get the idea."

"So, what do we care?" asked one of the pitchers.

"Well, you shouldn't. As long as you don't mind they called you bullpen boobs who couldn't hit a target to save your life." *If only*, Midnight hoped, *they could hit one now and save his.* "They said you couldn't hit water from a boat in the middle of the ocean. But, if you don't care, then I'll be on my way."

"Wait a second there, pal. *They* said that?"

"Don't kill the messenger," pleaded Midnight, backing away. "I'm just passing along what I'm hearing." He gave them each a Jawbreaker. "I'll bet you can't get it within a bat's length."

"Hickory or oak?" asked one of the pitchers, who wasn't particularly bright.

"Just throw!" Midnight said, annoyed he had wasted so much time already. The security guards were just a few yards away.

In sync, the half-dozen pitchers wound up and delivered. The Jawbreakers became some *real* hard candy, whizzing through the air at ninety miles-an-hour plus.

FWOMP! FWOMP! FWOMP! FWOMP! FWOMP! FWOMP!

It was two treats to the teeth for each. And though they

were caught off guard like fish biting bait, once the choking ceased, the guards settled contently. "Mmmm. Yummy, yummy in the t-t-tummy."

The pitchers returned to their bullpen bench satisfied and vindicated.

Midnight darted through an exit door to safety, as an angered manager grumbled off in the distance.

At the same time as Midnight was congratulating himself on his narrow escape from the TTT, Emma was being briskly escorted down a dark hallway by the press box bouncer.

"Come on, lady. Hurry up now." He wasn't physically pushing her forward, but with the boom of his voice and the hurried tenor of his footsteps, he might as well have been. "Keep going, now. You should know there are no women allowed in the press box."

"No women?" Emma asked. She had thought she had been taken away because she was a kid. Because she had been flirting and not working. Because she was blocking his view, or something. But because she's a *girl*?

"Of course. What do you think this is? Gossip group? Cooking club? Soufflé Society? No, it's a Major League Baseball game. There's no room for you here."

Emma's blood curdled at the man's conviction. She turned to give him one of her patented rants about equality, but he grabbed onto her shoulder and shuffled her ahead.

"I don't care where you go or what you do, little lady. But just stay **OUT OF MY PRESS B—**"

At that precise moment, the door beside them burst open like a sat-on bag of chips, and through it came a wild-haired wild man wearing half a Dodgers uniform.

CRUNCH!

He smacked directly into the press box bouncer, sending the man hard into the concrete wall, and releasing Emma from his grip.

"Midnight!" she shrieked. "You saved me!"

"I. . . I did?" he asked. He leaned over the man below him, who was knocked out like a hibernating bear—and about the same size as one, too. "Yeah. Right. I showed him!"

Midnight stuck his knee into the blacked-out bouncer's ribs for good measure.

"Come on Midnight. Let's find Charlie and get out of this place."

Charlie had been navigating through the dark back passageways of the stadium, following the blond boy.

"Dude, where are we going?"

"It's Don, not *Dude*. Don Ginmaster. Now, just go right through this door, and we'll be there." He pushed a door open, leading to the corridor where some fans were milling about. "Come on, follow me."

Charlie followed him along the walkway to a door that looked familiar. *Janitor's Closet*, it read.

"Wait! Don't go in—" But before Charlie could stop him, Blond Don opened the door, revealing the Flogtrac in all its glory. Don stared at the time-traveling transporter.

"Quick, hop in," Don said, striding toward the car without a moment's pause.

"What do you mean, *hop in?*" Charlie was getting a very odd feeling in the pit of his stomach. *Who was this guy? Why wasn't he surprised by the Flogtrac? And he's going to drive? How old is he, anyway?*

"There's no time to waste. Come on. You want to find your girl, don't you?"

"My girl?" Charlie asked defensively. "What do you mean *my* girl. She's just a friend. Uh... travel associate."

"Just get in."

"Where are you taking me?"

"To a galaxy far, far away. Now **GET IN!**" Don pushed Charlie into the passenger seat of the Flogtrac and slammed the door shut behind him.

Don buckled into Midnight's seat as Charlie's walkie-talkie chirped. "Charlie, where are you?" Much to Charlie's relief, it was Emma's voice crackling through the radio.

"I'm in the Flogtrac. We're coming." But before he could say more, the vehicle roared and Blond Don revved the engine.

"Wait a second," Charlie said with a sudden realization. "Where did you get the key to the Flogtrac?"

Don didn't answer. Instead, he pressed his foot to the accelerator.

"Well," Emma said, turning to Midnight, "I guess he's at the Flogtrac."

"You mean *they*," Midnight corrected her, looking concerned. "Charlie said *we're* coming, not *I'm* coming. So, *they* are at the Flogtrac, whoever *they* is."

"Oh my gosh, you're right," Emma gasped. "What if *they* is Charlie and the TTT?"

Without a word, Midnight and Emma picked up their pace toward the janitor's closet.

"Or," Midnight said as they jogged, "maybe *they* is just Charlie and Dr. Dingledinger."

Emma hoped Midnight was right. Just then, they arrived at the janitor's closet and Emma took a deep breath as she opened the door.

The Flogtrac was gone.

Before Emma and Midnight could figure out what to do

next, an out-of-control hot dog cart zipped up behind them with Dr. Dinglehopper perched on top. It turned hard, coming to a stop only by hitting the wall beside them. "Ye rang?"

"Dr. D! The Flogtrac's gone. And so is Charlie!" Emma squealed frantically.

"By golly, it's true," Dr. D said in his British accent, looking through the doorway. "Quick, hop in the Batmobile." He pointed to the back of the cart.

"*Batmobile?*" Emma repeated. "This is a hot dog cart."

Dr. Dinglehopper turned and looked back, lifting his inch-thick glasses. "Why yes. Indeed it is. What rubbish. I told them to give me the Batmobile. That thing flies faster than squirted sauerkraut. And *this* is what I get?"

Midnight lifted Emma up, sticking her by the ketchup and mustard spouts.

"Oh, and Mr. McLean? We're going to need a push."

Midnight dutifully pulled the hot dog cart away from the wall, shoving it into the closet toward the mops and buckets in the corner. At the last second, he jumped on, landing his buns by the buns and his feet by the footlongs, as a mysterious engine roared from the boiler below, shooting them through the time continuum.

Emma pulled her walkie-talkie out again, and spoke through the ketchup that had squirted on it in the turmoil. "Charlie, come in." She waited through a moment of static.

"Yeah, Emma, I'm here."

"Where are you going?"

"We're coming to find you," he said in a frenetic tone.

"What do you mean you're coming to find us?" she asked. "We're coming to find *you!*"

"I know you're in a galaxy far, far away, Emma. Don't worry. We're on the way."

"No, Charlie. We're in the time tunnel right behind you," she said, trying to put it all together. She knew something wasn't right.

"But *I'm* in the Flogtrac. How could you be?"

"We're traveling on a wiener and a prayer," Midnight shouted to the walkie-talkie from the back of the hyperspeed hot dog cart.

Not sure what to make of the conversation with Emma and Midnight, Charlie was about to ask Don what he thought, when he noticed the blond boy was using a transistor system of his own. Blond Don spoke subtly into his watch.

"It's time people," Charlie overheard him utter, as he pretended not to listen. "What do you say we make ourselves some *deep fried* chicken?"

Charlie looked down at his feathers and his wings and his webbed feet, acutely aware that Don Ginmaster wasn't talking about food.

CHAPTER 10

PROTECTION BY EJECTION

"**C**luck, cluck, WHAT?!" Charlie stuttered. "Where are you taking me? What's going on? Who are you?"

Don turned to him with a devious smile. "Oh, you'll have *plenty* of time to figure that out, my friend."

"But I haven't done anything," Charlie protested, wishing he'd never met stupid Midnight McLean in the closet. "I'm just a sixth grader with hopes and dreams and a long, colorful future!"

"The only colorful thing in your future is the moldy neon of Dung Geon. It doesn't matter what you've done or what rules you say you haven't broken. You know why? Because *I* make the rules, and *I* enforce them. And if I even *think* you're thinking about breaking one, then I will put you wherever I **DARN WELL PLEASE!**"

Charlie slumped in his seat in silence. Don Ginmaster continued giving instructions to who Charlie realized now must be the TTT through his transistor watch, as they cruised farther down the tunnel and closer to Charlie's demise.

Taking advantage of Don's momentary distraction, Charlie discretely whispered into his own walkie-talkie. "I thought we were coming for you, but this guy says we're headed to Dung Geon. What do I do, guys? There's no way out."

"Scream and cry like a little sissy baby and tell him you miss your mommy," answered Midnight, which Charlie didn't think was very helpful.

"Any *other* ideas?" he said, glancing over at Don to make sure he couldn't hear. "Midnight, is there anything in this stupid car that Don wouldn't know about?" Charlie held his breath, his fingers crossed. He felt helpless, hapless and hopeless.

There was silence on the other end of the walkie-talkie until Midnight gave a cry so loud that Charlie had to sit on the radio to muffle the sound. "Ah ha!" said Midnight. He was, after all, the creator of the Flogtrac. He knew all of its ins and outs—especially its outs.

"Charlie, under the seat, there's a special lever."

Charlie bent over and looked under his seat. Sure enough, between a few wires and some dust balls, there it was. It was a handle, brightly-colored and covered in skeleton images. He reached for it.

"Whatever you do Charlie, absolutely, positively *don't* even think about touching it!"

Charlie froze, slowly unraveling his hand and pulling it away. "So, what the heck do you want me to do with it then?"

"Just stay away from it. There's one just like it under the driver's seat, too. You have to get that Flogtracjacker to pull it. Trust me."

Charlie had no idea how he was supposed to get a guy who was sending him to a century in Dung Geon to do *anything* for him. He racked his brain, going over possibility after possibility that surely would not work.

Then, after about a dozen terrible ideas, something Blond Don did gave Charlie a good one. As they drove, Don whistled. As he whistled, he sang. And as he sang, Emma's model boy had to make sure he looked good.

Hi ho, hi ho, off to Dung Geon we go!
On our way: fast and fast and faster!
Hi ho, there's no escaping Don Ginmaster!

Don sang into the mirror, fixing a stray hair here and a stray hair there—his eyes more fixed on himself than the tunnel ahead. He slicked his hair back on both sides, and worked on the spikes up top, licking his fingers to get just the right point.

"You know," said Charlie, a plan forming, "my good friend Midnight is so concerned with *his* hair, that he keeps a special stash in a secret spot."

"Stash of what?"

"A little splash of gel, a splash of mousse, and a splash of cream to make it precisely perfect."

"And?"

"And. . ." Charlie tried to think of something that would make Don interested, ". . . some super-secret special spray stuff too. It's the magic ingredient. But he hides it in his splash stash, so nobody can look as good as he does."

"He couldn't possibly look any better than *this*, I assure you," Don claimed, admiring himself.

"Oh, but he does. Even better."

Don pondered the thought with an extra-evil eye. "And where, exactly, can one find this splash stash?"

"Oh, I could never say," Charlie insisted, settling back into his seat. *Take the bait, please take the bait.*

"Say it, or I'll turn your hundo into *two hundo*, pal."

"Okay, okay. Geez," Charlie agreed, putting his hands up in mock defense. "The secret splash stash is in a special compartment under the driver's seat. Okay? There, now look what I've done. Midnight is going to kill me."

Don looked in the mirror once more and fixed another stray hair just a fraction out of place. He gave Charlie a decisive look before reaching down under his seat. He felt around until he grabbed onto the lone lever. "Ha ha! I've found it! You see, when it comes to Don Ginmaster, the sky's the limit. There's no stopping me!"

Don pulled the lever, and. . .

FWING!

The sky turned out, in fact, to be his limit.

The ejection lever flung him right out of the driver's seat and up through the top of the time travel tunnel, leaving only his feet visibly hanging through.

"Midnight, it worked!" Charlie yelped through the walkie-talkie.

"Of course it worked. Have I ever come up with a plan that hasn't worked?"

Silence.

"Okay, well slow that flying Flogtrac down till we get there."

Charlie scrambled to the driver's side and found the brake. It didn't take long until the hopped-up hot dog cart zoomed up as fast as any food fighter jet could.

If only it could stop as quickly.

Dr. Dinglehopper shifted to the right, bouncing the cart off one wall, then shifted to the left, bouncing off the other. The cart spun 360 degrees to a screeching halt just inches away from the rear of the Flogtrac.

"Charlie, you're alive!" yelled Emma as she hopped into the Flogtrac, wiping mustard and ketchup off herself. She gave him a big hug. "I can't believe you made it."

Charlie hugged her back and then kissed her on the cheek in excitement. Realizing what he'd just done, he felt himself turn beet red as they both stepped back awkwardly.

"Oh, uh," Charlie hesitated, "that must've been, uh, the magnetic field. Yeah, that's right. Geez, all this magnetism. It's just so tricky," he laughed nervously.

Midnight eased the embarrassment. "Hey," he pointed up. "I wonder if those Air Jordans would fit me."

Hanging from above were the pair of feet belonging to Don Ginmaster. The other half of him was projecting through the top of the tunnel, dazed and confused from his surprise ejection.

"They definitely make you fly higher," answered Charlie.

"Wait a second," said Emma, looking closer. "I recognize those feet."

"Yeah, they belong to the monster who tried to take me to Dung Geon," noted Charlie.

"Those are Donny's shoes," she said, not realizing that the two were one and the same.

"Yeah, but *Donny* is also the dangerous-evildoer-guy who tried to send me away forever," Charlie insisted.

"*Air Jordans*," Emma said under her breath, realizing how distracted she had been by his looks. "Air Jordans didn't exist in 1947. I should've known," she added, looking disappointed in herself.

"Well, then, cheerio, my lads. On my way I go," said Dr. D, who got back in his hot dog cart. "Just make sure you don't lose sight of the clock. Four down, two to go. Tick tock, tick tock."

Midnight adjusted his bow tie and turned to Charlie and Emma. "Well, **YIPPEE!**" he exclaimed, catching them off guard. "We're bloody two-thirds there."

"'Bloody' is *my* word, bloke. And you might be more than half-done, but you still have plenty of work to do if you want to earn your wings. Just follow the rules and avoid those bad fools, and only *then* might you earn your travel tools," Dinglehopper instructed. "So, on your way you go. Just don't lose track of your hero."

Dr. Dinglehopper got behind his supercharged hot dog cart and pushed it with all his might, running it right into the side wall. **BONK!** "Oh, righto," he chuckled. "I guess it's *this* way," he pointed.

He turned the cart and pushed it again—this time down the actual solid tunnel path—scampering behind it like a bobsled runner. With enough momentum built up, Dr. D jumped up top, and the engine from below kicked in, shooting him off into the great beyond as fast as a corndog comet.

Midnight and Emma joined Charlie inside the Flogtrac.

"Alrighty. Number please," Midnight commanded.

"Number?" Charlie suddenly realized that with all the commotion—not to mention the feathers in his eyes—he hadn't made sure to remember the right number.

"Well, gee, Charlie, now we're going to be stuck here in this terrible tunnel forever. Great." Midnight wasn't being very supportive. "I hope you have the fortitude to endure such a fate," he sighed.

"Fortitude?" Charlie asked, something clicking in the back of his brain.

"That's what I said."

"Wait a second. Fortitude, *fortitude*," Charlie repeated. "Forty. . . two! That's it. That's our number. Jackie was wearing the jersey with the forty-two. Midnight, you're a genius!"

"Uh, I am? Why, yes," he postured. "Just as I keep telling you guys. You can't mess with a head like this." Midnight pointed to his wild-haired noggin.

"Will you just plug it in, already?" Emma pleaded. "If we spend another second talking about how crazy genius you are," she pointed to Midnight, "or what a dodo *you* are," she directed at Charlie, "then we can kiss goodbye any hope of earning our wings."

"Kiss? No kisses. I don't want to kiss *anything*," Charlie blushed.

Midnight didn't waste another second, punching the number forty-two into the EMC2.

Four numbers now filled the screen. Two spots still remained empty.

"Seatbelts, boys and girls!" Midnight tapped buttons in one computer, and then another. He pushed keys in the navigation system, switched a knob, punched a button and twisted a lever. "Off like the wind!"

The pager blared out, just as the Flogtrac took off. "Here, read it." Midnight tossed the device back to Emma. "Tell me the good news."

"Something's not right," Emma announced. "We're going backward."

"No we're not, we're headed straight as an arrow, right for that huge twisting cloud ahead."

"I think we're being sent back in our *own* time travels," she insisted. "Look!"

The 31ˢᵗ president was Herbert, that's 15 after Abe.
Go on to Hoover's time and find a lady slugger named Babe.

"We already found Babe Ruth," said Charlie.

"And as far as I know," Midnight mused, "he wasn't a lady. Nor the president, either."

The staggering cloud in their path stretched as far as the eye could see. There was, however, no stopping Midnight from pressing on.

"Midnight, what if we're not going the right way?" Charlie asked, feeling worried.

"No time to waste, my boy."

"Maybe time isn't all that important," hoped Emma.

"Not a second to squander, little lady."

"Yeah, well we don't know where we're going, and the only thing that's clear is that *that* way doesn't look like the *right* way. Why don't we just pull over?" Charlie asked, trying his hardest not to sound like he was begging.

"Oh, you want me to pull over?" Midnight said, as the monster cloud got closer and closer, louder and louder.

"Wow, that would be great Midnight." Charlie exhaled with relief, wiping his brow.

"Yeah, I'll pull over. . . when **RAINBOWS GET POLKA DOTS!** How is that one teensy-weensy little cloud going to stand in our way?"

That *one teensy-weensy little cloud* churned faster and faster as they neared, letting off a thunderous roar and flashes of electricity down through the tunnel ahead.

"Does that answer your question?" Charlie yelled over the sound.

BOOM! BOOM! BOOM!

Three more roars of thunder and flashes of lightning.

"Teensy-weensy?" repeated Emma, looking up to the twisting typhoon.

Out ahead, they could see a break in the clouds and suddenly Charlie realized, "This is no little cloud, Midnight. It's a hurricane!"

And in that cyclone's eye were bright colors—spotted colors—across a semi-circular arch.

Emma and Charlie yelled in unison, "Midnight, **THAT RAINBOW DOES HAVE POLKA DOTS!**"

But before Midnight could even think to turn back, his eyes widened as big as the bolt of lightning that struck them.

ZAP!

CHAPTER 11

A STICK OF DYNAMITE

In an instant, they were **POOF** and gone from the tunnel.

SHWOOP!

Bright lights zoomed by, but they weren't sure if that flash had turned them to ash, or the pop was a ticket to the next stop. It didn't take long to find out.

SHWOOP!

A small amount of light came through some misplaced wooden boards around them. They were not in a janitor's closet, nor an equipment room either—of that much they were sure.

"Well, isn't this just great?" Midnight said, agitated, as he stepped carefully out of the Flogtrac. "Why didn't somebody tell me we were going to get stuck in the pitch-black?"

"Yeah, who could've imagined trouble when you drove us into that giant hurricane?" Emma asked sarcastically.

They each got out, knocking over a few unidentifiable items here and a few others there. There was no light switch to flip. No light string to pull.

Charlie carefully backed up along the right side of the Flogtrac, feeling around for some sort of clue as to where they were.

Midnight slid backward along the left side, staring aimlessly into the darkness himself.

Charlie reached the back-right edge of the Flogtrac just as Midnight got to the back-left. They each cautiously turned the corner and. . .

PLUNK!

They backed right into each other.

"Jiminy Christmas!" shouted Charlie.

"Yeepers!" yelped Midnight.

They turned and gripped on to each other, spinning round and round in defense, knocking over who-knows-what and sending it who-knows-where in the darkness. Back-and-forth they went, until together, they slammed into a creaky old door that broke off its hinges and fell downward like a drawbridge. A plume of dust puffed up around them, leaving the two immersed in a cloud of dirt. And in sunlight, finally.

"Urrender-say!" pleaded Midnight in Pig Latin.

"Say what?" wondered Charlie.

"Surrender!" Midnight repeated, this time in human English. "Wait a second. . . Charlie?!"

"Who else would it be?"

"I don't know, some mysterious dust devil trying to swirl us into an alternate dimension of dirt?"

"It's just me," Charlie said, brushing himself off.

Emma walked outside from the old wooden shack unscathed. "Would you two get up? You're getting your suspenders filthy."

Charlie and Midnight looked at each other, then themselves. Each had on trousers and long-sleeved shirts. Their pants were, indeed, held up by suspenders, and their poofy newsboy hats finished the look.

Emma, Charlie noted, wore a collared blouse like something you might find on your great-grandmother, a long skirt down to her feet and black and white heeled shoes that looked hard to even stand in, much less move in.

"Hey!" called a young woman just a few yards away. "Yeah, you. Hurry on over here. We need some more players."

"But, we're not dressed—" started Emma.

"What are you talking about? What else would you wear for softball? Come on over."

Reluctantly, Emma led the way to the softball field. Charlie and Midnight dusted themselves off along the way.

"Go on, grab a glove. You two can be on my team," she told Charlie and Emma. "And you can be on that team," she told Midnight. "They need someone on the mound. Do you know how to pitch?"

"Do I know how to *pitch*?" laughed Midnight boastfully. "Do *I* know how to pitch? I've got an arm like a cannon, the determination of a bull, the passion of a tiger and a junk ball that's nastier than a caged carnivore at a meat market, lady. I'm lights out."

"Okay. A simple 'yes' would've done fine. I'll just be over here with my teammates." She backed away cautiously from Midnight.

"These gloves are flimsy and weak," said Charlie, picking up the glove he'd been thrown.

"What do you mean? That's the brand new **1932 WILSON 648 FIELDER'S MODEL**. It's perfect—some oversized fingers and enough padding so you shouldn't hurt yourself too bad," the girl said.

Charlie nodded.

"By the way, I'm Gertrude. But my teammates call me 'Coop.'"

Charlie looked up from his glove and noticed her from up close for the first time. He was speechless. She was beautiful and blonde, made even lovelier by her sweet smile. *And* she liked sports. Charlie figured she was about twenty—way too old for him, but way pretty, anyway. Too bad such a beautiful girl had such an unflattering name as Gertrude.

Since Charlie couldn't seem to speak, Emma did the introductions for them. "I'm Emma. That over there is Midnight. And this is—"

"I'm Charlie. But my friends call me 'Marl.'"

"No they don't," Emma laughed.

"Yes, they do," he insisted through his teeth, sticking out his glove for Coop to shake.

"Why, what leathery hands you have," she joked.

"Oh, uh, they're not normally like this. You know, it was just a little dusty back there," Charlie tried to explain.

"What do you say we get this game going?" she giggled.

As Midnight reached the mound, his teammates quickly closed in on him, huddling a little too close for his comfort.

"Where did *you* come from?" asked one.

"Yeah, it's almost like you just appeared out of thin air," observed another.

Their looks turned from semi-curious to semi-evil.

"Where, exactly, do you think you're going, Midnight McLean?" sneered an impossibly handsome blond boy, revealing himself from under a softball hat.

"I'm—" Midnight hesitated, wondering how this would-be model knew his name.

"We'll be honest. We never thought you'd make it this far, friend."

"Who's *we*? And who are you?" Midnight asked, before catching a glance of the boy's feet. *Air Jordans.* "Actually, never mind, *kid*. I've got you all figured out, but I thought we were done with you when we left you hanging high and dry back in that tunnel," Midnight said triumphantly.

Don was visibly embarrassed in front of his fellow TTT. "*Enough* of that. *I'm* done dealing with you three hooligans already. It's time for this whole shenanigan to end. What do you say, Mr. McLean? I think it's time we make a deal."

"Let's make a deal, huh?" Midnight said, curious now. "Only if the price is right."

"Oh, the price will be right, my friend. Who wants to be a millionaire?" Blond Don asked him, waving a sack full of cash.

"A millionaire? Hmm, the possibilities! Of course, I would be putting my integrity in jeopardy," Midnight pondered out loud, knowing that any sort of agreement with the TTT was not going to be as simple as it might sound.

"Not to worry, we'll take care of the details. You just deal with your little traveling troublemakers."

"How do you expect me to do that?"

"Are you smarter than a couple sixth graders?"

"I guess. What exactly do you have in mind with this deal of yours?"

"Here's what we're willing to offer. You want to win your silly little World Series game, right? We'll let it happen. We won't stand in your way anymore. No more interference from us. If you can earn your wings before the clock strikes zero, you can use them as you please."

"Or else?" Midnight asked, knowing he wasn't going to like what he was about to hear.

The group got even closer.

"Or else we'll take you into custody *right now* for malicious intent in violating the rules of the road."

"So, what if I agree to your proposition?" Midnight said, a plan forming in his head.

"You'll not only be able to play in your game—we'll also give you a million dollars."

"And?"

"And in return, we get to take your terrible twosome to Dung Geon for a fitty."

"A *what*?"

"Fifty years each. Hundo between them. That's it."

"Well, this is going to cause a Flogtrac family feud, I can assure you of that," Midnight said, realizing he wasn't being given any good options.

"No, Mr. McLean. You won't tell them a thing. You must follow our instructions. This is no game."

Midnight paused, contemplating what was being offered. The limitless possibilities of his time travel wings. The free and clear home stretch of their journey. The million dollars. And the 1994 World Series set up for him to win, once and for all. And *really*, what's fifty years to a couple of twelve-year-olds, anyway?

But he couldn't do that to them, *could he*? After all, they're his partners. His protégés. His responsibility.

"So, Mr. McLean, is it a deal, or no deal?" Don Ginmaster held up a jar of pepper to Midnight's nose. "If you agree to our terms, just say 'I do.'"

"AAACHOO!" he sneezed with all his might.

"Good enough for us," said Don. "Looks like our work's done here. Mr. McLean, we'll have your wings and your money when your journey is complete. Until then, we'll stay out of the way. Now, let's get some outs!"

The group backed off, returning to their positions on the field. Don returned to the dugout. Midnight was left alone on the mound, watching Charlie and Emma, clueless to what had just transpired.

"Come on," said Coop, standing by home plate. "Throw the thing already."

Midnight's attention turned to the game. He took a deep breath, focused in and toed the rubber.

Coop dug in to the batters box.

Midnight wound up, stepped toward home and fired a perfect strike right over the middle of the plate with the speed of a bullet. It felt good to throw like that again.

"STEEERIKE one!" he shouted, pumping his arm. "That's what I'm talking about! You can't touch lights-out Midnight McLean."

"Yeah, great pitch," Coop said with a friendly smirk. "But Miiidnight, this is *softball*, not baseball. You have to pitch underhand, silly," Coop laughed.

Coop may have been friendly—and pretty—but there was something about the way she had called to Midnight that made Charlie a little uneasy. The squeal of her voice just seemed so awfully familiar. He shrugged, and turned back to

the game, eager to see Midnight pitch again. For all his brag-
ging, the guy was actually incredibly good.

But Midnight didn't exactly master the whole underhanded throwing concept very well. On his next pitch, he held
onto too long, and the ball launched out of his hand, over
home plate, over the catcher, over the backstop and over the
dusty shed beyond. Ball one.

Underhand pitch two was released too early, and it
bounced by Midnight's feet, hitting just about every square
inch of dirt between there and home, rolling across the plate
for ball two. It looked like his only chance for a strike might
be if they set up bowling pins on the plate.

"By 'lights out,' did you mean you were going to put me
to sleep with your pitches?" Coop taunted. "Just pick something in the middle of those first two."

And Midnight did. He stepped back, swung his arm
around, and released a pitch headed right down Broadway.
Coop stepped, swung and smashed the ball out of sight.

Charlie looked at Midnight, who was standing on the
mound, looking flabbergasted.

Coop trotted around the bases to the cheer of her teammates.

"Way to go, Coop!"

"Another big shot!"

"Coop, you swing a stick of dynamite!"

The ball had flown off her bat like something explosive, for sure.

There in the dugout, the player sitting between Charlie and Emma spoke up. "She sure is good, ain't she? No one can match her at the plate, nor the mound neither. Well," she paused, "*almost* no one."

Just as Coop touched home, another young woman jogged up to the field seemingly out of nowhere. "Sorry I'm late, ladies. And gentlemen too, I see. Looks like we've got some new blood today, huh? Let's get this thing started for real. Everyone cheer, The Babe is here."

The Babe. Just like in the clue they'd received back in the Flogtrac. Charlie's heart pounded. This was who they were supposed to meet! He looked at her more intently. The Babe was strong and stout, about five feet, five inches tall and just plain looked strong for a girl. Charlie guessed she was around Coop's age—twenty or so—and had short brown curly hair down to her shoulders.

She dropped the big bag she had brought to the field, and riffled through it, pulling out a leather mitt. Babe jogged out to center field, where she took the position that nobody else dared try to claim as their own.

"Who's that?" Charlie asked the player next to him, playing dumb, hoping to get information that could help their mission.

"That's The Babe," she said, and before Charlie could interject, she waved her hand, "I know, I know—you're thinking 'that's not Babe Ruth!' But there's *that* Babe. And then there's *this* Babe. Babe Didrikson. Mildred's her real name. But she once knocked **FIVE** balls out of the park in one game, smashing it like Babe Ruth. And the name stuck."

"Mildred?" asked Emma, listening now, too. "And Gertrude?"

"Gorgeous names, huh?" her teammate admired.

"Um, they're something," Emma said, giving Charlie a *can you believe this* look."

"But that's not the only thing those two fight over. Who's got a neater name? Who's got the better bat? Who can swing faster? Who can throw harder? It's never ending with them. Then again, without their rivalry, neither of them would be as good as they are."

As if on cue, Coop called out, clearly irritated.

"Alright, can we get on with it already?"

"Don't get your skirt in a bunch. Let's play ball!" Babe yelled back as she settled into her spot in center.

The next batter stepped up to the plate, and Charlie turned to watch as Midnight focused in.

He whipped his arm around and fired the ball over the plate. One swift swing of the bat later, it was headed for a set of willow trees in right-center field.

Babe sprinted toward it like she was magnetized to the ball. It was sure to be a triple, maybe even a home run—if and when it landed. But Babe would allow no such thing. She swiped the ball out of the air just inches from the ground, making an incredible catch and rolling onto her back.

"Alright, one down," Babe announced, tossing the ball back in. She returned to center field like it was just another run-of-the-mill play.

Charlie was in awe. The look of horror on Midnight's face was enough to worry a warthog.

"Don't worry about the willows. The Babe has it all under control out here," Babe called to Midnight from the outfield, pointing her glove toward the trees lining the field.

The next batter didn't hit it to the willows. She barely hit it out of the infield. But once again, lights-out Midnight was like green-light Midnight. The ball—headed for short center field—looked like it was about to bloop in for a hit.

But on came Babe, charging from the outfield, diving forward, robbing the girl of her glory and saving Midnight's morale all at once.

"We've got to get one to drop in," muttered Coop, frustrated in the dugout. She grabbed a wooden bat from the dirt and smacked it repeatedly into the palm of her hand. "Babe Didrikson better not steal another hit from our team. Or else!"

Charlie noted her tenacity. Her conviction. Her pride. Her hand—and its undeniable sense of familiarity. There was *something* about her that he just couldn't quite put his finger on.

Babe didn't make another catch that inning. But she did do something even more impressive. Midnight threw the next batter his Cinderella Ball. Charlie only recognized it because Midnight had spent an agonizing ten minutes detailing its intricacies to him and Emma during a noticeably calm stretch in the Flogtrac. The Cinderella Ball was a pitch he invented in his playing days. It looks perfect at first, only to turn into a pumpkin patch of a pitch with a wicked drop at the end, hitting home just as the batter swings wildly out of her slippers.

But this time, he must not have calculated for the physics of the pitch coming underhand, and he left it just a smidge too high. The batter dinked the ball off the end of the bat, right through Midnight's legs, over second base and into center field.

"Finally," cheered Coop.

But her exuberance was short lived. Babe charged from center and picked up the ball on a sprint. She fired to first base from the outfield a throw that beat the runner to the bag, ending the inning just like that.

"That's it. She's in for it now," muttered Coop angrily, gathering her teammates around her.

"Alright, we're still up a run. Come on, let's shut them down and come back for some more runs next inning," she said before grabbing her glove and heading straight for the pitcher's mound.

Emma and Charlie were set for their first action in the game. They, too, grabbed gloves. Charlie started for right field, the position he usually played on his Little League team. He figured that was because nobody hardly ever hit the ball to right field in Little League. And he wasn't wrong.

Emma was headed for shortstop, but stumbled barely two steps out of the dugout. It turned out that not only was running in heels hard, it was even more difficult with a long dress dragging beneath.

Before she did her perfect Charlie Marley impression, tripping and actually eating dirt, she lucked out like a long-horn winning the livestock lottery. She landed in the arms of one masterfully timed tailor, Tex, who had appeared out of nowhere.

I tell you, little lady, whoever designed a dress with all this excess was a dang dingbat. We better do something 'bout this before you wind up tumbling like a weed in the prairies," he insisted in his deep southern drawl. Emma was so relieved, she didn't bother asking where he had come from. As if anything had made sense on this crazy journey anyway.

Tex pulled out a needle and thread to hem the bottom of the dress, while the rest of the team warmed up for their defensive half of the inning.

"While I'm making these measurements," he said, a needle between his teeth, "you might want to tap on that typewriter a tad and see what comes of it."

Confused, Emma looked around. There was a typewriter on the end of the dugout bench that she was quite sure hadn't been there moments before. But again, nothing surprised her anymore.

"This thing's pretty old-school," she said. The typewriter was big and bulky and its keys were raised level-by-level with the number keys much higher than the spacebar.

"Old school?" ol' Tex the tailor repeated. "Naw ma'am. That's the brand spankin' new 1932 Royal portable typewriter."

"Portable? Like a laptop?" "You try to put that on your lap top, little lady, and I'll tell you the pain in your legs will mega bite!"

As Emma's fingers neared the keys, the typewriter clicked out a note on its own, directed just for her.

"Hello there. So nice of you to make it," the machine typed onto the white paper curled through the top. "Please type your password or no message can transmit."

Emma typed in "Robinson" for their latest hero. R-O-B-I-N-S-O-N took about ten times longer to type on the machine than it ever did on a computer. And about fifty times longer than if she just could have texted it. But this was 1932. Punching the keys was her only option.

The typewriter hesitated. It shook. It spun the paper back and forth.

"Come on Eeemma, we need you out here," squealed Coop.

"Just a minute," she called, as Tex finished up his hem and the machine spit out its message.

There's a rivalry that's brewing and quite noticeably has drama.
Do the math and you'll find potential with commas.
There's softball and tennis and golf with no cart,
Swimming and diving, and that's just the start.
Basketball and track, billiards and boxing,
But only one can do these and earn medals with moxie.
Championships and golds give one a legendary feature,
While the other will be a hit. . . as your notorious teacher.

Emma read the message twice. Three times. Four. "Gives one a legendary feature," she repeated aloud. "The other, a hit as your—"

And then it hit *her.* Like a painful sensation. Or, more fittingly, like the Board of Education. She knew she had recognized that squeal. That intensity. That demand. That wooden bat beat against that hand.

Coop was the Poop Scoop! But *how?*

"Eeemma," Coop repeated from the mound. "Can we keep playing, or are you *history?* Should we *subtract* you from the roster?"

"No, no. I'm coming," Emma hesitated. *Had Cooper wanted them to find Midnight? Did she need her own second chance at changing history? Or was this just the coincidence of all coincidences?*

Tex had shortened Emma's skirt to just above the ankles, so at least she wouldn't fall on her face, even if it felt like the whole world had just turned upside down.

Midnight was leading off the inning for Babe's team, but as he stepped into the batter's box, jaws dropped all across the field. His pre-swing ritual was unlike anything any of them had ever seen before—on a softball field or anywhere on earth, for that matter.

He rolled up his long sleeves and dug his foot into the dirt. He twisted his toes back and forth, burrowing a hole as deep as the Grand Dirt Canyon. The bat was upside down in his hands, and he used it to clear out the filth from his shoes and his hat and his hips. Midnight flipped the bat right side up, twirled it around his back, tapped the plate and puckered his lips. He shook back and forth like he was doing The Twist.

He stretched down to tighten the laces on his shoes, then jumped up and down like a dang kangaroo. He pointed the bat to Coop on the mound and back he wound, ready for the pitch that was long overdue.

Coop stepped back for her windup.

"Wait! Timeout!" Midnight declared, stepping out of the box. "I forgot something. My apologies. Sorry about that."

He then began his tremendously tedious procedure from scratch. Only this time, somewhere between The Twist and the kangaroo, he added a dusty hand clap to complete the routine.

"Oh, and Coop?" he added with the bat wound back. "Do me a favor. What do you say you put one right here." Midnight pointed his bat right over the lower middle of the strike zone.

It looked to Emma like Coop wanted the challenge. Like she'd happily put it in that spot, but with every bit of power she could muster behind it. Coop wound back and delivered a fiery fastball right down the middle. Midnight unloaded on it like a tightly-pulled bow and arrow, crushing the ball high toward the clouds and well over the willows.

Charlie chased the ball as it bounced farther and farther away. When he finally got to it, he tossed it to the center fielder, who threw it to Emma, who was standing on second.

To Coop's delight and Babe's misfortune, Midnight had been so busy admiring his hit and so lousy running the bases that he only got as far as first base and had to settle for a snoozy single.

"Alright, Coop, you've got this one!" yelled Charlie from right field, acting confident. "And we'll take care of it if you mess this one up, too."

Coop squinted her eyes at him. "Thanks for the pep talk."

Please don't hit it to me. Please don't hit it to me. Please don't hit it to me, Charlie repeated in his head. *Please don't hit it to Emma, either. She wouldn't know what to do with it. But* **REALLY**, *please don't hit it to me!*

The crack of the bat was an answered prayer for Charlie—in part. The ball was not headed for him, he was relieved to know. But it *was* headed to shortstop, where Emma was positioned in her long flowing skirt, high heels and—since Charlie had never seen her play—assumed athletic cluelessness.

But Emma dove to her left for the ball, smoothly picking it out of the dirt with her glove. She jumped up, stepped on second base and threw to first for a double play.

Midnight was out by a mile at second, but that didn't stop him from sliding into the base anyway. It was so awkward and awful, it made the batter's box routine look polished in comparison. His body skipped across the dirt, landing in a heap a foot-and-a-half short of reaching the bag.

"Two outs!" Emma declared. "Come on, Coop. One more now."

Charlie was impressed, if perplexed. Where in the world did she learn to do that? She never played like that in gym *or* at recess!

As he looked in at Emma and Coop—his travel partner and his dream girl—he noticed the two exchanging an awkward look. Something seemed weird about it. He just didn't know what it was.

The next batter to the plate was a tall woman with a big loopy swing. But it was a powerful one.

Please don't hit it to me. Please don't hit it to me. Please don't hit it to me, Charlie thought again. *Please hit it to Emma. She knows what to do.* **REALLY**, *please don't hit it to me!*

No such luck. The batter popped the ball straight up to right field.

"I've got it!" Charlie yelled confidently, hoping he looked cool to his teammates—Coop in particular. "I've got it. I've got it. I've... **WHERE IS IT?**"

He lost the ball in the clouds and had no clue where to find it. *Who uses a white ball on a white cloudy day anyway?* he wondered.

"Use your eyes! It's right there," pleaded the center fielder.

Charlie used his eyes, but saw only clouds. He used his mouth to ask where it could be. And he used his nose to finally catch the falling ball. It appeared out of nowhere and slammed into his face, then into his glove.

But as he used the mitt to cover his sore snout, the ball fell out behind him.

The center fielder came over, picked it up, and threw it in to the infield, not even taking a moment to check on Charlie's condition. "Nice catch there, Bumpernose," she scoffed.

"I've been called worse," Charlie said, glumly.

There were still two outs, and now a runner on second. And thanks to Charlie's blunder, Babe Didrikson was headed to the plate, batting cleanup. Coop eyed her as she strode from the dugout. Babe stared back fearless and sure. She dug into the batter's box. Coop wound up and delivered a curveball. Babe swung and missed.

STRIKE ONE!

Another pitch high and the next one low, and it was quickly two balls and a strike.

Coop gripped the ball, wound up and delivered a specialty pitch. It headed right for the middle of the plate, and Babe swung with all her might. But just as she committed to the swing, the ball fell hard away from her, diving into the dirt. Her bat missed by a mile, and there were now **TWO STRIKES** against her.

"Coop throws a screwball of dynamite, too," the second baseman crowed.

"Yeah. She's a screwball expert, alright," Charlie heard Emma call back. He wasn't sure what she meant by that.

Coop needed one more perfect pitch to finish off The Babe. Charlie wondered what she'd go with. Sure, she could force a ground ball or maybe even a pop-up, but any pitcher facing their rival wanted the strike out. Could Babe hit Coop's fireball fastball?

The answer came with a crack—two cracks, in fact.

Coop got her sign from her catcher, then wound back to pitch. Babe coiled to swing. The ball sizzled in to the plate like lightning. But Babe's swing was **THUNDER**. She hit it spot-on, sending the ball off the bat like a rocket, headed not for the willows or the clouds beyond, but right back for the pitcher herself. It hit Coop in the face like she had a target on her forehead, first catching her by the eye, and then as she fell, hit her in the ear on the landing.

The group gasped as Babe ran straight for Coop. She was the first to tend to her. Coop groaned on the ground, gripping her eye and her ear. "Coop? Coop? Can you hear me? Are you alright?" Babe pleaded. "Somebody get a doctor!"

Both teams were huddled around Coop. Charlie and Emma were behind the others and couldn't see much, but there was plenty of worry from back there, anyway.

"Oh geez. I hope she doesn't get a black eye. I mean, with baby blues like those, it would be a shame," said Charlie.

"Charlie, she's—" Emma started, but Charlie was on a roll.

"And it better not have knocked out any of those perfect white teeth, either. I don't think I've ever seen a smile like that."

"Charlie, you've seen that smile before. Only, it was really more of a—"

"And that hair. When the ball hit her ear, it better not've made it all big and swollen, and screwed up any of that beautiful blonde—"

"Charlie," Emma said, interrupting his reverie. "Coop is *Cooper*!"

"No," Charlie said, seriously confused. "Coop is Gertrude."

"Coop is the Poop Scoop!" Emma was staring at him now, a serious look on her face. "Charlie, do you understand? Coop is Cooper. . . the Pooper Scooper."

He stared at her blankly. And then, the wheels started turning. "She's the— Are you saying— That beautiful creature is— **NOOO!**" Charlie couldn't believe it, but it made sense.

The closer he looked, the more he could see it now. It was, in fact, their grouchy, crotchety, curmudgeon of a sixth grade teacher—just about 100 years younger, a world prettier and significantly less wrinkly, like someone had gone and ironed her face.

Suddenly, there was movement from Coop in the middle of the group. "No, no, no. No doctor." She started to push herself up, as a giant lump was growing on her forehead. She stumbled to one side, then the other. Maybe it was her dizziness. Maybe it was the weight of the lump on her noggin. "You stole my signs, Babe. I know you did it," accusing her rival of knowing which pitch was coming. "I'm not going to be beaten by your cheating ways, Babe. I'm done. Done with you, done with your antics and done with this stupid game forever! Come on, guys, let's get out of here."

Coop summoned all of the players to follow her, leaving Babe behind by the mound. "**EVERYBODY** come on. Chaaarlie? Eeemma? Miiidnight? Are you coming?" she squealed.

"I have a history project," Emma blurted.

"Math homework for me," Charlie lied.

"Rocket science to practice," Midnight said, coming up behind them.

Coop and the rest of the group marched off the field, grabbed their gear, and left the dusty field behind. Babe Didrikson stood there with Charlie, Emma and Midnight, still unsure of what had just happened.

"Aw, she'll be back," Babe said, turning to the trio. "Right?"

Emma was very certainly sure Coop was gone for good— gone to a fate that will have them meeting again, one day far in the future. She pulled the typewriter's message from her pocket.

"Championships and medals will give *one* a legendary feature, while the other will be a hit as your notorious teacher," she read aloud.

"Well, she was, uh, *hit* alright," said Midnight.

"I've never seen Coop lash out like that," Babe added, still stunned. "I didn't cheat. You guys know that, right? I just hope this isn't the start of something new for her."

"I can just about guarantee she's going to hold a grudge for a long, long time to come," Charlie assured her.

"Well, I guess we can't play softball with just four people," Babe noted. "What do you say we try something else?"

She grabbed the big bag she had brought to the field, reaching in, making a clinking and clanking sound like it was full of tin cans.

"What do you have in there, Babe?" Charlie asked.

"What *don't* I have in here would be the better question. Here's a set of golf clubs, my tennis racket, a basketball, track shoes, pool cue, boxing gloves, a baseball bat." She rummaged through some more.

"Is that it?" Charlie laughed.

"And a sewing kit."

"Yippee ki-yay!" Tex popped out of nowhere from behind them. "Now here's a lady who knows how to thump a man's heart."

"Do you use that kit to fix up your uniform?" Emma asked.

"No, I'm not exactly the uniform-fixing kind," answered

Babe. Tex's head lowered sadly like he was just told his famous possum pie recipe wasn't really supposed to have roadkill in it.

Babe continued, "I actually won the Texas State Fair sewing championship last year."

"There's a Texas State Fair sewing competition?" Tex perked up. "By golly Miss Molly, I have a calling in this life! Babe, consider yourself challenged at the next meet. There are no fingers faster than ol' Tex the tailor's when it comes to southern sewing skills."

Babe abruptly turned her attention from Tex, tossing the sewing kit to the bag.

"What about all this other stuff?" asked Emma.

Babe grabbed the golf clubs and handed them to Charlie. "These are for the years to come, when I dominate professional golf." She flipped the basketball to Midnight. "This is from the AAU championship my team just won, and the three times I've been named an All-American." She gave the tennis racket and pool cue and boxing gloves to Emma. "These are what I do to relax." She took the track shoes out and put them on her feet. "And these are for running fast."

"Where are you running?" asked Charlie.

"Los Angeles."

"You're running to Los Angeles?"

"No, silly. I'm getting ready to go for the gold in the upcoming Olympics. And I'm not just running, either. There's the hurdles, then I've got the javelin throw and the high-jump in my sights, too."

"What *don't* you play?" Emma wondered.

"Dolls."

A piercingly loud beep interrupted their curiosity. It was coming from Midnight's pocket.

BEEP! BEEP! BEEP!

"What in the world is that beeping thing?" Babe marveled.

"A beeper," Midnight answered frankly.

"I guess I should've figured."

Midnight read the display:

What's all this ball talk and doll talk?
Don't get started with teddy bears and Raggedy Annies. You've
found your next clue, so move your little fannies!

"Well, that's awfully rude," said Babe to Midnight.

"It's not me," Midnight insisted. "It's the beeper that said that."

Babe looked confused at the idea that the beeper could say anything, but before she could ask, Emma jumped in. "The beeper, er, *Midnight* is right. Our schedule is super-tight, Babe, and if we don't get out of here quick, we're going to be grounded for good."

"And Midnight needs another shot at glory," Charlie cut in. "His last try was so embarrassing, it made switch-handed

Tee Ballers look like Hall of Famers. We've got to stay ahead of the TTT to make that happen," Charlie added and Emma groaned, hoping Babe hadn't heard anything suspicious. "Actually, where has the TTT been lately? It's like they forgot about us or something. You think they have some surprise attack up their sleeves?"

Emma realized Charlie was right. Where *was* the TTT? No one had tried to stop them or catch them since the Jackie Robinson game. Before she could say anything, though, Midnight quickly changed the subject.

"Alright, well I guess we'll be going then," he said, an oddly nervous look on his face.

"Wait, not so fast," Babe insisted, pulling out a driver from her golf bag. Emma hid behind Midnight, wondering if maybe *she* were TTT.

"You're not going anywhere. Not without a long-drive contest first."

Emma exhaled.

"You can't hit it farther than I," Midnight assured her, quickly taking up the challenge. "You're a girl."

"But I'm the *best* girl golfer you've ever seen."

"That's like saying you're the sharpest spoon in a drawer," Midnight answered, not-very-nicely.

"Well, you saw how hard I hit it off Coop's face. If I just readjust a few degrees here and redirect a little up there, you don't stand a chance."

"Oh yeah?"

"Yeah. I've always known I'd be the greatest athlete who ever lived. And unless you, Mr. Longshot, do something to prove me otherwise, I'll keep that dream alive."

Emma nudged Charlie. "We *have* to go. We don't have time for a golf contest."

"We don't even have time for a blinking contest. What does Midnight think he's doing?" Charlie said.

Babe teed up a golf ball at home plate and took a couple practice swings.

"Did you hear what she called me?" Midnight smirked to Charlie and Emma. "'Mr. Longshot.' Just wait to check out how long this shot's really going to be. She won't believe her eyes."

"When she called you 'Mr. Longshot,' I don't think she meant—" Emma started to explain that it wasn't a compliment, but gave up. It wasn't worth crushing Midnight's dreams. "Uh, good luck."

"Yeah, just hit the heck out of it, and get us the heck out of here," Charlie pleaded.

Babe set up for her shot. "One swing, all the pressure. Got it?"

"Absolutarific," agreed Midnight confidently, as he started into an awkward and bizarre stretching routine with his club over his head and his legs outstretched into the splits.

Midnight had seen Babe hit a softball. But he had never seen her hit a golf ball. And if he had, he almost certainly would not have agreed to the competition in the first place. Babe swung back and unleashed on the ball like she was a ticking time bomb waiting to explode. It took off into the clouds, flying three times the distance of the willow trees, and landed smack dab in the middle of a dirt pasture far beyond.

"That was a long shot," Midnight uttered.

"And the chances of you hitting it any farther is a long shot, too," answered Babe. "So, like I said, prove me wrong."

Midnight suddenly looked a little more uneasy, but Emma didn't care. She had one thing on her mind, and that was getting out of there, and quick. Charlie, she noticed, wanted out too. He was dancing around in anticipation like he had ants in his pants. Emma took the time to plot their retreat to the Flogtrac.

Midnight began a pre-swing routine that made his softball warm-up seem quick and boring. By the seventh time he half-swung back and shimmy-shook his hips like an electrified ape, Charlie reached his breaking point. His ants-in-his-pants dance turned into a full-out body boogie, and his patience became as thin as a piece of paper.

"HIT IT ALREADY!" Charlie exploded.

And he did. By accident. The ball might have gone farther had Midnight just sneezed on it. It dribbled weakly out onto the infield and stopped wearily in front of the pitcher's mound.

"Well, I guess that solves that," said Babe proudly. She walked out to retrieve the balls.

Midnight just stood at home plate aghast, before Emma and Charlie took the opportunity to drag his still-stunned self to the dirt-filled shed behind the field.

"Looks like I can out-putt your long drive too, Mr. Long-shot," they heard Babe call from behind them. "Emma? Charlie? Mr. Longshot? Little strange old Texas tailor?" But the traveling trio was already back in the shed, where they got their first full glimpse at the Flogtrac in its present form. The light from behind them flooded onto the vehicle.

Charlie and Emma hopped in quick, but Midnight paused, thunderstruck by the sight before him. "Now, this car is hot."

"That's because it has flames on the sides. Duh," Charlie pointed out. The Flogtrac had, in fact, become a 1932 Ford Coupe with custom flames painted from front fender to back bumper.

"Midnight, if you don't get in by the time I count to three," Emma started. "One, two..."

"Okay, okay!" Midnight got in the front seat of the Ford Coupe Flogtrac and pouted. "Who are you, my mother?" "Midnight, we're this close to being permanently grounded. I'm not going to let you blow your opportunity over a couple cool running boards and a flaming paint job."

Midnight focused in. He pulled a knob and twisted a lever. He punched some buttons on the dash computer. He flipped a switch and turned the key in the ignition. "What have we learned here today, kiddos?"

"That Coop the Poop Scoop was actually not always the devil of a teacher we know her to be," said Charlie.

Emma did some math in her head. "And, that if the Pooper Scooper was in her twenties here in the '30s, that's got to put her. . . into the triple-digits as we know her."

Charlie continued, "And that there's a reason for her bad hearing and terrible eyesight."

"And that she swung a stick of dynamite," added Emma, recalling what her teammate had said, and what she witnessed for herself.

"So, if she ever wanted to whack us with the Board of Education, we can expect some power behind those crusty bones. *That's* what we learned."

"No," interrupted Midnight. "No, no, no, no and no. What we learned here is that if someone says you swing like a girl, you better hope you swing like a girl like *that*!"

"What number am I supposed to plug in to the EMC2 for a woman in a dress?" asked Emma.

"Her name's 'Babe,' because she hit five home runs in a game. Try that," said Charlie.

Sure enough, Emma plugged in a 'five' into the fifth spot in the EMC2, and within seconds, it lit up green, leaving just one final missing piece to the puzzle.

As the EMC2 flashed, the pager beeped again.

Move, Move, Move!
Get on the path before all your dreams go bye-bye.
Off you go to a hardwood court where man can fly.

Midnight gripped the steering wheel for departure, looking deep in thought. "Wait a second. Hardwood court. Man can fly. What if this is all a trick?"

"How do you figure?" Emma said.

"Think about it. There's no way it's legit. Do you really think the Wright brothers played basketball?"

"The Wright Brothers?" Charlie asked.

"They invented the airplane. They can fly. Slam dunk. Easy peasy, simple as that."

"What do you say we trust the pager? It's gotten us this far, right? After all, we only have one more stop to go, and by my calculations, less than thirty minutes to get it done," said Emma.

"Alright!" exclaimed Charlie. "What the heck are we waiting for, then?"

"Not a darn thing!" shouted Midnight with seemingly restored confidence. "Let's rev this monster up and leave this scene."

In his excitement, Midnight gripped the elastic suspenders hanging tightly over his shoulders and snapped them like rubber bands. "Yowzers! My arms!"

"What is it, Midnight? Are you okay?" asked Charlie anxiously.

"No. I'm not. My stinking arms are numb. And I can't drive without my arms."

"Well, we can't just sit here," insisted Emma.

Instinctively, his feet took over. Midnight stepped on the accelerator, which shot the Flogtrac forward and through a pile of brooms and mops and buckets in the shed.

There was a **SPARK**, a **BOOM** and a **BAM!**

And through the bluish force field they went, heading for one final stop before getting their shot at their travel wings.

The question, though, was whether they would even get there, veering as erratically as a brainless bee on a honey high.

Their fate was firmly in Midnight's hands. And his teeth, for that matter, which were now tightly secured to the Flogtrac steering wheel.

CHAPTER 12

HIS AIRNESS

The Flogtrac pinged and ponged off the walls of the winding tunnel like it were stuck in a particularly peculiar pinball machine.

"Midnight, straighten up!" Charlie demanded as they bounced off another wall.

"Mmm Ppp Fff," said Midnight.

"How about taking the steering wheel out of your mouth?"

He did, leaving a trail of slobber behind. "My posture is fine," he shouted back.

They hit another wall. Steering *without* his mouth didn't help anything.

"I meant straighten up the Flogtrac. If we hit another wall. . ."

CRUNCH!

". . . I might lose my marbles."

CRUNCH!

"Or my lunch."

"Looks like we're losing more than that," noted Emma. They had left a zigzag trail of Flogtrac fragments in their wake with every bang and bump.

After one final hit, they screeched to a stop unceremoniously in the middle of the tunnel. There weren't many parts left for them to drop, nor were there many parts left for them to continue.

"I'm sure I needn't remind us of what we're facing," Emma pointed to her watch.

"What options do we have?" asked Charlie.

Midnight, who finally regained the feeling in his arms, said nothing, but reached out of the Flogtrac, apparently immensely interested in a shiny spherical object that lay beside them on the path. "Charlie, did you say you lost your marbles?"

The small sphere was just out of Midnight's reach. But whereas any rock you've ever seen would just sit there like an inanimate object should, this one had movement to it—an eruptive kind of movement like it was on the brink of something explosive.

Midnight reached a little farther out, just barely short of touching it.

"Midnight, what are you—" started Charlie.

"Yeah, I wouldn't—" added Emma.

But there was nothing they could do to stop him. And

there was nothing he could do to stop the massive volatility of his decision.

The moment Midnight touched the marble, it erupted in a **BIG BANG** of universal proportions, combusting with so much power they were thrown into incomprehensible disarray—not that there was any time to comprehend it, anyway. Instantaneously, out of that marble shot a now-familiar tiny bluish force field that sent them into the path of brilliant lights that illuminated their atmosphere.

SHWOOP!

Emma's and Charlie's hair now looked as if it had been blown with a cosmic hair dryer. Albert Einstein would have been proud. And jealous.

SHWOOP!

Charlie was the first to see Midnight's face, which had been torched in the explosion. "Are you alright up there? Your grill looks char-broiled."

Midnight tried to look at his face too, but since his eyes were already on it, he had no luck.

Emma couldn't see how wild her own hairdo was, but judging by Charlie's, she feared the worst.

"Thank goodness we're here." Charlie squirmed out of the Flogtrac, relieved to touch solid ground again.

"Yeah, but where *is* here?" Emma said, patting her tangled mane.

Charlie looked around for a moment, trying to find an answer. All he saw were pictures of big red horned creatures on the walls. "Spain?" he guessed.

"For what?"

"The running of the bulls?" Charlie knew he was grasping at straws.

Emma wasn't convinced.

Charlie's eyes were drawn back to the Flogtrac and its long sleek new look. "Viper!" he pointed.

Midnight almost leapt out of his loafers. "Yikes! Where? **WHERE?!** I hate snakes more than I hate Brussels sprouts."

"No, the Flogtrac," Charlie said to assure him.

"What?! A **VIPER** in the Flogtrac?" Midnight pulled himself up into a ball, gripping his knees into his arms in the front seat. "Ewwy! Ewwy! Get it!"

"Midnight, I think Charlie means the Flogtrac has turned into a Viper. You know, the car model? Not the snake." Emma got out of the Viper Flogtrac, leaving Midnight still scared stiff inside.

"We have less than thirty minutes to go, Emma. Still one more number to get," noted Charlie.

"I know, I don't even have enough time to make fun of that ridiculous velvet red suit you're wearing. If only I had a few extra moments to tell you how bad that big bowtie looks on you, too. I wish we had just a little time to spare. Then, I could point out those silly shiny shoes you've got on. Too bad we don't, though."

Charlie looked down and saw what he was wearing. He, too, was suddenly thankful there wasn't enough time for her to throw any insults his way.

He grabbed the door handle. "Oh, and Midnight? I'm betting I'll get horns before you're right about the Wright brothers." Charlie made imaginary horns with his fingers, as if they were jutting out of his head. He didn't imagine he was going to grow them anytime soon, nor that Midnight was on the right track with his assumption.

Charlie opened the door and was about to turn to let himself out of the room to wherever his velvety red threads were going to take him when Midnight cried out, **"BULL!"**

"Nope, I'm dead serious," said Charlie. And as he turned, he suddenly realized that his bright red outfit was infinitely more dangerous than just as a fashion crime. There was—as Midnight indicated—a big red bull awaiting him on the other side. Charlie braced himself for certain death, but instead, the bull spoke—and in a very calm voice at that.

"His Airness expects you," said the bull.

It took Charlie a minute to come to grips with reality. After all, he had never known a mascot to speak, which is, it turned out, what the bull was. The giant red fake furry animal had huge white eyes, a big black unibrow and a Chicago Bulls basketball uniform across his chest.

"His. . . *Airness*?" Charlie repeated. "Did that explosion drop us into some twisted dimension where big cartoon

"Just follow Benny the Bull, pal," said the bull semi-annoyed. He would have rolled his eyes if they weren't sewn tightly to his face. He led Charlie through a tunnel and out to a hardwood basketball court surrounded by a full house crowd in a frenzy. There must've been 20,000 people dressed in red and black, Charlie thought as he looked up at them. "Follow my lead."

Benny the Bull ran down the tunnel, cartwheeling once, twice, then backflipping and sliding across the court into a smooth pose at center court to the delight of the crowd.

"The hardwood court where man can fly," Charlie repeated to himself. He had found the *wood*, but Benny the Flying Bull didn't exactly qualify as a *man*.

Charlie noted the giant scoreboard that hung overhead. The third quarter had just ended, and the fourth was set to start.

CHICAGO BULLS - 67

SEATTLE SUPERSONICS - 58

"Twelve minutes to go!" Charlie heard the play-by-play announcer exclaim from the side of the court through a microphone headset. "It's the Bulls up by nine, and one quarter away from hoisting the **1996 NBA CHAMPIONSHIP TROPHY!**"

He then heard a different voice coming from someone actually standing on the basketball court. "Almost there. If we can just hold them off." Of all the imposing figures they had run into in their travels, none was taller than the one standing over him now.

The player looked to Charlie.

"I'm supposed to find someone called 'His Airness.' Do you know where he is?" Charlie asked.

"I sure do," said the giant man. "He's right here."

"Here, like in this arena? I mean, it's a pretty big place with lots of people. Does he have a throne or a special viewing box or something?"

"He's got an even better seat than that."

"Well what, exactly, does he look like?" Charlie asked, peering around. "Does he have a crown on his head?"

"Nope. Nothing on his head. But he can jump out of his shoes. Super-acrobatic. And, by the way, he's a Bull."

Charlie looked out on the court where Benny continued his energetic high-flying exhibition of skill.

"*Benny* the Bull?" he wondered.

"No, Michael the Bull," the basketball player was smiling huge now.

"Oh, I haven't met him yet," Charlie said, confused.

"Yes you have."

Charlie looked up at the player. He was bald—nothing on his head. He hadn't jumped out of his shoes though—they were still on his feet. And his acrobatics were still to be determined. But he was wearing the number twenty-three on his jersey with **BULLS** displayed across the top.

"Are... *you* His Airness?" Charlie ventured, still uncertain.

"Michael 'Air' Jordan at your service. Benny out there thinks he can be like Mike, but he's got a long way to go," Michael laughed. They both watched the mascot, who was dumping popcorn on an unsuspecting SuperSonics fan.

"So, can you... fly?" Charlie asked.

"Some seem to think so. Let's just say I can jump pretty high and pretty far."

"So, what am I supposed to do for you?" Charlie asked. "Why do you need me here?"

"Well, with that bright velvet suit, I shouldn't have much trouble picking you out of a crowd. That's just what I'm looking to do. I need you to go up and make sure nobody sits in that seat right there." Michael pointed a few rows up in the stands.

"That's it?"

"That's it."

"Why?"

"That's where my dad used to sit—but he's no longer with us. It's been three years and I always look up to that seat and think of him. But if anybody sits there, I get completely thrown off my game. So, all I ask is that you usher people away."

"Have you kept that seat open every game for the last three years?"

"Of course not," said Michael.

Charlie nodded his head. After all, it would seem like there'd be a lot of seat switching and way too much velvet wearing involved.

"Because I've been playing pro baseball instead."

Charlie was as confused as a bookworm in a school of fish and he must have looked it too, because Michael continued to explain.

"After we won three NBA championships here in Chicago, and my dad was killed, I wanted to play the sport he always loved. But now, I'm back. And *we're* back," Michael pointed to his teammates. "And if we hold on for one more quarter, we'll win our fourth title. This one in Dad's memory. On Father's Day."

Right there in the middle of the arena, surrounded by those thousands of fans, Charlie opened up to Michael. "I've never even knew my real dad," Charlie told him, feeling a little more comfortable on the subject after sharing it with Babe Ruth earlier in his journey. "I was an orphan when I was little." He never let it really bother him, given that it was out of his control, but it was still part of who he was.

Michael nodded in understanding.

"Well, I'll protect his seat for you, Your Airness," Charlie said with confidence. "You can count on me." He turned to go, not noticing the giant foot of Benny the Bull stationed behind him. He promptly tripped right over it, tumbling back into the tunnel from where they had come in. *His Gracelessness* gave Michael little assurance.

"It's a good try," shouted Benny, "but when I told you to 'follow my lead,' I meant cartwheels, not somersaults. Keep working on it, though. You'll get it!"

Charlie was settled in a heap of velvet and popcorn halfway up the tunnel.

"You know how hard it is to get butter stains out of velvet?" Coach Stinkysox stood over him with folded arms and a tapping foot.

"I hadn't thought of it," Charlie groaned, at this point not even surprised to see him here.

"Well, kid, lucky for you, we have more pressing issues. You needn't me tell you that time is of the essence. So, let's get you to work."

Up above, Emma pursued the press box. She was planning on getting in and out in a flash unnoticed. She was hoping for a hit-and-run operation—and she was unsuccessful on all fronts.

"There is absolutely, positively, unmistakably no chance I will let a little *girl* into the big boy press box. Not now. Not soon. Not **EVER!**" an imposing figure with a big body and a disproportionately small head shouted from behind the press box door before slamming it shut in her face.

Emma had to come up with another plan. Time wasn't just ticking down on their journey. It was ticking down on the game.

"Charlie?" she chirped into the walkie-talkie. "Charlie, come in. I'm stuck."

"Stuck in what?"

"Stuck *in* nothing. Stuck *out* of the press box."

"Well, sneak in if you have to," Charlie's voice sounded exasperated when Emma assured him the likelihood of getting into the press box past the daunting doorman was slim-to-none.

"There isn't much choice, Emma. You'll just have to wait for the right moment and go."

Emma sighed. Like *that* was helpful advice. She looked at her watch. Twenty minutes remained.

Charlie made it to the stands, and headed toward the chair Michael had asked him to keep clear. It was, however, suddenly anything but clear. Wedged in that special stadium seat sat a monstrous man as stuck as a hippo in a hula hoop.

His Airness was watching the action as Charlie approached the guy and because of it, "Air" Jordan turned into "Error" Jordan, turning the ball over in the distraction.

"Excuse me, sir?" Charlie asked, timidly.

The massive man just dug deeper into his pool of nacho cheese and watched the action on the court, while his dip dripped from his chin.

"Sir?" Charlie said, a little louder this time. "This isn't your seat."

"How do you know?" the big guy shot back, not even turning to look at him.

"Because this is a special seat."

"Well, it ain't *that* special. Needs more cup holders." The dude had three jugs of soda balanced on his lap.

"I'll see what we can do about that. But, in the meantime, I need you to pop out of this chair."

The gargantuan guy looked at Charlie like he was considering eating him, and then chomped on a candy bar instead, turning back to the game.

The crowd groaned as Jordan had the ball stolen again, distracted by the commotion in his dad's old section.

Seattle had tied the game.

Charlie tried to budge the man out of the seat while the Bulls' coach called a timeout. He tried to yank on his arms. He even tried to bounce him out by jumping on his balloon belly, which had unintended consequences. Charlie was propelled up onto the outstretched hands of the nearby fans from which he crowd surfed all the way across the section, passed from fan to fan, down to the next aisle over, then promptly dumped like last week's trash into the walkway.

Fifteen minutes to go.

Charlie wondered what else he could do to get the big fella out of Mr. Jordan's seat so Michael could get back to championship form. He hoped Emma was faring better on her quest to get their mission's message. And he hoped maybe even Midnight could be of some service to their dilemma. But he soon found out that good ol' Midnight had a dilemma of his own.

"Ladies and gentlemen," the PA announcer proclaimed during the timeout. "It is time for the biggest giveaway in NBA history. If our mystery contestant can make just *one* half-court shot, he'll win this incredible brand new 1996 Dodge Viper! Would you believe it, folks, we just found this beauty moments ago in a storage closet here in the arena? How about that!"

The crowd roared. Charlie gasped.

"The Flogtrac. They're giving away our Flogtrac," he said, barely able to believe it.

"The fan we've chosen for the chance to own this new Viper is... McNight MidLean!"

"MCNIGHT MIDLEAN?!" Charlie repeated. *No way.* Midnight McLean was about to step out to center court and jeopardize their whole journey in one fell swoop. Going out in the middle of 20,000 people—any or all of whom could be TTT—under a spotlight no less, wasn't exactly a real strategic way to stay under the radar at this stage in the game.

How could he stop him?

Twelve minutes left.

A hush fell over the crowd. Both teams left their time-out huddles to watch. Midnight grabbed the ball and licked his finger to test the wind. Of course, as he was standing in the middle of an indoor stadium, there wasn't any. The lights dimmed. The spotlight shined.

Benny the Bull stood behind him, pumping his fist, digging in his foot and lowering his head like he was going to charge.

Maybe it was the horns. Maybe it was the look in his sewn-on eyes. Maybe it was the way he wagged his stuffed tail. Something just didn't seem right, and Charlie looked around frantically for help.

To his relief, Coach Stinkysox came to the rescue.

Just as Midnight stepped back for momentum and ran forward for that dream shot, he was flat out wham-bam-slammed to the ground. The basketball launched out of his grip defectively diagonal, rolling feebly off the court like a mislaunched cannon ball. Midnight himself hit the hard-wood with more force than the ax of a lumberjack.

The old coach had come out of nowhere.

The tackle knocked off Midnight's shoes, the landing dislodged his lab coat, and the coach's grip ripped his pants, revealing his bright pink boxers with bright white hearts beneath.

Charlie heard Midnight's voice crackle like a sparkler on the 4th of July.

"Stinkyface?!"

He couldn't believe the wimpy-looking man wearing headphones and a rainbow visor with a neon green see-through brim could have packed such power.

"Yes, Mr. McLean, I gracefully accept your debt of gratitude."

"Debt? Gratitude? I think you mean *upset. . . attitude!* Because that's all I've got for you." Midnight got back up on his feet and lunged for the old man.

Despite his age disadvantage and seeming physical shortcomings, Coach Stinkysox was amazingly agile. The chase that ensued around the court was something like a flashy neon version of cat and mouse and the crowd gasped with every turn of the action—like when Midnight dove for the coach, only to go head-first into the base of the basket. Charlie watched, horror-struck, as Midnight trailed him across the scorer's table, knocking off every last thing in their path: pieces of equipment, pieces of paper and peace of mind all together.

"I don't know what's in that crusty head of yours!" Midnight yelled ahead.

"You were going to get gored by that bull!" Stinkysox shouted back.

"That *bull?* That bull isn't real! I just wanted to win that car in front of all these people. It could've been all mine!"

"That Viper IS yours, you doofus! Whoever's in that bull costume might be TTT. My quick thinking saved you," Coach Stinkysox gasped, out of breath.

"That bull wasn't TTT, I guarantee it. That was stinky thinking, Stinkybreath," Midnight said with a certainty that struck Charlie as odd as he watched, entranced from the aisle.

Eight minutes to go.

"Emma!" Charlie shouted into his walkie-talkie. "If there were ever a time to sneak in, now's it. Are you seeing what I'm seeing?"

Emma, still stationed outside the press box, didn't hesitate for a second. She gripped the handle to the door and carefully turned it, unsure of what might greet her on the other side. But just as Charlie thought, there was never a better time to get in. Everyone in the room was hovered by the window, peering down at the craziness on the court.

They laughed. They pointed. They were oblivious.

Emma tiptoed in and swiftly located a special computer in the back corner of the room. She noticed a sign on the top of the monitor: *Now with access to the World Wide Web!*

She plugged in "Babe" for the password, but the computer froze. She tried again, but the computer screen didn't budge. She moved the mouse, but the cursor went nowhere either.

"Come on, you hunk of junk!" Emma whacked the side of the computer, sending a loud thud throughout the press box. She felt the eyes of the room before she even turned around.

Sure enough, dozens of reporters and press people had turned their attention away from the window and to her.

And so did one really angry and really out-of-position doorman.

"What did I tell you, little girl, about coming into the big boy press box?" he demanded as he neared. "This isn't the place for you. As if you have any idea of how to handle the complexities of the media, not to mention this advanced integrated equipment."

The computer had unfroze with Emma's smack. She heard the printer furiously churning behind her, and slowly crept back away from the doorman toward it.

"Little girl, you wouldn't know a newspaper from printer paper, and I'll bet—"

The doorman was now within feet of Emma, and Emma was within inches of the printer. She whisked the sheet off the top and then bolted for the exit, but stopped short, indignant. "You think *I* don't know newspapers? As lead reporter, I can assure you the *Eureka Enquirer* will be launching a full investigation into your discrimination practices, mister. And, by the way, I can *guarantee* you I at least know more about computers than you know about manners."

With that, she turned and ran.

By the time she made it down the corridor and into the clear, some semblance of order had returned to the basketball court. Midnight and his bright pink boxers with bright white hearts had chased Coach Stinkysox and his neon green hat across every inch of the hardwood, only to finally dart up the stadium stairs and out the exit to the boisterous applause of the crowd.

After all, the fans had come to see basketball and while the timeout entertainment was comically compelling, there was a championship on the line.

The game resumed, but the interloper in Mr. Jordan's seat remained put.

"Charlie, I've got it!" Emma wheezed into the walkie-talkie.

"You've got a way to move the human boulder from his seat?" he said, sounding hopeful.

"No, I've got the message," Emma said in between gasps for breath.

"You sound like you're running a marathon. What'd you find?"

"Not sure. I haven't read it yet—too busy escaping the *big boy* press box." Emma unfolded the clue and read aloud:

> *Your hero has tried his hand at diamond dirt,*
> *Only to find it's hard being a b-ball convert.*
> *But no win here and as far as he thinks,*
> *It's better to quit and head off to the links.*
> *Victory means three more titles to show,*
> *If he can't swing it, he's off to play golf as a pro.*

"His Airness can't quit again," insisted Charlie. "Unless he's piloting a blimp, he can't fly on a golf course."

288

Down on the court, Michael dribbled through his legs, jumped up and passed the ball to Benny the Bull, who was at that moment standing on his head in the third row. Benny, unfortunately, was out of bounds, ineligible and a terrible shot anyway. Another turnover.

Things were getting ugly, and only four minutes remained in the game. If Michael didn't snap out of it—and quick—his status atop the basketball world would be sunk like a shanked shot into a water hazard. He'd be trading in his jump shot for a chip shot, and when it came to winning there, he might very well have *no* shot.

Six minutes left.

Charlie was in no mood to screw around. He already had a popcorn butter stain across the front of his velvet jacket, and his crowd surfing gaffe had landed him in a pickle—a pickle pumpkin pie, to be exact. Who would ever have such a thing at a basketball game, Charlie couldn't figure. But it made for quite the stench as he stomped up the stairs and back around to Mr. Jordan's seat.

"I'm going to tell you, and I'm going to tell you one more time," Charlie demanded, pointing at the intruder. "This. Is. Not. Your. Seat. It is a very important seat. And if you don't get out of the seat by the time I count to three, I'm going to turn you into mincemeat."

"Mincemeat?"

"Yeah, you heard me."

"Does it come with hot fudge gravy?" the man said, licking his lips.

"Huh?"

"And what's that scrumptious smell? Is that. . . pickles? **AND PUMPKIN?**" The big guy followed his nose and thrust out of the chair, making the sound of a cork popping from a bottle. His crumbs rolled off into a pile by his feet.

"And that's not all," Charlie said, backing away.

"Yeah, you're right. I smell popcorn and pie. **OH MY.**" He started rumbling toward the little usher. Up one step, two steps, three steps. Every step Charlie took, the monstrous man lumbered behind, chasing that staggering scent his nose simply couldn't resist.

At the top of the stairs, Charlie backed into a railing with nowhere else to go. He cowered into a little ball against the wall as the man closed in on him. "Here. Take it!" Charlie offered, holding up his crud-covered velvet jacket. "Please don't eat me!"

The colossal ogre grabbed the coat and took in the wonderful whiff of pickle pumpkin pie and popcorn goodness. He felt something in the pocket. "Mmmm. Jawbreakers. Yummy yummy in the tummy!"

Where did those come from? Charlie thought before shrugging. At least that'll keep him busy for a while.

CRUNCH, CRUNCH, CRUNCH.

"All done. What else do you have?"

"How about a knuckle sandwich?" Charlie said, hoping he wouldn't take him up on his offer.

"Mmmm. I love *every* kind of sandwich! I love a pastrami and papaya sandwich. A peanut butter and cheese sandwich. A chimichanga chili sandwich. A buffalo wing and jelly sandwich. A shrimp shish kabob sandwich. . ."

Charlie took his opportunity, while the big guy continued down the list, to sneak back to special seat duty.

Three minutes were now on the game clock.

Michael did a double-take looking at his dad's old spot. No intruder. Nobody replacing his irreplaceable biggest fan.

Seattle's star came in for another steal. Michael shot one last glance at the seat and flung the ball around his back, through his legs and drove for the hoop. It was like the whole court had cleared out for him. His Airness took off from beyond the foul line, flying toward the hoop and hanging like he was in slow motion. His tongue was stuck out in his signature pose as he slammed the ball through the basket, bringing the crowd to its feet and the game back into his control.

Michael was barely halfway back down the court when he stepped in for a steal, gliding back to his hoop for another breathtaking high-flying dunk. He was back in form, and the Bulls were back on top.

Charlie brushed off Mr. Jordan's seat, though his eyes were totally diverted to the court. He couldn't believe what he was witnessing. *The* Michael Jordan, shining in his prime. Leading his team to victory. Outmaneuvering anyone who might try to stop him from doing so. While Charlie kept his eyes on the court, he cleared away the remaining debris left behind by the trespasser. The cleaner that seat got, the higher Michael seemed to fly.

The time travelers had three minutes left. There was a minute left on the game clock. Seattle had one final shot to get back within reach. Michael jumped like he had springs on his feet and blocked the shot with ease. Back down the court, he relied on his most crucial teammates. He dished the ball behind his back to Scottie Pippen, his right-hand man. Scottie tossed over to Dennis Rodman, whose bright-colored hair distracted all comers. Dennis fired a perfect pass back to His Airness, who finished the job with a long leap and model Jordan jam to seal the deal.

The buzzer rang out and confetti rained down on the Bulls—the NBA champions again.

Charlie could barely see through the falling sparkles, but as he looked back up the stairway, he saw the hungry hulk still rattling off his favorite sandwiches to nobody in particular, while concurrently trying to eat the falling paper from above.

Charlie looked down to Midnight, who was leaning against the Viper Flogtrac courtside with his ripped pants hanging loose and bright pink boxers with bright white hearts hanging out.

Emma came zipping down toward Charlie, grabbed his arm and yanked him toward the Flogtrac. "Have you looked at the clock? We've got less than two minutes left for time travel!" Emma cried as they ran across the court through the players and the confetti, nearly running smack into MJ himself.

"Hey, kid," said the man of the hour. Still attached at the arm, they stopped and turned to Air Jordan. "You did good. And it looks like you got the girl, too."

Charlie blushed and tried not to look to Emma. She pulled her arm back away and gave him a weird look.

"I wish we could stay, Mr. Jordan. But we gotta fly," Charlie muttered.

"You're a little short, Charlie. But keep working at it. Someday maybe you can be like Mike."

Charlie started to explain that his kind of flight was less foot-powered and more Flogtrac-powered, but he didn't have the chance. Emma gripped back onto him—by the shoulder this time—and whisked him away.

"Midnight, let's get this thing outta here! We've got like two minutes left," she cried.

"Oh?" said a still-dazed Midnight.

"And we still have to plug in a number to the EMC2, find the closet and somehow drive into the continuum, all before time expires," Emma urged. "And if you don't get in the Viper Flogtrac right this instant, I'll turn it into a viper-*filled* Flogtrac."

"Ewwy, icky, yucky!" Midnight squealed as he hopped into the driver's seat like his feet were on fire. "You know how I feel about those venomous vermin." He shook his whole body to get the ick out quick.

As Midnight punched buttons on the computer and tapped the keyboard above the wheel, Emma reached out to the final box in the EMC2 and tapped a two and a three for Michael Jordan's jersey number twenty-three, and the device glowed like the Christmas tree in Rockefeller Center. The lights throughout the stadium flashed in tandem.

With the turn of the key, the Flogtrac roared to life right there courtside amidst the massive championship celebration.

"Can you even see where you're going?" Charlie yelled over the crowd. "It's raining confetti."

"Ah, my little backseat driver, the great Midnight McLean is prepared for even the most unlikely of scenarios. Let me just activate the READY STEADY CONFETTI CATCHER 3000."

Midnight flipped a switch on the dash, activating a robotic vacuum funnel that popped up through the hood of the Viper Flogtrac. It sucked up all the confetti falling in front, to the sides and above them, taking the little papers through the body of the Flogtrac and spitting them out in a **POOF** behind them.

One minute remained.

"Midnight, do you mean to tell us you invented a feature on the Flogtrac *specifically* for the case of raining confetti?" Emma asked.

"Of course not. That would be ridiculous," Midnight rolled his eyes.

"It also acts as the READY STEADY *SPAGHETTI* CATCHER 3000 too, just in case it rains pasta. Now buckle in the seatbelts, boys and girls!" Midnight hit the accelerator, weaving in and out of the players and personnel who were headed through the tunnel for more locker room celebration.

"Someone's trying to steal that Viper!" the public address announcer shouted over the PA system.

Midnight turned the Viper Flogtrac around the corner, toward the time continuum closet. But something stood in the way.

Stationed in front of the closet door with his flimsy rubber horns, intimidating eyes and mightily menacing unibrow was Benny the Bull. Apparently, they weren't going anywhere if the bull had anything to say about it. "Nobody steals from us!" a voice said from within the mascot uniform.

Midnight revved the engine. Benny pawed the ground.

Their dilemma was interrupted by a familiarly excruciating squeal.

BEEP! BEEP! BEEP!

Midnight couldn't believe he was receiving a page at a time like this. But he knew he couldn't ignore it.

There are no buckets nor mops nor brooms out here, but look for an alternate path to steer. Get there before all your hard work is nixed. 10 . . . 9 . . . 8 . . . 7 . . . 6 . . .

"What are we going to do?" asked Charlie. "We can't go around him."

"And we sure can't go over or under, either," Emma noted. "That doesn't leave us with many options."

"Certainly you haven't considered *all* our options, kiddos." Midnight popped open a compartment and gripped a dial. "Like I said, I've come prepared."

He held onto the wheel and shot the Flogtrac forward. Benny darted toward them full bore for what was certain to be a catastrophic collision.

But just in the nick of time, Midnight twisted the dial, and from beneath the front of the Flogtrac popped up a pointed tool that poked a hole right through the middle of Benny the Bull. It stretched him wide open enough for the Flogtrac to shoot through, exposing the bluish force field in Benny where his number used to be.

As they slammed through, the Theory of Bop Mucket Continuumumum held true, and they were swallowed up in a flash.

There was a huge **SPARK**, a thunderous **BOOM** and a gargantuan **BAM!**

"Now, that's what I call good drive-through service," declared Midnight, as they shot down a winding galactic pathway.

"Holy cow!" Charlie finally blurted out.

"No," corrected Midnight. "Holey *bull*."

"Midnight, you even have a Flogtrac feature for run-ins with bulls?" asked Emma.

"No, no, no. The Wham Bam Thank You Mammal 4600 isn't just for bulls. It's also for camels. And for bison and rhinos and elephants and lions and whatever other prey might stand in our way."

They zoomed down the familiar winding tunnel, suddenly amazed at the position they were in. Nobody behind. Nothing in their way. And an endless path ahead.

"Now what?" Charlie uttered.

"Now, we take what we've earned," answered Midnight. He looked to the EMC2, which had altered its display from its six square front to show a destination location situation. With one eye on the pathway and one hand on the wheel, he plugged in the time and place he'd pursued from the invention's foundation.

"Are you ready, kiddos? '94 Series, ere-hay e-way ome-cay!"

It was like the announcement of a shuttle launch—with the anticipation of some sort of blast-off. And then they waited. And drove. And waited. And drove.

It was excruciating.

"Hmmm. Not quite as I calculated," Midnight said to their chagrin.

"Did we. . . make the countdown cutoff in time?" wondered Charlie, finally uttering the question they all were thinking. "Or, are we. . . *stuck* here?"

"Let's hope we don't have to find our own way back," noted Emma. "I get the feeling we're still a *long* way from home."

Midnight remained patient. "Let's just trust it, kiddos. I'm sure everything is just fine." He jabbed his elbow into the EMC2 to shake it up. And not a moment later, a giant beam of light shined down from above.

Their Flogtrac floated up, leaving the pathway and zooming vertically, being pulled by some force out of their control.

They peered up to the sight of a spaceship-looking unit and an open hatch that sucked them closer and closer.

Did the TTT have an alternate arrangement in the works?

Or was it some sort of climactic galactic vacuum ending their journey with a single swipe?

Perhaps they were just being extremely inconveniently abducted by aliens?

Just as they neared the door, they got their answer. There was the welcomed sight of a tiny bluish force field waiting above.

SHWOOP!

It sucked them through, into a path of incredible brilliant lights surrounding them in every direction—more brilliant than any they had seen thus far.

SHWOOP!

They arrived to a sight more incredible than anything they'd expected. There, in front of the Flogtrac, stood Cornelius, the tiny travel troll with an off-center red baseball cap, tuxedo t-shirt, giant ears and big floppy feet.

And next to Cornelius was a tall, terribly tricky boy with spiky blond hair and a bright red sweatshirt.

Don Ginmaster and Cornelius the travel troll were side-by-side.

"How about *this* senseless spectacle?" marveled Blond Don.

Cornelius stopped him. "Welcome, travel friends. You're right on time. Come on over here a little closer." In his hand,

Charlie thought he got a glimpse of something sharp, but Cornelius quickly hid it before he could get a better look.

CHAPTER 13

MIDNIGHT'S MOMENT

Midnight stepped out of the souped-up golf cart first, sliding down long side panels that now attached the Flogtrac to the floor. The panels extended out from the base, making the Flogtrac resemble the kind of rocket ship Cornelius had flown earlier.

"Those will help you chop frrriction as you cut across time frrrequencies," noted Cornelius, rolling his tongue with vigor.

Midnight gave Don a suspicious glance, and then looked awkwardly away. Charlie and Emma both noticed him trying to avoid eye contact. *Why was he acting so weird?*

Emma slid out of the Flogtrac, down the left panel. Despite knowing his imperfections, she still wanted to get near Don. She gave a guilty shrug as she got closer to him.

Charlie, meanwhile, slid down the right panel, catching one ankle beneath the other, spilling sideways into a stack of boxes that tumbled on top of him.

"Wow, did you have a good *trip?*" Blond Don mocked.

"Fine trip. Incredible people. Learned a lot. Thanks for asking," Charlie grunted, pushing his way out from beneath the pile.

"How about we get on with it, travel troll? I have things to do, places to be and extragalactic girlfriends to see," Don whined impatiently.

"Extragalactic girlfriends?" Emma repeated, backing away from the evil enchanter. "I hope they reject you like we already *ejected* you."

"Alright, you three, come in close," Cornelius announced. "Let's get right to the point."

"You have fulfilled the requirements of learning the time traveling ways. You have honored the rrrules of the rrroad all day. You now know why the rules that are written are quite so demanding. And you must continue to follow them to stay in good standing. The TTT will keep an eye out if you stray from these things. But now, I present you with your time travel wings." Cornelius gripped onto Midnight's shirt, pulling him close and stabbed a pin through it.

Ah, thought Charlie. *I knew he had something sharp.*

"Owwwy wowwwy!" Midnight yelped.

"Oh, you big wimp. I barely nicked you." Cornelius adjusted a bright golden wing-shaped badge pinned to Midnight's shirt, which he patted proudly.

He pinned a set of golden wings on Charlie, and then Emma too, ceremoniously tapping each on the shoulders with his walking stick the way a king might honor a knight.

His big flopping feet echoed off the walls, and the stick doinked with each subsequent tap on the shoulder.

FLIP FLOP DOINK, DOINK.

FLIP FLOP DOINK, DOINK.

FLIP FLOP DOINK, DOINK.

"Welcome to the club," Don sneered, visibly unimpressed. "Just remember that the TTT keeps a constant watch out for time crime crooks."

Cornelius lightened the mood. "Mr. McLean, what do you say we get you off to your game and looking the part?"

"Yeah, take this," Don offered, pulling a duffel bag off his shoulder. "It's got all you need to fulfill your fantasy. And if all goes as planned, it's yours to keep." He raised an eyebrow at Midnight, handing it over.

Midnight grabbed the bag from Blond Don, peeking inside with eyes that got as big as saucers. He looked to Charlie and Emma, then back inside the bag, before Cornelius led him through a door to the locker room.

"What's in the bag, Midnight?" Emma asked. But she didn't get an answer before he was totally out of sight.

"I'll take care of these two," Don called to the travel troll. "They'll be in good hands, I can assure you." He pinched Charlie and Emma's shoulders, and led them through another door to a corridor lined with frantic baseball fans.

"Can you believe it?" they overheard one fan ask.

"I know! Game 7! All tied up! World Series!" cheered another.

"And don't forget who we've got in the bullpen to turn out the lights," added a third.

Charlie whispered loudly to Emma, "Wow, they're actually talking about Midnight."

Charlie squirmed out of Blond Don's grip in the middle of the walkway. "Hey, do you think you can loosen it up a bit back there? We've earned out wings fair and square, so cut us a little slack. Alright?"

Blond Don just stared back crookedly.

306

Emma ducked out of his clasp too. "Yeah, who do you think you are, leading people around like this? And leading people *on* like—"

"Listen, you two. You screw around, you bend the rules. You walk around like getting here was all up to you. It's time you know the truth. It's time for me to step in and pooh-pooh your ill-advised confidence."

"Did. . . you just say you're going to step in poo-poo?" Charlie asked.

"No, I said I'm going to step in and pooh-pooh—"

"I'm pretty sure you just said it again. You're going to step in poo-poo."

"No, uh— That's not what I— I didn't mean—"

Don's fuming face was redder than his strawberry-colored sweatshirt.

"Do you have any idea what Midnight just got in that closet?" Don questioned, his menacing tone returning.

"Yes, a sharp poke," Charlie answered.

"What else?"

"A pair of shiny golden wings."

"What *else*?"

"A bag?" Emma jumped in.

"And do you know what was *in* that bag?" Don's eyes were glinting in a way Charlie didn't like.

Charlie and Emma could have guessed all day, and never would've gotten close to the answer.

"Benjamin Franklin."

"You had Benjamin Franklin in that bag?" Charlie squealed. "Please tell me you poked holes so he could breathe."

"No, dingbat. There were 10,000 Benjamin Franklins," Don retorted.

Neither Charlie nor Emma knew what to make of this.

"Benjamin Franklins," Don repeated. "Hundred-dollar bills. Ten thousand of them."

"Why would you give Midnight a million dollars?" asked Emma, doing the math.

"Because we had a deal, and that was my end of the bargain."

Charlie turned to Emma, feeling confused and betrayed. By the look on her face, she felt the same way.

"And your friend, your buddy, your *pal*, Mr. McLean, is going to hold up his part. He'll win the World Series."

"But that's what he's wanted all along," Charlie said, still confused.

"True. But we're allowing it. He gets his dream. And we get you two," Don said smugly.

"What do you mean you *get* us two?" asked Emma, narrowing her eyes.

"A fitty each. That's the payment. And you got off lucky. Fifty years in Dung Geon really isn't that big a deal. We almost nabbed you for a hundo, but that Midnight McLean drives a tough bargain."

"Midnight negotiated our time in Dung Geon?" Charlie said, his stomach sinking. "*Our* friend Midnight?"

"Believe it. He almost had a sneezing attack he was so excited about it. Didn't you think it was weird you didn't see a single member of the Time Travel Troop over your last two stops? That's awfully generous of us, wouldn't you agree?"

"Yeah, super-generous," Emma muttered angrily. "So, what happens if he doesn't win the game?"

"You think after all this, there's any chance he *wouldn't* fulfill his dream of winning the World Series? With a million dollars in one hand, you think he won't want a championship ring on the other? If he screws this up, he's dumber than the dirt he'll be eating all over again."

"So there's still a chance?" Charlie asked, with a glimmer of hope.

Instead of replying, Don grabbed their shoulders again with a clasp like a vice grip. It was clear—they weren't going anywhere he wasn't leading them.

"Listen, little traveling troublemakers, what do you say we turn those frowns upside down and go watch some baseball? There's a World Series to win. You wouldn't want to miss *that*, now would you? After all, it's the last fun you'll be having for a long, long time."

Emma peered over to Charlie. "I hope Midnight electrocutes himself on Benjamin Franklin's kite."

At that very moment in the locker room, Franklin's kite—of course—wasn't flying anywhere, but pictures of him were. Midnight was showering himself in hundred-dollar bills like they were a giant pile of fall leaves.

"Great balls of honey, look at all this money, money, money!"

Cornelius eyed Midnight in his stupor. "And what, might I ask, do you plan to do with all this money, money, money when you're all-doney, doney, doney?"

Midnight turned his attention from the pile of cash. "Look, little travel troll, I appreciate your concern and I appreciate your assistance in getting us here. But I've waited a long time for this, and all I want is to walk out of here with the game-winning home run in the bottom of the ninth inning of Game 7 of the World Series, a giant diamond-covered championship ring and this great big pile of cash to buy great big piles of things. Is *that* so much to ask?"

It was hard to take Midnight seriously with all those bills hanging from his hair, lodged in his belt and stuck to the spikes on the bottom of his shoes.

"It is when you sell your soul for it," Cornelius noted.

"I didn't sell my soul for it. I sold two other people's. That's not the same thing... right?"

"So, this whole trip, this whole journey, this whole adventure: it was all for you and nobody else?" Cornelius said, giving Midnight a reproachful look.

"It's just that it's time for me to get the recognition I deserve. The home run. The World Series. The big money."

"Did you ever hear the expression, Mr. McLean, that money can't buy happiness?"

"Yeah, well *this* much can." Midnight reached down and threw another pile of cash into the air.

Cornelius sighed. "What do you say we get you out to the bullpen before you miss your mighty moment, Mr. Moneybags?"

"It's alright even if I do. I'll just travel back a few minutes and do it again," Midnight noted, patting the golden wings pinned to the front of his baseball jersey.

Up above, Blond Don led Charlie and Emma out to the stands, frog-marching them all the way down to their reserved seats in the front row, right behind home plate.

Looking left, they saw a conglomerate of terribly tense troopers. Every member of the TTT was in attendance, watching spitefully as their leader placed the two travelers in their seats.

Looking right, they saw familiar friendly faces—a decidedly more distracted group. Mr. Muffin was on one end, chomping on french fries from one hand and french toast from the other.

Coach Stinkysox was right next to him, folding a pile of handkerchiefs. His goal was to manage the grease disbursal from the food that dripped down to Mr. Muffin's shiny black shoes.

Ol' Tex the Tailor was equally intensely focused on the game on the field and the project in his lap. He furiously knitted away at a pair of mittens as quick as a Texas tick.

Dr. Dinglehopper was admiring the flower pinned to his surgical scrubs, when he suddenly took interest in Tex's project, too.

"What the bloody heck are those? A couple boxing gloves?"

"No, you twit, they're mitts," ol' Tex retorted. "Why don't you go back to watching the game and quit botherin' me?"

"What bloody game?"

"The one right in front of you, Dinglebat."

"Oh, righto. Who's playing?"

It was now the top of the ninth inning, tied at five. Midnight's team was in the field.

The pitcher on the mound sweated profusely, gripping his shoulder. He was tiring, and it was showing with every pitch he threw. The first batter dinked a blooper into right field for a single, and the second ripped a double to left, leaving runners on second and third. The next hitter never took the bat off his shoulder, watching four balls outside the strike zone, sending him to first with a walk.

With the bases loaded and no outs, the manager had seen enough, but the pitcher, it seemed, refused to go anywhere. He demanded one more chance to finish the job, and the manager reluctantly let him have it. Only, the hurler didn't know just how off his aim had drifted. The next pitch, targeted right down the middle, instead hit the batter's backside, bringing in the go-ahead run, making it a 6-5 game.

It was then that the crowd had seen enough. They called for the one and only closer who could pull them out of such a jam.

"LIGHTS OUT! LIGHTS OUT! LIGHTS OUT!" they chanted.

There was no choice but to make the move. The manager motioned to the bullpen for Midnight McLean.

The door opened, and Midnight entered the field as confident as could be, knowing his opportunity had finally come again. He had mapped out the perfect pitches to throw. He had the game-winning power in his bat. He knew exactly how to change his fate forever.

Midnight floundered out of the bullpen to the chants of the crowd, running like he had flippers on his feet. No matter how great a pitcher Midnight might've been, or how far he could've hit a ball, he still bounded around like a bumbling clown, but it only pumped up the crowd more. Their star pitcher could do no wrong. He was their guy. Their lights-out machine. Their hero. Even if he did run like a loon on the moon.

When he finally reached the mound, the stadium was shaking like a brimming blender. And for Midnight, all the ingredients were in place.

He toed the rubber as the next batter stepped up to the plate. With the bases loaded, there was no room for error. Any small mistake could let in another run, or more. But Midnight, of course, already knew that. He wound back for his first pitch, stepping and delivering a fireball strike right down the middle, surprising the batter with its staggering speed. The catcher clutched his hand in pain despite all the padding in his glove.

"Steeerike one!" Midnight shouted, pumping his arm. "You know it!"

The hitter didn't stand much better of a chance on the second pitch either. Midnight threw a nasty curve that started out above the guy's head and then dropped down well below his knees for strike two, right past a mighty and fruitless swing.

"Steeerike two!" Midnight announced, shaking his hips. "Can't stop me!"

But he changed things up for the 0-2 pitch. Midnight wound back and delivered an off-speed floater that brutally fooled the batter. He swung so early, he had enough time to reload and swing again, but the changeup pitch drifted into the catcher's mitt unharmed.

"Steeerike three!" Midnight declared, boogying like a belly dancer. "You're outta here!"

There was one out now, and the bases remained loaded. And Midnight remained crazy.

The next hitter lurched up to bat, unsure of what to expect from the closer. The crowd, meanwhile, knew exactly what they wanted to see. And Midnight, as he toed the rubber again, was certain they were going to get it.

A slider started it off, headed for the batter's knees, sneaking across the plate for a strike.

"STeeeRIKe UNO!" Midnight yelled, shooting his fingers to the catcher like they were guns. "Just getting started."

He followed it up with a pitch that flew without much direction. It was a knuckleball that floated and fell, then rose back up. It darted right, then left, and confused the catcher so much, he didn't even catch it with his glove. Lucky for him, it fit perfectly in the grill of his mask. For the batter, it was like swinging at a bumble bee with the wrong end of a fly swatter.

"STeeeRIKe DOS!" Midnight proclaimed, spinning in a circle like a top. "Here we go again. . . *again*."

The next pitch he threw was the best Midnight had. It was his signature. His specialty. His go-to finisher. And that's just what his junk ball did. It spun, it stopped, it jumped and hopped, and finished off the batter like buttered kelp at a high cholesterol crab convention.

"STeeeRIKe TReS!" Midnight barked, tossing his glove up into the air and landing it on his head. "Two down, one to go!"

The crowd fueled the fire, continuing to chant, "LIGHTS OUT! LIGHTS OUT! LIGHTS OUT!"

While at the plate, the batters could only watch stupefied, behind the plate, Charlie and Emma looked on, mortified.

"I wish someone would actually turn the lights out so we didn't have to see this," Charlie hoped, thinking about the fate that awaited them once the game was all said and done.

Emma's eyes were squinting with spite. "It's like watching a train wreck. Only, the conductor's a circus clown, and we're stuck on the tracks."

Down the third base line, the TTT seemed impressed by the colorful and effective display Midnight was putting on. On the other side of the field, the reaction was an array of excited, analytical, distracted and confused.

Mr. Muffin applauded by smashing together his french fries and french toast at every strike thrown. He had a handful of mashed potatoes and french pancakes by the time the third batter stepped into the box.

Stinkysox listened to the broadcast through his headphones, analyzing each element of the game as the action evolved.

It didn't seem to be of much interest to ol' Tex, though, who was frantically fitting the mittens to precise perfection. Or to Dr. Dinglehopper, who didn't seem to quite get, for some reason, that they weren't at a cricket match. "Come on," he called out. "Get it through the wicket, mate. Throw him a blimey wicked googly!"

Midnight was quick to get back to the work at hand. One more batter to face, and everything would be in perfect place for his righteous redemption.

He finally took the glove off his head, and focused on getting the third out.

The batter dug in. He swung with all his might as Midnight's next pitch headed straight down Broadway. But when the ball got halfway there, it split in two like a chopped orange, and not knowing which to hit, the batter whiffed right down the middle. Both halves came back together and dropped in the catcher's mitt whole once again.

"**STeeeRIKe-A-one!**" Midnight whooped. "Now, *that's* a splitter no hitter can touch."

The batter had no more luck with the follow-up, which was as fitting as anything in Midnight's arsenal. He wound back and delivered a ball that started way outside, and darted back across the plate against all reasonable laws of physics. No other screwball but Midnight could pull off a screwball pitch like that.

"**STeeeRIKe-A-TWo!**" Midnight hollered. "Zip it, curve it, now *strikeout*, 'cause you deserve it!"

The batter looked at him, confused as ever. What else could Midnight possibly have up his sleeve?

With the count 0-2, everyone expected no less than an over-the-top fastball with all the bells and whistles you get with a Midnight McLean delivery. But as Midnight set up to pitch, he delivered something that nobody had seen before. At least, not in the World Series, and certainly not for a long, long time, anyway.

Midnight wound up, reached back, twirled his arm and served up an underhanded sluggish slow-pitch, floating it up over the plate like a lollipop pie. But it was the hitter who turned out to be the real sucker. His eyes got so big, his heart pounded so hard and his arms tightened so tense that he threw his bat at the ball while it was barely just reaching its peak.

It missed by a country mile, but did hit another target slap-happy and solid: Midnight's head. He was knocked out stone cold before the umpire could even call **STRIKE THREE.**

The entire stadium gasped in horror. Charlie and Emma jumped out of their seats and rushed onto the field before Blond Don could stop them.

"Midnight! Midnight! Can you hear me?" Charlie yelled as he reached the mound. He slapped him a couple times to see if that might help. It didn't.

"Hey, you big dummy. Looks like someone's stealing your duffel bag full of money," Emma lied.

Midnight started to come to. "What? Who? Where?" he mumbled groggily.

"So, it *is* true? You really sold us off to the depths of a galaxy far, far away for a little bag of money?"

"It was a big bag, actually. With a million dollars inside. And don't forget I still get to hit my big home run, too," Midnight said, looking sheepish.

"Midnight, how could you?" Charlie demanded.

"To tell you the truth, I never *technically* agreed to the deal. I just ended up blowing snot on them when they asked. But once that dreadful Blond Don showed me the gold pot at the end of the rainbow, I'll admit, I was reeled in, hook, line and sinker."

"Did the bat knock any sense back into you?" Emma asked.

"Who, me? What bat? How many *cents* are we talking about?" Midnight stood up to the raucous applause of the crowd and moved toward his team's dugout. He raised his hat up into the air in acknowledgment and went to look for a batting helmet that might fit over the new giant bump on the top of his head.

Charlie and Emma looked around for some sort of exit plan, but a giant shadow lurked over them. Blond Don got his grip on their shoulders before they could even think to make a move. He retreated with them back to their seats.

The score remained 6-5, and Midnight's team was set to take its final shot at winning the World Series.

Midnight was scheduled to bat sixth, and he was ready for his big moment from the second he got to the dugout. The bases would be loaded. There would be two outs. There would be a full count. And the game would be in his hands.

The pitcher took the mound and the leadoff batter entered the box. No outs, none on. Five batters to go.

Strike one, strike two and strike three took care of out number one.

The second batter, knowing a single run would tie it, tried to do it all with one swing of the bat. He crushed a high fly ball deep down the left field line on the very next pitch and began his trot around the bases like it was a done deal. But it wasn't. A gust of wind curled the ball left of the foul pole, and out into the crowd for a long strike one.

The batter fumingly returned to the batter's box, but his strategy didn't change. This time, he waited just a fraction of a second longer and ripped one deep down the right field line—a goner for sure, if not for the most untimely nuisance night owl catching the ball mid-flight and carrying it across the foul line, then out of the stadium. Strike two.

He couldn't believe it. Nor could the crowd, many of whom threw popcorn and ice cream cones at the owl in frustration, inadvertently landing most of the delectable projectiles on the heads of other even angrier fans.

Since left field didn't work, and nor did right, he aimed for center and sent the very next pitch to the deepest part of the park, more than four-hundred feet away. No pesky bird stole it this time—but an agile outfielder did. The center fielder leapt up onto the wall, stood up, reached back, and hauled in the sure home run for the second out.

The batter fired his helmet into the dirt and tore out chunks of his thick brown hair by the handful.

"There's nothing to worry about," muttered Midnight. "It's all under control."

There were two outs and nobody on. Midnight's team was down to its final out, with still three batters to go before he was up.

The crowd was on its feet, trying to initiate the increasingly improbable comeback.

Charlie and Emma were on their feet too, but they were hoping that by some miracle it wouldn't play out the way Midnight told them it would. If Midnight never got his shot to win the World Series, then maybe they would be spared from their dubious fate. All the other team had to do, after all, was get one measly out.

And on the very next pitch, they suddenly believed in miracles. A slow ground ball toward first base was dinked off the hitter's bat. It bounced through the infield like a frolicking frog and right to the first baseman. But, just as it hopped in front of his glove, it clinked off a dirt rock, sending it clumsily through the fielder's legs, allowing the batter to reach the base safely. The tying run was quickly on first.

"How's that even possible?" Charlie groaned. "That was the most routine ground ball I've ever seen."

Emma didn't have an answer, but her eyes were drawn to a familiar tuxedo t-shirt-wearing travel troll beyond the right field wall. Cornelius was standing on top of the bullpen dugout, shaking his hat toward first base, as if he were casting some sort of slip-up spell.

Emma nudged Charlie, who also saw Cornelius, but didn't catch on quite as quick. "What, do you think Cornelius had something to do with that play?" he asked.

"Maybe after all Midnight's done to get here, Cornelius is gonna make sure he gets his shot," Emma shrugged.

But the very next batter confused them even further. It was a pop-up right to the pitcher's mound. The third baseman called for it. The second baseman did, too. The first baseman called them both off, but the shortstop decided he would just take it himself. None heard the others, and they all collapsed onto the pitcher at once, simultaneously falling back like they had run into a cylindrical brick wall.

The pitcher was so dazed, he couldn't decide which of the three balls he was seeing he should try to catch. The real ball bounced off his face and dropped onto the mound, allowing the hitter to reach first, and the runner to move to second.

Two on, two outs, one batter to go.

Surely that had to be Cornelius' doing too. But when Charlie looked over, he was just sitting quietly atop the bullpen dugout stroking his long white bushy beard. They looked to his associates, but Mr. Muffin had his French-food-filled hands still occupied, Stinkysox was busy pondering the amount of bleach all those dirty uniforms would need, ol' Tex was focused on the finishing touches of his magical mittens and Dr. D was reading. The fact the *Surgical Sentinel* was about two inches from his face and upside down assured Emma and Charlie that he, too, had nothing to do with any sort of spell.

They looked to the row of TTT, but they all seemed too distracted by a tall pretty redhead sitting in the second row to pull off any tricks.

That only left one person. Don Ginmaster was rubbing one hand through his spiky blond hair and pointing the other trickily to the pitcher's mound. That was definitely fishy.

"Are you *helping* Midnight?" Charlie asked point blank.

"Who, me?" Don played stupid.

"I thought rule number one was that you couldn't change history," Emma reminded him.

"I don't know what you're talking about. Can't a guy put his hand through his hair and point deviously to a baseball field without getting accused of something?"

"Not when your hair is gelled up solid as a rock," Charlie shot back. "There's nothing normal about that. There has to be another reason, Blond Dummy."

"You want to know the truth?" Don asked. "The truth is if you don't turn around right now, I'll take you two out of here before your precious Midnight even gets the chance to betray you. Understand? You might as well enjoy your freedom while you've got it."

They couldn't argue with that.

Midnight was on deck. His helmet sat high on his head, atop the bump from the flying bat. His warm-up routine was frighteningly familiar to Charlie and Emma by now, yet still weird to witness nevertheless. But it got him focused, and that's all that mattered with the World Series on the line.

"First pitch will be high by the eyes. Lay off it," Midnight called out to the batter before him. Sure enough, it sailed in up by the hitter's face, high for ball one. He looked at Midnight surprised, but figured it for a good guess.

"This one's outside and even colder. Keep the bat parked on your shoulder."

And once again, his memory served him right. The hitter didn't move, as the pitch zipped out of the strike zone and outside for ball two.

"This one's a curve. It'll drop in for a strike. But you can't hit a curveball to save your life."

The pitcher wound back and delivered a perfect looping strike to move the count to 2-1.

The batter stepped out of the box and looked to the on-deck circle. "How do you know these things, McLean? It's like you have ESP or something."

"Actually, I have ESPN. . . Classic. I've watched this stinkin' game more times than I should admit. Here comes a low slider, so don't try to hit it," Midnight said, not noticing the batter's confused stare.

Sure enough, a slider headed to the outside corner, and dove in the dirt for ball three.

The batter looked to Midnight for his next pitch prediction.

"It'll look outside like it's another ball, but trust me my man, you won't like the call." The pitcher delivered a fastball to the outside corner of the plate. Like Midnight said, it looked like ball four, but the umpire thought differently, and called it a strike, causing the angry crowd to roar.

"Don't worry, dude, leave it up to me," Midnight assured him. "Here comes ball four, don't you dare swing at strike three!"

As the 3-2 pitch came, it looked mighty sweet from the start. It was right down the middle, and left the hitter wondering how he could hold back. But keeping his faith, he trusted the advice, and it paid off in spades. It was the pitcher's fireball specialty, stopping mid-flight, dropping to the ground and rolling into the catcher's glove. But it wasn't even met with so much as a check swing, and loaded the bases for the long-awaiting Midnight McLean.

The crowd exploded in excitement as their star closer came to the plate. They knew his potential, and they could see the opportunity before him.

Bases loaded. Down by one. Two outs. Bottom of the ninth in the World Series. A hit would do the trick, period. A home run would put an exclamation point on it.

Midnight adjusted his helmet as he strode to the box. The single biggest moment of his life was finally here. Again.

He eyed Charlie and Emma sitting behind home plate. They stared back with angry looks. He broke eye contact, and considered all that he had sacrificed to get back to this very moment. And *everyone* he'd sacrificed too.

He noted the entire roster of TTT down the third base line. They gawked back with evil eyes. He turned to the associates behind his own dugout. They looked on with eager eyes. He checked back to Blond Don and his deviant eyes, and out to the bullpen and Cornelius' expectant ones.

Midnight rolled up his long sleeves and dug his foot into the dirt of the batter's box. He twisted his toes and burrowed a hole all the way down to his socks. He took the upside-down bat and gave his shoes, his hips and hat a tap. Then flipped it around his back, knocked the plate and puckered his lips, before shaking around like he was doing The Twist. He slapped his hands together for a dusty clap or two, and then stretched down to tighten his laces on his shoes, before jumping up and down like a hopping kangaroo. He pointed the bat to the mound, and back he wound ready for the pitch, since his warm-up routine was finally through.

The first pitch was inside, brushing Midnight back off the plate. His foot was burrowed into the hole enough that even though he knew where the ball was going, he still barely got out of the way.

"Ball one!" called the ump.

Midnight reset himself and began his routine all over from scratch. He dug in even deeper. The crowd was getting restless. The pitcher was already on edge.

The next pitch was a fastball low and outside, but in the strike zone. Midnight figured he could crush it, but once again, he couldn't pivot his foot out of the deep hole he'd dug. He laid off the pitch, and took it for strike one.

Another one to the outside followed, with hopes that Midnight would chase it. But he knew better and took it for another ball to get ahead in the count, 2-1.

Midnight was starting to suspect trouble. He hadn't remembered having footing problems the first time he'd gone through this. But with every warm-up ritual, his foot dug deeper into the box. By the next pitch, it was like quicksand, and even if he wanted to hit the ball, he couldn't get the leverage he needed.

Right down the middle, a fastball put Midnight behind, two balls and two strikes.

The crowd groaned, knowing they were down to their final strike.

"Don't worry," Midnight muttered. "This one won't even be close."

And sure enough, it wasn't. The pitcher was so amped up, so excited, so pumped with adrenaline, that the would-be World Series winning pitch almost landed in the stands, forcing dozens of fans to dive out of harm's way. But lucky for him, it bounced off the protective screen and ricocheted back to the catcher, preventing the tying run from scoring from third.

Three balls, two strikes, two outs: the scenario that Midnight had dreamt about, had anguished over, had risked his and Charlie's and Emma's lives for, was right in front of him once again.

He was ready. But his foot wasn't. It was now completely immobilized by the batter's box dirt. It was like an anchor, keeping him from straying away—or even worse, swinging away.

Midnight called timeout, straining and pulling and doing everything he could to work his foot loose. But this time, the dirt was too thick—almost cement-like—and no matter how hard he yanked, he remained fastened to the batter's box.

He looked all around for an idea, but could think of nothing. His eyes were drawn to the outfield bullpen. Cornelius was shaking his hat toward him. Was he trying to tell him something?

Midnight looked back for some sort of answer toward Charlie and Emma, and there was Blond Don behind them, rubbing one hand through his prickly blond hair and pointing the other trickily toward him.

Apparently both the forces of good *and* evil were scheming to control the fate of Midnight's foot, not to mention everything that would result from its freedom.

Midnight swung his bat down on his shoe. No luck. He reached down and tried to pull it out by hand. Couldn't get through the muck. He leaned back to let gravity work it loose. Still stuck.

He was out of answers. Out of hope. And wanted to just get out of there. If only he had a pair of wings.

"Wings!" Midnight shouted to nobody in particular. He reached up across his jersey and unpinned the golden wings Cornelius had attached to him. "I've earned 'em. I'm going to use 'em!"

He employed the sharp end of the golden badge as a cutting tool and sliced into the muddy mound immersing his foot. A few swipes around the outside of his cleat and he was home free, wiggling loose from the grasp of the binding batter's box.

He could now finally focus on the task at hand. This time, he piled the dirt *up* and pounded it back down instead of digging through it. And he initiated his warm-up routine one final time, from The Twist to the taps to the hopping kangaroo, ready to finish what he came here to do.

The crowd was riotous, chanting for Midnight to put an end to the game with one swing of the bat. The pitcher focused in, searching for the perfect throw.

The fielders got into position, ready for whatever was to come.

Both teams climbed their dugout steps, anticipating the celebration.

Charlie and Emma covered their eyes, peeking through just enough, expecting the worst.

Midnight looked back one more time to his traveling teammates. And then over to his baseball ones.

He'd told Charlie and Emma that if he knew where a pitch was coming, he could hit it the length of the Mississippi River. And being that he'd been there before, he had the distinct advantage of knowing precisely where this one was headed.

The pitcher wound up. Midnight wound back. The pitcher let it go. Midnight let it go.

The ball started right down the middle like a fastball, and just at the last moment, took a ninety-degree dive down.

Midnight uncoiled his bat and swung at the ball with everything he had, using his perfectly-planned leverage and unbelievably explosive power.

And his bat made spot-on solid contact with. . . nothing but the back of his own helmet.

The force sent him spinning around, twisting his ankle, buckling his knees and crashing into the dirt with the weight of the World Series on his back.

STRIKE THREE. GAME OVER.

WORLD SERIES LOST. AGAIN.

The catcher snagged the ball and jumped with joy, landing right on Midnight's pitching hand with the heels of his cleats.

"Ouchy, ouchy, ouchy!"

The pitcher met him at home plate, followed by their ex-
uberant teammates, who jumped one-by-one into a dog pile
right on top of Midnight.

Up behind home plate, Don Ginmaster failed to grasp what he was seeing. He also failed to grasp the shoulders of his two prisoners.

Emma and Charlie ran down to the field to Midnight.

It was hard to maneuver through the pile of players celebrating on top of him, but they reached underneath and dragged him to freedom.

"Midnight! What did you do that for?" charged Charlie, ten-percent angry, and ninety-percent relieved. "You had the World Series in your hands, and you missed by a mile. I mean, *thank you*, but you blew it. Again!"

"Nah, I didn't blow it," Midnight said, gingerly pulling himself up to his feet.

"After all our work, and all your dreams, and all your slimy deals with the the TTT, why didn't you hit your stupid home run?" asked Emma.

"Because it would've been just that. Stupid. I couldn't let my two travel buddies get taken off to some horrible galaxy far, far away. For what?"

"But that's what you invented the Flogtrac for," said Charlie, realizing that Midnight had flubbed on purpose. "Why you went on this whole trip, anyway. It was your only shot at glory."

"Oh, Charlie, I never could have invented the Flogtrac if I weren't an inventor in the first place. And I wouldn't be an inventor if I'd gone and hit that home run. There's a good reason for the first rule of time travel. Change history, and life as you know it will never be the same. Anyway, there's something much more important that comes from this little mishap, I'm pleased to say."

"Excuse me. Excuse me," commanded a woman, pushing her way through all the players and personnel on the field. "Excuse me, are you alright?" she asked as she reached Midnight. "I'm a doctor—Dr. Hildegard. Let me take a look at that hand. . . and that arm. . . and that leg!"

Midnight grimaced like the pain was throbbing even worse than it was. Although, something about this tall redheaded woman with pigtails made the pain almost disappear completely.

"Looked like you got trampled on pretty hard there."

"Oh, it was nothing," Midnight lied. "Nothing a little TLC can't cure."

"And a cast, some ice and a lot of rest," Hildegard assured him.

Emma pulled Charlie aside. "There's something that's kind of weirding me out here."

"Yeah, I know. A tall redhead with pigtails. I thought that was the weakness of the TTT."

"That's not what's weirding me out, Charlie," Emma said. "Look at her. If you added red hair and stilts to *yourself*, it'd be like you were looking in a mirror."

Charlie turned to Hildegard and gasped. She did, in fact, have eyes just like his, ears just like his and freckles just like his too. She looked like she could've been his mother.

"Do you think this all—" Charlie started, looking around trying to comprehend everything that was running through his head. "What if she's my—" he paused, looking at how Hildegard held Midnight's hand. "That means my real dad is—"

"Midnight, come on," Hildegard said, pulling him slowly to lead him away. "Let's get you taken care of." They took barely three steps before she tripped over his bat that had been dropped by home plate, falling hard onto the dirt.

"I'm okay," she laughed, brushing herself off. "It happens all the time."

Midnight, mesmerized by Hildegard, was startled by a tap on the shoulder. "Hey, *you* said we had a deal." It was a fuming Don Ginmaster—backed up by dozens of TTT henchmen behind him.

"Well, I guess the deal's off, Don," Midnight shrugged, grimacing with the pain of his newly-broken limbs.

"That's not what was agreed to. We give you freedom. We let you get your home run. We give you a million dollars. You have to let us take those two little troublemakers to a galaxy far, far away."

"Something about that deal just never felt right," said Midnight.

"But you agreed to it."

"Well, young Don, not exactly."

"I was there. I asked, you agreed. Do you really think you can get away with this?"

"AAA. . . AAA. . . AAACHOO!" Midnight sneezed on him with all his might. "That was your answer then. That's your answer now. Looks like your work's done here, boys. You can find Benjamin Franklin and his nine thousand friends in the clubhouse."

"You mean ten thousand."

Midnight took his helmet off to scratch his head in mock bewilderment, but when he did, $100,000 poured out from underneath. "Yes, ten. That's what I meant."

Blond Don collected the cash and used it to wipe the sneeze juice off his face as Midnight and Hildegard started to leave the field with Charlie and Emma following closely behind.

"Stop them!" Don commanded to his TTT sidekicks. But none of them did. They were frozen, staring hypnotically at the beautiful tall redhead with pigtails, leading their adversary away.

Farther down the left field line, the time travelers were, in fact, stopped in their tracks. "Not zo fazt! How about offering madame a znack?"

"Monsieur Moofyay?"

"For zee madame." Mr. Muffin passed Midnight some mashed french fries, which he happily extended to Hildegard with his good hand.

"And a handkerchief to dab away the grease?" followed Coach Stinkysox. "Feel free to use it to take care of that goo on your face, too."

"Thanks, Stinkysnot."

"My good Lord, it's a mighty cold October night. Reminds me of a cow drive on a two-dog Texas night. Perhaps some finely customized mittens might keep the gal warm?" said ol' Tex the tailor, sidling up to the group.

"And to top it off, the scent of a lovely red rose for the lady," presented Dr. Dinglehopper, taking the flower that was pinned to his scrubs.

"Thanks, Dilbert. But it's white. And it's a lily." It didn't really matter to Hildegard, who welcomed it cheerfully.

FLIP FLOP DOINK, FLIP FLOP DOINK.

Two gigantic feet, a walking stick and a tuxedo t-shirt emerged from behind the others.

"Well, well, well, Cornelius. Mission accomplished, huh?" Midnight hoped.

"Indeed, young man. I think we can close the book on case 112679. Wings earned. Lessons learned."

"So, what now?"

"Well, Mr. McLean, let me just say this: Since Emma equals Midnight times Charlie to the power of 2, Cornelius is here to be of assistance to you. You've found the code to becoming a hero as agreed, by following the rrrules of the rr-road: one, two and three. I'll take these two back to the realm of the Pooper Scooper, 'cause you get on the wrong side of that one, and she's worse than a Time Travel Trooper."

Charlie and Emma followed Cornelius to center field, as Midnight tipped his cap to the trio. "I'll be back before you know it."

"Alright, Clumsy. Alright, Red," summoned Cornelius. "Get rrready for the rrride of your life."

CHAPTER 14

RE-ENTRY TO EUREKA ELEMENTARY

Right there on the field pulled up a shiny spectacle of flashing red, white and blue lights, twirling pinwheels, whirligigs and sparkly streamers that looked more like a techno-disco party than the time traveling rocket ship that it was.

"Here you are, sir," stepped out a speedy driver. "Victor Valet on the job without delay." He handed the keys to Cornelius, who took his spot behind the wheel.

"Well, are you two coming? The Pooper Scooper won't wait. And you know your fate if you're a second late."

They climbed in, past the shiny horns that lined the side of the vehicle. Cornelius revved the screaming engine, bursting smoke out of the back of the space rocket.

He pushed a button, twisted a lever and switched a knob. He pressed keys in one computer and, into another, punched in the 3.14159 frequency of the intergalactic system where they were headed.

He pointed the rocket ship to a pile of rakes and hoses and tarps. "Ready, ready, sit still and steady!"

The rocket ship shot right through the pile in an instant, initiating a **SPARK**, a **BOOM** and a **BAM!**

It sent them into a winding tunnel at a speed the old Flog-trac never dared reach. And it was a good thing, because at this velocity, their heads were spinning like a tilt-a-whirl at supersonic hyper-speed.

They twisted and turned through the tunnel, flying through a spectacle of stars, bright lights and incredible colors in all directions.

"Beautiful ride, eh?" Cornelius posed.

"It...would...be...better...if...I...didn't...feel...the...need...to...blow...chunks," grunted Charlie, holding on for dear life.

"We gotta step on it," Cornelius insisted. "Don't forget: your project's still due, and this travel troll's work is never through!"

"Yeah...but...do...you...really...need...to...drive...like...a...maniac?" groaned Emma.

"With feet like these, Red, there ain't much choice in the matter." Cornelius accelerated down and launched the rocket ship even more hazardously along the path.

Off to the left, Charlie and Emma could see a flurry of meteors, comets and asteroids shooting every which way. To the right: a mishmash of galactic tornadoes, hurricanes and sun rays exploding all around.

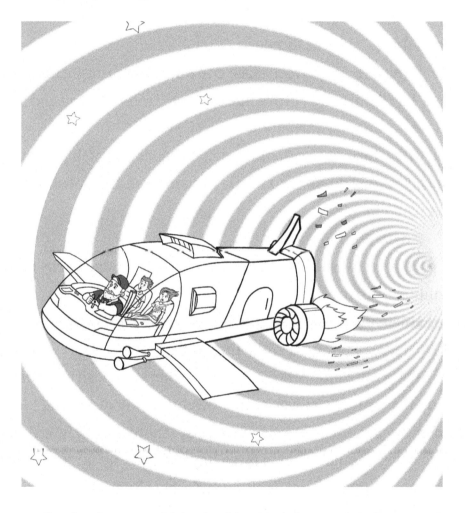

If only they would be lucky enough to get taken out by one of them—they prayed—they could end this vomit voyage once and for all.

A large structure, positioned directly down the winding pathway, finally gave them some hope.

"You. . . see. . . that. . . big. . . barn. Right. . . Cornelius?" Charlie wondered.

"Please. . . tell. . . us. . . there's. . . a. . . time. . . continuum. . . in. . . there," wished Emma.

"Quite the perrrfect place for a homecoming, wouldn't you say?" Cornelius broke out in song. "After all, *you and old McLean had some fun getting by the E.I.E.I.O.!*"

They flew through the open barn doors at breakneck speed, and straight into a tiny bluish force field positioned perfectly inside.

SHWOOP!

Their atmosphere was illuminated by a spectacle of a million brilliant lights zooming by.

SHWOOP!

There it was again—one final time.

They were stopped. The space rocket was positioned inside the janitor's closet in the lower hallway of Eureka Elementary School. Just a few feet away, there was a sight they had never thought they'd be so happy to see again: the chalk eraser thingymagiggy, looking superbly situated, surrounded by all those spilled erasers.

"Well, I'd say that was one radical ride," said Cornelius, turning back to look at Emma and Charlie.

"I'd say it was one ralph-a-rific ride," Charlie moaned, holding his stomach and quickly exiting the space rocket.

"Full of regurgitation stimulation," added Emma, getting out and happily touching earth with her own two feet.

"Well, you better hop, skip and jump on up to that classroom before you give the Pooper Scooper any more inspiration to wield that Boarrrd of Education."

They didn't need any more motivation than that. After all, they knew exactly the force she was capable of bringing.

"Wait Cornelius, what about Midnight? Will he make it back?" Charlie asked.

Emma started to pull him by the arm.

"Midnight will find his way back when the time is right," Cornelius assured him.

"And what about you?" Charlie called out.

Emma pulled him to the door through the pile of erasers.

"Oh, don't worry about me," insisted Cornelius. "I'm off to party with the stars. A celestial celebration awaits."

"Celebrating our journey?"

"Actually, a milestone birthday. Old Cornelius is turning the big 4-5-8 today."

"Since when is that a milestone birthday?"

"After you hit 400, my friend, *every* birthday is a milestone birthday."

Emma finally dragged Charlie through the door, which shut with a thud behind them.

"Emma, wait. There's one more thing."

"What is it?"

"Midnight and Hildegard. I have to know. Are they who I think they are?"

Emma agreed, and they turned to open the door. But it wouldn't budge. They twisted the handle and pushed the panel, but couldn't move it a single inch. The closet door was locked.

And then, the bad news got even badder. Charlie was shoved sharply in the back. He slowly turned to the sight of spiky brown hair and a scowl nastier than a honey badger's.

"Buster!"

The bully's dim-witted duo of sidekicks, Dizzle and Rocky, stood right by, as if they were all attached at the hip.

"You better get up to class," Buster breathed odorously, forcing Charlie and Emma to hold their noses. "The Pooper Scooper sent us to find you, and you already know she's in one of her moods."

Dizzle jumped in, showering them with saliva. "And if we don't bring you back by the time she counts down to zero, there'll be trouble of *preposterous proportions*."

Rocky lisped logic in a way only he could. "We figured at leatht we could adminithter a wedgie or two for our troubleth."

The triplets spread out, surrounding Charlie and Emma.

"I think the *Eureka Enquirer* would be very interested in

a feature on you three," Emma said. "I can see the headline now: 'The Triplets: Tricked, Tripped and Trapped.'"

Buster wasn't quick enough to realize it wasn't a compliment. "Everyone knows that nobody messes with the Oakley tripl—"

Before he could finish, Emma flipped like a gymnast, kicking him with a swift strike to the stomach.

Charlie pointed off in the distance, distracting both Rocky and Dizzle. While he called his shot, he jumped in the air, clotheslining one and landing awkwardly onto the ankle of the other.

All three brothers were on the ground—incapacitated, outraged and humiliated.

Charlie and Emma stepped over them and headed back to class.

"Where did you learn to flip and kick like that?" Charlie wondered.

"Secret skill. I use it when I need it. Keep it between us?"

"Sure. Between us. I've got secret skills too," Charlie insisted.

"Oh yeah? Like what?"

"Like bike riding skills. I'm a magician on two wheels."

"Isn't that your Gnarly Harley right out there?" Emma pointed through the hall window to his mashed up bicycle.

"Well, I've got other skills, too," he said, turning red.

"I'm sure you do."

They picked up the pace as they rounded the corner to their classroom's hallway and heard a squealing sound more painful than fingernails on a chalkboard.

"Fiiive... Fooour... THReeee... Twooo... onnne..."

They turned into the room just in the nick of time.

"Weeell, Mr. Marley. Weeell, Ms. Mayfield. It's about time you returned to class," screeched Mrs. Cooper. "But I see you've returned empty-handed."

"We've got something even better, Pooper—, uh, Mrs. Cooper," Emma declared.

"Something better than a perfect pile of clean erasers, eh?"

"Coop, we're gonna knock your socks off," asserted Charlie.

Mrs. Cooper gasped and Charlie grinned, knowing it was likely because nobody had called her by her nickname in decades.

Charlie had learned plenty about Ruth's called shot and the band, perfect tens and the barrier-breaking man. Of course, there was new knowledge of the guy who could fly, the lady Babe and where Coop's past went awry.

Emma had her computers and the press, and the old era cars to address.

Their history reports were set to impress.

"Weeell, you two, you better not disappoint."

"I'm sure we won't, *Coop*," Charlie said again. He saw something of an inviting eye coming from the old Pooper Scooper, as if she figured they knew something everyone else didn't.

"Alright then, Mr. Maaarley, you're up," Mrs. Cooper said, giving him a curious look.

Charlie took his place in the front of the class. "Hey, everybody, take a look at Brace Face Chase."

The entire class turned to look at the boy, who froze like a prison escapee in a spotlight.

"You see that candy bar he's sneaking?"

Everyone giggled as Brace Face Chase tried to hide the evidence in his mouth.

Charlie picked up the wrapper off of his desk, as Chase chomped away.

"Look, a Baby Ruth."

Mrs. Cooper did not look happy with Brace Face, nor impressed with Charlie.

"Let me tell you about another Baby Ruth—better known as The Babe. The Great Bambino. The Sultan of Swat. The greatest ball player who ever lived. The man who swung a stick of dynamite."

The Pooper Scooper gripped The Board of Education like a softball bat, and set it on her shoulder. She drifted off into Charlie's story, flashing back to a whole 'nother era. And, for the first time in a long, long time, cracked a lovely sweet smile that Charlie could not have more effortlessly coordinated.

CAST OF CHARACTERS

GEORGE HERMAN "BABE" RUTH, JR.
FEBRUARY 6, 1895 - AUGUST 16, 1948
6'2" 215 LBS
#3

Babe Ruth was the greatest baseball player of his time. He transformed the way the game was played, in part by the astounding number of home runs he hit. The Babe led the Major Leagues in homers a record twelve times, set hitting records that stood for decades and was inducted in the Baseball Hall of Fame in 1936.

Ruth was a pitcher early in his career—the winningest left-hander in baseball from 1915 through 1917. But he was such a good hitter, he was moved to the outfield so he could play every day. Babe hit 714 career home runs, a record not broken until Hank Aaron in 1974. He hit a record sixty home runs in one season, 1927, which stood until Roger Maris hit sixty-one in 1961. In 1920, he hit fifty-four, which was more than almost every other whole *team* in the Majors.

The Babe played for the Boston Red Sox, New York Yankees and Boston Braves in his twenty-two year career, winning seven World Series titles.

Yankee Stadium, opened in 1923, was nicknamed "The House that Ruth Built."

Ruth's final World Series came in 1932 as a member of the Yankees. In his second at bat in Game 3, after already hitting one home run earlier, he pointed to center field with two strikes against him. On the very next pitch, The Babe hit a long shot over the center field fence, which many believed he had predicted with the point. The Called Shot only added to the lore of the legendary hitter.

JOHN ELWAY, KEVIN MOEN & THE STANFORD BAND PLAY NOVEMBER 20, 1982

The Stanford Band Play has to go down as one of the most incredible and bizarre in all of sports history.

The 85th Big Game between archrivals Stanford and Cal was also the final college game for Cardinal quarterback John Elway. After Stanford kicked a field goal with four seconds left on the clock to take a one-point lead, it looked poised to send their star quarterback out with a big win over the big rival, and earn a berth in the Hall of Fame Classic bowl game.

But on the ensuing kickoff—in those final four seconds—pandemonium took over. Cal's Kevin Moen received the ball and started a string of five laterals—keeping the ball, the play and the game alive.

On the third lateral, it seemed Dwight Garner's knee may have been down before he passed the ball back to his Cal teammate. That appeared to be the go-ahead for the Stanford Band to come onto the field to celebrate the victory. Only, it turned out Garner wasn't called down, and the play continued with the band on the field.

Moen received one final lateral at the Stanford 25-yard line, and then ducked and dodged his way through the band to score the game-winning touchdown, giving the Golden Bears an improbable 25-20 victory.

Elway's college career was through, but he went on to one of the most illustrious NFL quarterbacking careers in history, throwing for more than 50,000 yards and 300 touchdowns. He was the NFL's Most Valuable Player in 1987. He also led the Denver Broncos to five AFC championships, winning two

Super Bowls in 1998 and 1999, before retiring. In the 1999 Super Bowl, he was named the MVP.

Elway was inducted into the College Football Hall of Fame in 2000 and the Pro Football Hall of Fame in 2004.

After the controversial play, the announcer of the Big Game, Joe Starkey, called it the most amazing, sensational, dramatic, heart-rending, exciting, thrilling finish in the history of college football!

MARY LOU RETTON
JANUARY 24, 1968 –
4'9" 93 LBS

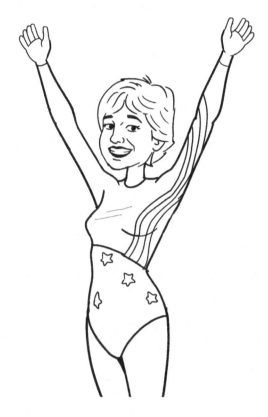

Mary Lou Retton was only 16-years-old when she made her historic mark on the world of gymnastics. She won a number of big competitions before the 1984 Olympic Games in Los Angeles, including the American Cup Championship, the American Classics Championship and the U.S. Championship.

But it was her performance at the '84 Games that made her the most popular athlete in America.

Trailing Romanian Ecaterina Szabó for the All-Around gymnastics title, Mary Lou executed a performance on the floor exercise that earned a score of a perfect ten, bringing her within 5/100ths of a point of first place.

Needing another perfect ten in her final event to win the gold medal, Mary Lou nailed a flawless vault. Thanks to her two back-to-back perfect tens, she became the first American woman to win the Olympic All-Around title, and the first American woman to win *any* gymnastics gold medal, for that matter.

She also earned two silver medals and two bronze medals at the '84 Olympics. Her five total were the most medals won by any athlete in those Games.

Mary Lou Retton was just seventeen-years-old when she retired from gymnastics in 1985. She was inducted into the USOC Olympic Hall of Fame that same year, and into the International Gymnastics Hall of Fame in 1997.

JACK ROOSEVELT "JACKIE" ROBINSON
JANUARY 31, 1919 - OCTOBER 24, 1972
5'11" 204 LBS
#42

Whites played in the Major Leagues, and blacks played in the Negro Leagues. That was before Jackie Robinson.

On April 15, 1947, Jackie took the field for the Brooklyn Dodgers as the first African-American in the modern era to play in the Majors, breaking the color barrier that stood in baseball for more than six decades.

When Dodgers general manager Branch Rickey chose Jackie to help integrate baseball, he knew there would be tough criticism and ridicule ahead. He told Robinson that he would have to promise to keep his composure and not fight back when dealing with racism.

Jackie dealt with bigotry not only from fans, but even from many of his own teammates at first. However, the Dodgers stood by him, and he gained the support of his fellow players.

Despite suffering through an 0-for-20 slump during his first two weeks in the Major Leagues, he went on to hit .297 with twelve home runs that season, led the National League in stolen bases and helped the Dodgers win the NL pennant. He was the first person ever named Rookie of the Year.

In 1949, he won the batting title, hitting .342 with sixteen home runs and again led the NL in stolen bases. He was named the National League's Most Valuable Player.

Jackie stole home plate nineteen times in his career. He helped the Dodgers win six National League pennants and the 1955 World Series.

Before he made it to the Majors, Jackie was the first person to earn varsity letters in four sports at UCLA: baseball, basketball, football and track.

Fittingly, he became the first African-American inducted into the Baseball Hall of Fame in 1962. In 1972, the Dodgers retired his number, 42. In 1997, on the 50th anniversary of Jackie breaking the color barrier, Major League Baseball retired his number all across the league.

MILDRED ELLA "BABE" DIDRIKSON ZAHARIAS
JUNE 26, 1911 - SEPTEMBER 27, 1956
5'7" 115 LBS

Babe Didrikson was a superstar golfer. She was a super-star track and field athlete. She was a superstar basketball player, baseball player, softball player, tennis player, swimmer, diver, skater and bowler too.

She was voted by the Associated Press as the greatest female athlete of the 20th century, and six times was AP Female Athlete of the Year. No one else—male or female—has received the honor in their category so many times.

Babe won eighty-two golf tournaments, but didn't even take up the sport until after she was a national star in other sports already: as an All-American in basketball and an Olympic track and field champion.

In the 1932 Olympics, she won gold medals in the javelin throw and 80-meter hurdles, and tied for first—but received the silver medal—in the high jump.

She took up golf as a new challenge after the Olympics, and went on to help pioneer the Ladies Professional Golf Association (LPGA), winning thirty-one events on the tour. As an amateur, she won seventeen-straight tournaments including the U.S. Amateur, British Amateur and the All-American. She even twice played in the men's Los Angeles Open. Babe won her tenth major championship, the U.S. Women's Open, in 1954. That came just one month after cancer surgery. Cancer took her life two years later.

She was inducted into the World Golf Hall of Fame in 1951, the National Women's Hall of Fame in 1976 and the LPGA Hall of Fame in 1977.

Babe got her name because of her abilities in baseball. In one game, while playing with boys, she cracked five home runs, and earned the nickname of the legendary slugger, Babe Ruth.

How competitive was Babe Didrikson? In addition to all the sports she excelled in, she even claimed to have won the sewing championship at the State Fair of Texas in 1931.

MICHAEL JORDAN
FEBRUARY 17, 1963 –
6'6" 216 LBS
#23 AND #45

He was perhaps the greatest basketball player to ever take the court. He was the world's most recognizable athlete. He redefined his era. His nickname exemplified the very place he most impressively made his mark.

Michael "Air" Jordan won six NBA championships with the Chicago Bulls and an NCAA championship at the University of North Carolina. For Carolina, as a freshman, he hit the game-winning shot that gave the Tar Heels the national title. He also won two Olympic gold medals—one in 1984 and one in 1992—the latter as part of the original Dream Team.

Michael led the Bulls to championship three-peats twice: 1991-93 and 1996-98. After the first set of championships, he surprised everyone by retiring from basketball and taking up a career in professional baseball, playing for the Birmingham Barons, a minor league affiliate of the Chicago White Sox.

Michael's toughest challenge, and something that may have led to his first retirement, was the murder of his father, James Jordan, in 1993.

But after a year away from the game, MJ returned to basketball and led the Bulls back to glory. In his first full year back, Chicago posted a record of 72-10—at the time, the best season in NBA history, and the first of three more consecutive championships.

Jordan was a five-time NBA Most Valuable Player, a record ten-time scoring champion, Rookie of the Year in 1984-85, a fourteen-time All-Star (named game MVP three times) and was the NBA Finals MVP in each of the Bulls' six championships. He finished his career with 32,292 points, an average of 30.12 a game, which is the best in NBA history.

One of the most amazing stories about Jordan is that the young man who would go on to one of the greatest careers in basketball history wasn't even on his high school's team his sophomore year. He was cut in tryouts.

CHARLIE MARLEY
12 YEARS OLD
4'11" 105 LBS

If you're looking for someone to carry a crystal platter across a shaky tight rope without letting it shatter or splatter, Charlie Marley would probably be the last person you'd call—or even think of, for that matter.

To say that Charlie's kind of clumsy is to say that Daffy Duck has a bit of a saliva malfunction. Charlie's coordination is as spotty as a leopard's skin.

The twelve-year-old has messy brown hair and freckles. He is a sixth grader at Eureka Elementary, home of the fighting Dust Devils, and has never been picked first for a recess football game. Ever. Even that one day that almost every kid in the school was home sick with the measles, and there were only two players to pick from anyway, he was still picked last. Charlie tends to melt in clutch situations like a Hershey bar in a microwave.

But what he lacks in sure-handed skills, he makes up for in sports intrigue. Intrigue, however, doesn't exactly prevent you from getting thumbtacks strategically placed on your seat on a daily basis.

Charlie is responsible for bringing the news to the people of his hometown of St. Albany. He delivers the *St. Albany Daily News* on his paper route every morning before heading to Mrs. Cooper's sixth grade class. And he could not do so without the aid of the coolest bike on earth, Charlie Marley's Gnarly Harley.

At home, Charlie has a younger sister, Sasha, who is nine, and two loving parents who tend to be paralyzed in wonderment at Charlie's tardy tendencies and mind-boggling gracelessness. Charlie was adopted as a young boy, but never knew who his real parents were.

EMMA MAYFIELD
12 YEARS OLD
4'8" 95 LBS

The *Eureka Enquirer* would not be the first-rate elementary school newspaper it is without its lead reporter, Emma Mayfield. The twelve-year-old sixth grader with long red hair and freckles digs for facts deeper than a delving excavator.

Emma is almost as inquisitive as she is environmentally aware. Little gets her colder than the issue of Global Warming. But as focused as she appears on such issues, she has other interests that few people know about. It's not easy to avoid picking up a few competitive skills with two brothers around the house.

While Emma refuses to waste her time with the Eureka Elementary recess football game, she would probably be the best player on the field.

She has a knack for computers, the curiosity of a cat and a deep determination to uncover the truth. But she refuses to adhere to all of the rules set out by authority.

A wearer of tie-dyed shirts and long skirts, and a scholar of 1960s peace rallies, Emma is well aware of the importance of standing up for what she believes in and not allowing anyone have the upper hand in dictating her actions.

There is little that can be done to throw Emma off her game. But a pair of piercing eyes and a couple of distinct dimples are a good place to start for anyone aspiring to break through.

MIDNIGHT MCLEAN
42 YEARS OLD
6'2" 175 LBS

Few people remember the details of one of the greatest pitchers in baseball history. They forget his nasty junk ball. They forget his quirky running style. They forget his ability to hit a ball the length of the Mississippi River. But they don't forget his one World Series appearance. After all, following a wildly nonsensical swing that lost the 1994 Series, no other player had ever been so brutally beat down by another team's celebration.

Midnight McLean is now an inventor, who created such useful contraptions as the READY STEADY CONFETTI CATCHER 3000 and the WHAM BAM THANK YOU MAMMAL 4600. He is also responsible for the advent of the armored padding many professional baseball players wear today that would qualify them for most medieval jousting matches of centuries past.

Midnight's sleek lab coat and bow tie are in stark contrast to his wildly erratic white hair and whimsically naïve persona.

He is bilingual, specializing in both English and Pig Latin, a skill rivaled only by his expertise in antique automobiles.

While Midnight is best known for his World Series failure, he was still one of the best in the game when he was in his prime.

His quirky rituals on the mound and at the plate were just as distracting as a misdirected knuckleball in a blustery ballpark. To put it simply, for almost anyone who faced Midnight McLean, it was lights out.

ABOUT THE AUTHOR

ANDREW LURIA is a six-time Emmy Award winning sports and news anchor, and a father of three kids who are just about your age! He played college baseball and football at Cornell University, and has reported on just about every sport there is. He loves stories for kids, which is why he decided to make one of his own—this one! He also loves teaching kids, which he does as a baseball, basketball and football coach, and in the elementary school broadcasting program he runs in his free time. *(Wait, I thought you said he had three kids. What's "free time?!")* He lives in Carlsbad, California with his wife, three kids and two dogs: Archie and Henry. At one point or another, his family also had dogs named Charlie, Emma, Cooper, Muffin, Oakley, Buster, Dizzle, Rocky and Midnight. Do those names sound familiar?!

TWITTER & INSTAGRAM: @ANDREWLURIA

WWW.CHARLIEMARLEY.COM

WWW.BEACHSIDEPUBLISHINGCO.COM